THE FALCONER'S STAIRS

Glimmer Vale Chronicles #5

MICHAEL KINGSWOOD

CONTENTS

ABOUT THIS BOOK

Jared Tolburt twice almost cost Raedrick Baletier and Julian Hinderbrook their lives: once when he turned on them while they were fleeing the Army, and again when he unwittingly led a group of bandits into Glimmer Vale.

Now, Tolburt intends to search out a hidden and well-guarded magical treasure, and Melanie Klemins has offered to accompany him.

Unwilling to trust Tolburt with Melanie's safety, and with Raedrick unable to travel due to his wife's pregnancy, Julian has to do the last thing he ever wanted: travel with and help the man he trusts least in the world.

Far from home and beset with dangers of all kinds, Julian, Melanie, and Tolburt will have to depend on each other even to survive, let alone succeed in their quest for The Falconer's Stairs.

The Falconer's Stairs is the fifth book of the Glimmer Vale Chronicles, a far-reaching quest through a world of valor and magic.

Enjoy the book!

After you're done, please come to Michael's website and sign up for his mailing list at www.michaelkingswood.com/newsletter-signup/.

Guaranteed to be spam free, he uses it to announce new releases and special promotions for his fans.

MAP OF GLIMMER VALE

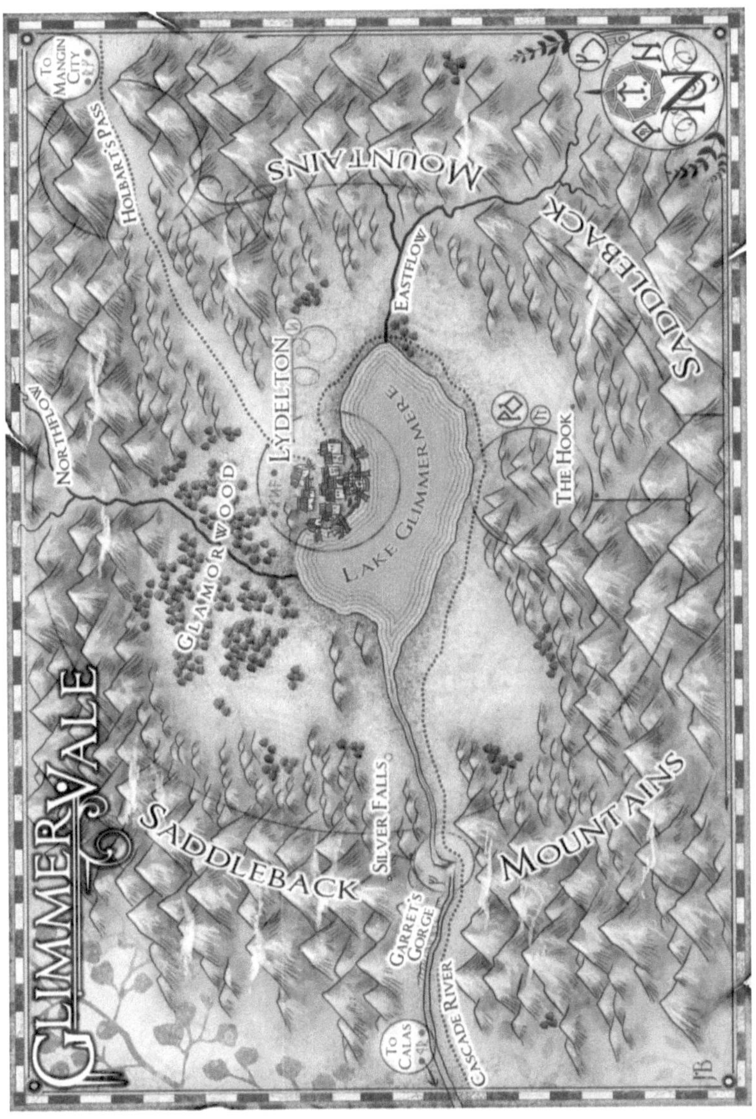

❦ I ❦

REBUILDING

The sound of hammering rang out clearly, overwhelming the other, softer noises of the valley. Although, truth be told, there were not many other noises to drown out.

The valley, all the way up to the small cove where a party of men were busily at work constructing a modest structure, was filled with char and wreckage. Burnt stumps and charred limbs were all that remained of the forest that once stood here, between Tollard's Peak and the brisk current of the Northflow, thanks to a band of wicked men.

The destruction had been complete, but even as men were now rebuilding, so the forest was as well. Grass and bushes had grown where the evergreens once had been, and saplings could be seen here and there, poking up through the underbrush. In a few years, the place would almost be as it was.

Almost.

Julian Hinderbrook looked away from the remnants of the forest and back toward the construction project, and memories flowed into him from the desperate few days he had spent up here last winter, trying to evade Geoff's band of robbers and get back to town with his party's skins intact. The hunting lodge that had stood here had been their shelter for the night, and then later Geoff had tried to use it as a weapon against them by burning it down, and lighting the entire forest ablaze at the same time.

I

Holb, and a number of woodsmen who frequented his tavern, had built that lodge and used it during the warm months. They had lost a lot of money and effort when the lodge burned down.

And it was all Tolburt's fault. If he hadn't led Geoff's accomplice into these mountains in search of treasure, the rest of the bandit party wouldn't have followed. And then...

Intellectually, Julian knew it wasn't fair to blame Tolburt for what happened. Not all of it, anyway.

But Tolburt had earned Julian's scorn through deeds a thousand times worse than those, so he didn't feel too bad about it.

Standing beside Julian, Raedrick Baletier, his friend and fellow Constable, crossed his arms over his chest. Like Julian, he was dressed down to his shirtsleeves on account of the growing heat of early summer and he wore their badge of office on his left breast: a silver fist holding a set of scales. Unlike Julian, who was wearing white, Raedrick's shirt was a deep blue. His khaki-colored breaches were tucked into black boots, and he wore a curved sword on his left hip. As always, his shoulder-length black hair was tied back into a ponytail at the nape of his neck, and his goatee was freshly trimmed.

As he surveyed the scene, Raedrick rubbed at his chin with the fingers of his left hand and frowned thoughtfully. "Seems like a lot of extra effort to rebuild here. Why not further upstream, past where the fire burned?"

He was right. The construction crew had a system set up to minimize the inconvenience of having to trek upstream more than a half mile to get good timber, but all the same that added a lot of time and effort to the rebuilding.

Despite that, the lodge was proceeding nicely. Already the stilts that held the living area aloft over the flood-prone ground on the edge of the little cove were in place, and the main structure looked to be completed in just a few days, from the look of it.

It also looked like they had taken the opportunity to expand on the earlier structure, make it bigger and nicer.

Not a bad idea, that.

"No better spot on the river to dock boats," said the man to Raedrick's right. Shorter than both Julian and Raedrick, bald, and powerfully muscled, he wore worn leathers that had clearly seen many days out in the wild, and smelled the part. "That, and we like that little cove." He grinned broadly. "Good fishing."

Julian also grinned. He got what Povol was saying. Just because some bad guys tried to make him leave, no reason he should.

"Your boy's doing alright," Povol added. "Been a big help."

That wiped the grin from Julian's face. He didn't trust himself to not say something nasty, so he kept his mouth shut and just watched the construction efforts.

A tall, thin man with a mop of black hair and a close-cut beard, in particular, held Julian's attention. He was stripped to the waist in the early summer heat, and was helping another man maneuver a particularly lengthy piece of wood into place.

From the no-so-softly spoken curses coming from them as they worked, it wasn't going particularly smoothly.

"Holb told me similar about his work at the bar," Raedrick said, a certain satisfaction in his voice as he, too, observed Tolburt's labors. "Do you consider his debt paid, then?"

Julian looked back at Povol out of the corner of his eye, and saw the mountain man's lips compress into a scowl. He flexed the fingers of his right hand—only three of them, thanks to an arrow from one of Geoff's men—and the scowl deepened.

But after a few seconds, Povol let his hand drop down to his side, and he made a quick, clearly reluctant nod. "Aye, I suppose. Soon as the lodge is rebuilt." He paused a second before adding, "He offered to help train my new dogs up, come next snow. You know that?"

Raedrick shook his head, and Povol snorted out a laugh.

"Not like he'd know how. But it was good of him to offer."

"Good to know." Raedrick gave a satisfied nod—disgustingly satisfied—and turned to regard Povol more fully. "Let us know if you need any more help up here?"

The mountain man grunted and nodded, but his expression said he would do no such thing. But then, that was his way.

"We'll be off then. We'd best get back; we have a meeting with the Mayor in the morning, and I don't want to be out too late tonight."

Povol grinned slyly. "You mean you don't want that bride of yours to be lonely in bed, eh?"

Raedrick did not reply, but Julian thought he flushed ever so slightly, and his lips turned downward.

Julian couldn't blame him for being cross. Povol was at best uninhibited in his speech, and some things just were not meant to be discussed in public. At least, not so crassly as that.

Povol seemed to notice Raedrick's disapproval, and his grin slipped a little. "Meanin' no disrespect to the Mistress of course, Constable."

Raedrick made a dismissive wave of his hand. "Good day, Povol."

"Aye, you as well."

The two clasped hands, and then Julian did the same with the mountain man. Then he and Raedrick left the construction site and walked over to the other side of the cove, where they had tied up their canoe.

During the spring thaw, the Northflow was a torrent of rapids between here and Lake Glimmermere, but now that it was getting on into summer, the current had subsided enough that the upstream trip was navigable. Good thing, too, because it would have take the better part of a day to hike here over the mountains.

Julian was just as happy to not have to deal with that.

As they approached the canoe, he asked something that had been irking him for a while now. "What's your plan with Tolburt now?"

Raedrick glanced sidelong at him and shrugged. "As far as I'm concerned, that's up to him."

Julian was afraid he'd say that. "You ask me," he said as he took hold of the boat's stern, "it's about time we sent him on his way."

Raedrick paused in climbing aboard to shoot Julian a look that said he was being obtuse before settling onto the little bench in the boat's bow and taking up his paddle.

"What? You want him to stay here?" Julian shoved the boat fully into the water, hopping into the stern a moment before it floated out of reach. He settled down on the stern bench, and started rowing in unison with Raedrick up forward. "We don't need his kind of trouble any longer than we have to."

"He's caused no trouble, and you heard Povol. He's earned the respect of many people in this town over the last few months."

Julian just snorted at that.

They left the shelter of the cove, and the Northflow's current nudged the bow downstream. Shortly, they were floating easily on the current, making good time toward the Lake, and then home in Lydelton.

"Well, when he causes mischief again, don't say I didn't warn you, Rae."

From the bow, Raedrick just shook his head and chuckled indulgently.

2

GLAD TIDINGS

Five days later, Tolburt walked into the Constabulary.

Julian and Raedrick's office was in a small one-story building a block north of Main Street in the heart of Lydelton. They had a little eight-room cell block in back, and a cozy little office up front. Julian's desk sat opposite Raedrick's, nearest the wood stove that stood in the left rear corner of the room.

It wasn't much, but it worked for what they needed in a quiet little town like Lydelton.

When Tolburt came in, clad in a faded brown shirt that he had left untied to halfway down his chest and slightly darker pants that hung loosely around scuffed black working boots, Julian was at his desk reading through a report the local judge's clerk had sent over about their recent case load, with recommendations on how to deal with the "rash of crime" that had befallen Lydelton in the last year.

Julian snorted and set the report down in exasperation. As though there was anything they could have done to avoid that. All of the major crimes the clerk wrote of were caused by elements outside of Lydelton's normal population, so what exactly did he think would be accomplished by his hair-brained schemes?

Julian suspected the judge was just jealous. Since many of the cases were severe enough that he was not empowered to hear them, Julian and Raedrick had to transfer them down to the court in Mangin City for final dispensation.

Had to rub the judge raw, come to think on it. And the gods knew he and Raedrick would prefer that their judge was fully empowered. But it wasn't up to them.

Well, that report represented half an hour that Julian would never get back.

When the door swung open, he for a second had hope that perhaps something interesting was about to happen.

Alas...

"What do you want, Tolburt?" He didn't try to keep the scornful "We don't serve your kind here" tone out of his voice. The rat deserved it.

Tolburt looked quickly around the room and frowned. "I'm looking for the Corporal."

Julian rolled his eyes. "*Constable* Baletier is tending to some personal business. So. Again. What do you want?"

"Lodge's built. I've kept up my side of the deal, so I've come to check out with him."

Well, maybe this visit would yield something worthwhile after all. "Leaving town then?"

Tolburt nodded. "Soon as...Constable...Baletier gives the ok." He flashed an eager smile. "I've got a treasure to find."

That again. The same convoluted bit of chicanery that had drawn the little weasel up into their town in the first place. Of course, there was nothing to go on to find that particular fantasy than a cryptic letter Raedrick and Julian had found in a magically-protected chest in the back of a cave upstream from...

Wait a minute.

"What do you mean?"

Tolburt just grinned broadly. "If you see him before I do, ask Constable Baletier to come by Mistress Klemins' shop after lunch."

"Wait. What - ?"

But he had already turned and walked back out the door.

Son. Of. A. Bitch.

"I don't like the sound of this," Julian said as he and Raedrick approached Melanie's Mystical Crafts.

"Peace, Julian. At least hear him out before you assume the worst," Raedrick replied.

Julian frowned, grinding his teeth in irritation.

Situated on the east side of Lydelton, only a couple blocks from the edge of town, the shop resided in the lower level of a two-story building that resembled pretty much every other in Lydelton: sturdy construction, with a high-peaked roof designed to minimize snow accumulation in the Vale's lengthy winters.

But that was just the outside.

As they went within, the feeling of sameness fled completely. Mystical symbols and words of power were painted along the walls, just beneath the ceiling. The lighting was subdued by translucent shades over the windows, and the place smelled of a musky incense. An array of shelving stood in the center of the room holding various books on all manner of mysticism, charms, and trinkets that Julian presumed had some pseudo-magical significance. The far wall was covered in hooks, from which dangled pendants and other symbols of power next to various herbs that had varying degrees of medicinal utility. Off to the left, at the rear of the store, stood a long counter where Melanie kept court. Behind the counter, a doorway, partially blocked by dangling strings of multi-colored beads, led deeper into the bowels of the building.

Julian had no idea what lay back there, besides the stairs leading to the second level and Melanie's living quarters.

As usual, Melanie Klemins was sitting on a stool behind the counter, reading a small, leather-bound book. She wore a deep green, loose-fitting dress that was embroidered with yellow flowers on the bodice and along the ends of her sleeves. It was a far cry from the nearly-regal attire she usually wore, but Julian supposed allowances had to be made for the heat.

It was very warm outside. It was stifling within. But somehow it didn't look like she was sweating at all.

Mages and their tricks.

The bell mounted above the entrance jingled as they stepped inside, and Melanie looked up from her book. She arched an eyebrow and smiled in that almost sultry way she had sometimes. "You're late."

Raedrick blinked, then grinned back at her. "I didn't know we had a set appointment."

Melanie inserted a bookmark and snapped her book shut, then placed it down atop the counter. She shrugged, and the waves of her dark brown hair bounced slightly. "We didn't. But you're still late." Her eyes twinkled in the subdued light, and her smile grew a tad bit deeper for a second. Then it faded, and she was all business. "But Jared is, apparently, even later."

Julian snorted. Hardly a shock that Tolburt—he hadn't thought of the man by his given name in years—was proving unreliable. Again.

No sooner had that thought passed through Julian's head than the bell over the door rang out. He looked over and, sure enough there was Tolburt, wearing the same attire as before, as well as an eager but smug grin.

"Good, everyone's here," he said, rubbing his hands together as he approached. His eyes moved from Raedrick to Julian, then hurriedly to Melanie. "Ready, Mistress Klemins?"

Melanie sniffed softly. "We've been waiting on you, Jared." An arched eyebrow accentuated the words, and Tolburt's grin slipped ever so slightly. Then the moment of irony passed and Melanie's expression became all business. "You'd better grab a seat, gentlemen. This will take a while."

3

HISTORY LESSONS

"My contact down in Mangin City came through," Melanie said. She reached down behind the counter and produced a hefty tome that was bound in ancient-looking brown leather. When she set it down atop the counter, Julian thought he could see little puffs of dust wafting out from between the pages, it looked so old. But that was surely just his imagination.

"That one of the books that came in the first caravan?" he asked.

She shook her head and let out a soft, slightly annoyed sigh. "No. Nor was it on the second." She turned a level gaze on Julian, then the other two men sitting next to him on stools in front of the counter. "You fellows have cost me a pretty penny on this research project."

Tolburt snorted softly. "I tried to tell you you didn't have to do it."

"We all know full well what would have happened had I not."

"Yes," Raedrick replied. "You would have driven yourself nuts from unsated curiosity, Melanie."

He got that level stare all to himself, but Raedrick didn't budge. He just looked back at her with an expression that seemed to say, "Prove me wrong." Finally, after a long moment, Melanie made a wry little smile and a small shrug.

"Perhaps. Regardless, I finally found it." She laid her hand gently atop the tome. "This dates back five hundred years."

Julian blinked. "The Kingdom didn't even exist then."

"You are a keen student of history, clearly." That wry smile returned, a bit broader this time. "You're right, of course. Back then this part of the world was ruled by numerous petty warlords. And Kalem, it seems, was the son of Botreaus Hevergod." She paused, looking at them as though expecting a reaction.

Julian looked over at Raedrick, who returned his gaze and shrugged. Tolburt clearly had no idea who that was either.

Julian cleared his throat. "Who?"

Melanie rolled her eyes. "Like I said, a true student of history. You've heard of the Butcher of Mardez?"

"Of course. Who hasn't?"

"Same person."

That set Julian back a tad. The Butcher was notorious, even all these years later. Julian had grown up with stories of his many atrocities: dead children by the thousands, women defaced and ravaged, men gelded or impaled. To defy the Butcher was to suffer a horrible, lingering death. If you were lucky.

Or at least, that's what the stories said.

"I never heard he had a son," Raedrick said, leaning forward with evident interest.

"Well, I think we can all figure out why that is," Melanie replied. "Obviously this Kalem did not collect his birthright, or else you would not have found that note to him."

Raedrick winced slightly at the mention of the note, and Julian couldn't blame him. The magic protecting the chest with Kalem's note had very nearly drained Raedrick of every last bit of warmth within his body. It made Julian shiver just thinking about it.

Melanie went on, "I think we can presume he died in the attempt. In his father's eyes he would have died a failure." She arched another eyebrow. "And tyrants are not known to record their failings for posterity to remember."

Raedrick nodded, conceding the point.

"But someone *did* record it," Tolburt piped up. His eyes glimmered with eagerness.

"Yes. This," she patted the book lightly, "is a history compiled by one of Hevergod's rival warlords. He clearly felt no compunction about discussing his rival's flaws."

Julian supposed that made sense. And the magical trap around the chest had begun to make sense as well. "They say the Butcher had powerful mages in his employ."

"They were called sorcerers, not mages, back then," Melanie said, "but yes, he did. And more than that, in addition to being a cunning war leader, he was quite possibly the most power sorcerer of his day."

"So what does that book say about Kalem?" Raedrick asked. He was definitely interested; he was leaning well forward, his elbows resting on the counter as he listened closely to the story.

"Evidently he was a cunning warrior, very charismatic. While Hevergod's people respected him, it was more out of fear than love. But according to this account, Kalem was different. His people held him in high esteem, and his men loved him. Despite this, or perhaps because of it, his father apparently treated him cruelly. It didn't help that, despite his skill at arms, he never acquired his father's talent for magic. The book doesn't quite say that Hevergod was looking for a way to get rid of Kalem, but it is strongly implied."

"Sounds like a swell guy," Julian said, earning soft snorts and bemused glances from the other men.

That set Julian's teeth on edge. Raedrick, he could take that from, but Tolburt? He was about to put the rat back in his place, but Melanie kept right on going as though he had not commented at all.

"Apparently, Hevergod decided to test Kalem, to make him earn the right to be heir. He and his closest sorcerer advisors constructed a series of physical and magical obstacles that Kalem would have to pass. If he succeeded, he would earn his father's regard and find the key to his realm."

"Does it say what that key was?"

Melanie shook her head. "From what I've learned of Hevergod's predilections, I can only presume it was a magical item of some kind."

Julian groaned. "I think I've had about enough of those. No end of trouble from them." He almost reflexively moved his hand down to his left knee. He had assisted Melanie in crafting a magical wedding gift for Raedrick, and had injured his knee in the process. It had healed, but sometimes he still felt a twinge from it. "And wouldn't the Magestirium have the cussed thing anyway? You said they have them all locked up in their vaults."

"Not all, Julian. If you recall, I said they keep all of the constructs they are in possession of in their vaults. That does not even include all the constructs they are aware of, despite the Magestirium's best efforts."

Raedrick raised an eyebrow. "How's that?"

"The Magestirium's writ does not extend to the entire world, Raedrick. Other nations have different policies, and many have managed to keep the Magestirium's grasping hands at bay." She sounded distinctly satisfied at that. "And besides, the only clues to the key's whereabouts were the map that Jared had," she nodded at Tolburt, who managed to look smug, "and the note you two found." Melanie shook her head briskly. "No, there's no reason to think the Magestirium has it, or even knows where to begin looking for it."

Raedrick narrowed his eyes. "But they know about it."

"Almost certainly. Their libraries are truly vast, and there are men in their number who do nothing but pour over the old tomes."

That evoked a frown from Raedrick, and Julian couldn't blame him. If the Magestirium knew of this thing, whatever it was, they probably would be extremely interested in finding it. And if he knew one thing, it was that he did not want to cross that bunch, not if he could help it. Not again. He, and Raedrick and Melanie as well—Melanie in particular—had done enough to put themselves in their bad graces. No need for anything more.

He shook his head, then reached over and clapped Tolburt on the shoulder hard enough that the little rat winced slightly. It was petty, perhaps, but Julian got a bit of satisfaction from that. "Too bad, Tolburt," he said. "No treasure for you after all."

Tolburt looked at him quizzically.

"What?" Julian said. "You heard her. That thing's magical, which means it's Magestirium business." He shook his head again. "Not something we're going to get involved with."

Tolburt took a second to respond, but his expression remained the same. "Who said anything about we? I've got the claim, I'm going to claim it."

"Oh for the love of... Tell him, Rae." Julian looked over at Raedrick, expectantly.

And found his partner frowning at him in disapproval. "He's got the right to it."

"You can't be serious."

Raedrick shrugged. "I checked with Povol. The lodge is finished;

his debt is paid. Tolburt upheld his part of the deal, so he's free to go." His glanced sidelong at Tolburt and seemed to mull it over for a second, then added, "I'd say his claim on the key is better than just about anyone. The Butcher's line ended with him, and that was five hundred years ago."

Julian threw his hands up. "But the Magestirium - "

"Has no claim on it."

"Come again?"

Raedrick smiled in that infuriatingly calm way he did when he was being clever. "As Melanie pointed out, even now the Magestirium's authority is not worldwide, and it didn't even exist when the key was made. How can it have claim over something that predates itself?"

Julian just stared at him. That was… It was…

Actually, it was a fair point.

And what did he care anyway? If it got Tolburt out of town, it was all to the good.

He nodded acquiescence and said, "Alright then," then managed a grin for Tolburt that probably didn't succeed in being encouraging. "Well, good luck finding it, I guess. Just have to figure out what the Falconer's Stairs are and you're all set, eh?"

Tolburt smirked at him, and Melanie cleared her throat softly.

"I was just about to get to that," she said.

She reached beneath the counter and withdrew a second book, smaller in every way and very clearly newer. The pages were hardly discolored at all, like it was only a few years old at most. "The answer was in here." She turned it so the cover was plainly visible.

A Geologic Survey of the Upper Saddleback Mountains.

Melanie looked from Julian to Raedrick and back, clearly expecting a reaction of some sort. For his part, Julian wasn't sure what she was looking for. The book had a boring-sounding title. That was not so unusual. It was a part of Melanie's library now, after all.

She rolled her eyes, managing to look amused and irked at the same time. More amused, from the tone of her voice when she spoke again. "The team that did this survey was quite detailed, and extremely organized. It didn't take long to find the answer." She opened up the book to a page that had been marked with a small scrap of paper, then read from it. "The formation, called the Raptor's

Ascent by residents of the region, is nondescript unless viewed from the northwest. From that angle, it takes on the appearance of a carved set of stairs, curving up the side of the mountain, that end at the feet of a bird of prey with wings extended."

She looked up from the book, smiling triumphantly.

Raedrick's eyebrows climbed high on his head. "The Raptor's Ascent… The Falconer's Stairs… It fits."

Melanie nodded. "The name would have shifted over the centuries, but the formation itself, apparently, did not."

"Hold on a second. Wind and rain and snow would have worn it away," Julian said, confused.

"Magic, remember?" Tolburt said, his grin matching the triumph in Melanie's, except it just made Julian want to hit him. More.

"Does it say the formation's location?" Raedrick asked, either missing the smugness in Tolburt's tone or not caring about it.

Melanie nodded. "About seventy-five to eighty miles north and east of Mangin City, in the eastern spur of the mountain range."

That was music to Julian's ears. "Well, I guess that's it then." He returned Tolburt's grin with another of his own. "Have fun on your treasure hunt, Tolburt." And don't waste any time in leaving town, he didn't add.

Raedrick nodded, looking almost wistful as he turned his attention away from Melanie and fully on Tolburt. "Yes, good luck, Jared." He extended his hand and, after a second, Tolburt clasped hands with him. "You did well by us here, and you'll always be welcome if you wish to return."

Julian wasn't so sure of that, but no need to ruin a nice, and hopefully quick, goodbye.

"Truth to tell," Raedrick added, "I wish I could go with you. It will probably be a fascinating trip. But…" He trailed off.

"You can't leave your wife with the baby due in a few months," Tolburt said, almost as though chiding him for even considering doing such a thing.

Raedrick nodded, that wistful look still his his eyes.

Julian found himself rolling his eyes. "When are you heading out?" he said, to get the conversation back to its important point.

Tolburt shrugged. "Now that I've got leave to go…" He trailed off and looked over at Melanie, questioningly.

She pursed her lips for a moment, considering. "I should be ready the day after tomorrow, if that works for you."

"Absolutely," Tolburt said.

"Whoa, hang on." Julian narrowed his eyes at Melanie, incredulity mixed with dread suddenly filling him. "You're not - "

"Going? Of course I am."

"Magic, remember?" Tolburt said. Again.

Julian about hit him, but Tolburt slid off his stool and began sauntering away toward the door before he could do more than think about it.

"I'll see to the supplies then," Tolburt said, pausing at the door and looking back at Melanie. "First light?"

She nodded. "Agreed."

Tolburt left without further discussion, the tinkling of the bell the only evidence he had been there.

Son. Of. A. Bitch.

❧ 4 ❧

PALAVER

"**A**re you nuts?"

Melanie regarded Julian with a frank stare. "I beg your pardon?"

Placing his hands atop the counter, Julian leaned in slightly and gave her a hard, level look. "You aren't really planning to go off on a journey with *Tolburt*?"

Melanie sniffed softly and slipped the mark back into her geology book, then set the book down atop the ancient history. Adjusting her seat on the little stool she liked to perch on behind the counter, she returned his look with equal accusation.

"Is there some reason I should not? And more to the point, what concern is it of yours?"

Julian felt his mouth drop open. What concern was it of his? Why, she was… He was…

She raised an eyebrow, and Julian forced his mouth shut. He ground his teeth for a second before finally speaking.

"He's an untrustworthy rat. No telling what he'll do when he's alone with you."

The accusing stare faded a bit, and Melanie began to look amused. "Really." She gave a little toss of her head, and her hair settled more evenly about her shoulders. "So I'm incapable of taking care of myself, is that it?"

Julian knew better than that. If anything, Melanie was one of the most capable women he had ever met, if not *the* most. "Of course that's not what I'm saying. But you can't keep an eye out forever. He'll - "

"He'll what?"

"I don't know what exactly, but it won't be good. He can't be trusted, Melanie."

"Yes, you've made that abundantly clear."

"So you won't go, then?"

Melanie turned her eyes skyward, and for a second Julian got the distinct impression she was making an appeal to the gods. When she looked back at him, her expression had lost most of its amusement, becoming sternly determined.

"Whether I go or remain here is not for you to say, Julian."

He opened his mouth to reply, but she held up a silencing hand, and he stopped.

"You don't give him enough credit, Julian," Raedrick said, his tone dripping disapproval.

"Credit? After what he did to us?"

"His debt to the town is paid, and there's not a man in Povol's or Holb's groups who doesn't speak highly of him."

Julian scowled darkly at him. "That's not what I'm talking about, and you know it."

Raedrick said nothing, just returned his stare with a firm set to his jaw that broadcast entire levels of disapproval.

From the corner of his eye, Julian could see Melanie's confused frown. "What *are* you talking about?"

"You going to tell her, Rae, or should I?"

Raedrick's lips compressed for a second. Then he visibly relaxed and he nodded, gesturing with his left hand from Julian to Melanie.

"He sold us out," Julian said, his gaze still locked onto Raedrick's. "Not long after we all ran away from the Army. He found a patrol that had been searching for us and led them right in, to save his own skin."

Raedrick's lips turned downward into a little scowl, but he said nothing.

Julian snorted. "Didn't do him a lick of good, though," he continued. "They trussed him up with the rest of us. We lost...two? Three?...good men when we managed to make our escape."

"And we left him behind." Raedrick's voice was soft, sad.

Not this again. Julian jabbed an index finger toward his old squad leader. "And you beat yourself up over that for almost two years. I still can't figure why."

"He was one of my men."

"Bollocks. He stopped being your man when he betrayed us. Everyone thought he got what was coming to him. Everyone but you, I suppose."

Melanie frowned, tapping at her lips with her index finger. "That's why you were so determined to go up into the mountains after his friend last winter.'

Raedrick nodded.

"And you almost got the lot of us killed over it," Julian growled. When Raedrick didn't immediately respond, he turned away from his friend and regarded Melanie frankly. "You see why Tolburt can't be trusted?"

"I see why you would think so."

Julian gaped at her. Had she not been listening at all?

"I understand he hurt you, Julian."

"Hurt me? He didn't hurt me, he - "

"Yes, yes." She made a dismissive wave of her hand. "Regardless, I have never seen or heard of him behaving except as a complete gentlemen since he came here. He's going to chase after this regardless, and it is all but certain, given what you two encountered in that cave and what I've learned about Hevergod and his sorcerers, that he will not survive whatever traps and tricks they left at The Falconer's Stairs without the help of a practitioner."

It was difficult to see the problem with that arrangement. He opened his mouth to say so, but Melanie continued speaking, trampling over his reply before he could make it.

"And even were that not the case, I have a responsibility. This construct, whatever it is, is likely very powerful. It should not just be left lying around where the gods know who might obtain it."

Julian snorted again. "The hell you do. That's the Magestirium's job, not yours. Besides, you just said any random fellow who tried to get it would most likely die. It's lasted there for five hundred years already."

Melanie's eyes narrowed. "The Magestirium does not have the information we do."

"All the same, Julian's right," Raedrick interjected.

They both turned surprised eyes on him, and he made a little shrug to match a wry half-grin. "Well he is. And besides, your truce with the Magestirium carries the stipulation that you not leave Glimmer Vale."

"I'm aware of that."

"Loran Haversted said he had used tracers to follow Telurian here. They probably have similar spells set to monitor you."

"There are ways around those sorts of spells."

"But you won't know for sure if you were successful until they come for you again, will you?"

She shook her head.

"Then why take the risk?" Raedrick must have seen the incredulous look on Julian's face, because he grinned a little bit more broadly. "Don't misunderstand my meaning. I thank you for your willingness to help. But you could do as much, maybe more, if you just sent a message to Haversted. I could hold Jared here until they send someone to assist, or maybe they could meet him in Mangin City." He raised an eyebrow. "You don't need to risk yourself over this. So...why?"

Melanie met his gaze coolly and replied, "Just because I am not a member of the Magestirium does not mean I don't have responsibility here, Raedrick." She drew a quick breath. "One thing Timon taught me early on is that all practitioners have a duty to the art, and to its posterity. That includes a duty to prevent its side-effects from adversely affecting the un-initiated." Her cool facade faded, slightly, as she grinned all of a sudden. "But beyond that... Well, I want to go for the same reason you do."

Raedrick blinked, and Melanie chuckled softly.

"Come now, you're curious about what Hevergod left behind for his son." She glanced Julian's way and arched an eyebrow. "You both are."

That was true enough. Julian had certainly pondered the puzzle a few times over the last several months. He grudgingly nodded. "I told you that before. But that doesn't mean I want to run off...with Tolburt...to find the bloody thing. Or that you should, either."

"I would go in a heartbeat," Raedrick said, "except - "

"It'd be a trip of three to four months at least, and you can't leave Lani for that long," Melanie finished for him. "No man worthy of being called one would." She drew herself up. "Look, you boys are not going to talk me out of this, so you'd best get used to the idea."

Julian knew that look on her face. He had seen it before, that tightness in the lips, the sharpness in her eyes. She wasn't going to budge on this one.

Looking back at Raedrick, he saw that Raedrick had come to the same conclusion. The other Constable shrugged slightly and spread his hands in a gesture that shouted helplessness.

Damn it.

Julian pushed himself up off his stool and, muttering under his breath, started toward the door.

"Where are you going?' Melanie sounded suspicious.

He sighed. "To pack." As he reached for the door latch, he looked back at her over his shoulder, and was amused to see the look of disbelief on her face. He put on his most winning smile. "You didn't think I was going to let you go off with Tolburt by yourself did you?"

Shaking his head in mock disbelief, he threw her a wink, then he pulled the door open and left her store.

As the door shut behind him, he let the act go. He ran his head through his hair and sighed, hardly believing that he was about to do this thing. And with Tolburt, of all people!

This was going to be a bad few months.

GOODBYES

J ulian pulled his mail over his head and rolled his shoulders a few times to coax it into settling more comfortably around his frame.

Not that it was ever actually comfortable, especially when the weather turned toward heat. But it beat being skewered. Most days.

Once the mail was situated as best it could be, he pulled on a dark green shirt overtop the linked rings and looped his baldric and sword scabbard over his shoulder. Then he buckled on his belt and checked himself in the little mirror he had mounted on the wall of his flat.

Nothing seemed too out of place, so he picked up his bedroll and lifted his saddle bags over his other shoulder, then he left.

He stomped down the staircase that led from his front door down to street level, then he set out for The Oarlock, where he kept his horse stabled.

Twenty minutes later, he tied off the horse's reins on the hitching post out front of the Constabulary and went inside.

Despite the early hour, Raedrick was in. He stood next to his desk on the right-hand side of the room, dressed in blue shirtsleeves and grey leggings. As usual, his badge of office was pinned to his left breast, and he had his sword belt on, though the scabbard was unhooked and leaning against the wall behind his desk, next to a dozen other blades that rested in a rack there.

"The others should be here any minute, Rae. Last chance to call this thing off."

Raedrick sniffed, but his grin was cheerful. "You know better than that. Jared's earned his freedom, and this chance."

Julian shrugged. No sense re-arguing the matter. All the same... "Can't blame a man for trying."

Raedrick just chuckled.

"How'd the Mayor take the news?"

Raedrick's mirth faded a bit. "He wasn't very happy about you going, but it's not like he can readily object as long as one of us remains in the Vale." He hesitated for a second, then added, "However, he was adamant about one thing: the town's not going to pay you while you're away."

"Come again?"

"The Mayor says since this does not fall under official Constable duties, so he considers it an unpaid leave of absence."

Julian winced. "Guess I should have seen that coming." He drew himself up. "No worries. I've got a fair amount of coin saved away. Paid my rent already for the time I'll be gone. It'll be tight on the road, but we'll make do."

Raedrick nodded. "Melanie doesn't seem to be lacking, anyway."

That much was certain.

The two of them stood in silence for a long moment. As the silence dragged on, the room seemed to get more and more stifling despite the sun having barely peaked above the western mountains.

Julian cleared his throat.

And was interrupted by the door swinging inward to admit Tolburt.

The rat was dressed for the road in loose-fitting plain wool, a patchwork of yellows and browns that didn't make him look especially well to do. Which, Julian supposed, was appropriate.

Tolburt grinned broadly, nodding to Raedrick in greeting before turning his gaze on Julian. "Ready?"

Julian tried the stern stare, but Tolburt's grin did not falter in the slightest. Finally, he just nodded.

"Let's get going then. Daylight's wasting." He turned to exit, but was brought up short when Raedrick spoke up.

"Hold, Jared."

Tolburt looked back at Raedrick, an eyebrow raising.

"So we're clear." Raedrick took two steps over and stopped directly in front of Tolburt. He looked straight into his eyes, and Tolburt's grin faded. "You're free to go on this trip, but Melanie and Julian are in charge."

"But - "

Raedrick held up his hand, and Tolburt shut up. "That's how it is. What's more, if the key you're seeking is as Melanie suspects, some powerful magical item, she'll be taking custody of it."

Tolburt's nostrils flared and he leaned forward, toward Raedrick. "Now see here. It's my claim, and I - "

" - Are entitled to any treasures you find there. Except magical ones." Raedrick smiled ever so slightly. "I've thought it through again, and I was wrong. The Falconer's Stairs are within the Kingdom's borders. The law is clear: any magical constructs, especially ones as powerful as Melanie thinks this is, are the property of the Magestirium. She will collect it, and then will make sure it gets put into their hands."

Tolburt clearly wasn't buying that notion at all, and for his part, Julian did not either. What, was Melanie just going to mosey on down to the Magestirium's headquarters and give it to them? Even if she had a messenger ship it to them, how would she explain acquiring it?

But Julian wasn't going to bring that up, not while Raedrick was laying down the law like he was. And not when Tolburt had no knowledge of Melanie's...special...relationship with the Magestirium.

Tolburt scowled, but after a few seconds' thought, he nodded acquiescence.

Raedrick's smile broadened, becoming more warm. "Do you have everything you need?"

Tolburt's eyes flicked to the side and he licked his lips. "Now that you mention it, I could use a sword."

"You've got to be kidding me," Julian said.

"There are bandits on the road, Constable," Tolburt said, looking askance at Julian, "and I lost mine a while back."

Raedrick studied Tolburt for a second, then nodded, gesturing toward the sword rack.

"Thanks." Tolburt retrieved one of the blades, and a scabbard, then he took a moment to unbuckle his belt and get the weapon into place on his hip.

"Good luck, Jared," Raedrick said, and the two men clasped hands.

After Tolburt had left, Raedrick looked Julian's way. "You're not going to have a problem with him."

It was a statement, but Julian couldn't help but hear a hint of a question in there, too. He shook his head. "Long as he doesn't try anything, should be fine. But I don't intend to let him out of my sight. You may trust him, but I don't."

If Raedrick wanted to press the issue, he didn't show it. Instead, he nodded and took Julian's hand in a firm grip.

"Be careful. There's no telling what the Butcher left there."

"Don't need to worry about that. I remember our cave all too well." Julian released Raedrick's hand and grinned. "Try not to burn the town down while I'm away, will you?"

Raedrick chuckled. "I'll do my best."

Julian laughed as well. But as he left the Constabulary, he couldn't help but wonder whether this was going to be the last time he laid eyes on the place. After all, you didn't go down in history with the nickname Butcher unless you've swam in a lot of blood.

One thing was for certain: Tolburt was definitely going to be on point for this operation.

❧ 6 ❧

OUT OF TOWN

Melanie was waiting, mounted on her black mare and dressed as though going to a ball, when Julian stepped outside. Her dress was cream and blue, divided for riding, and she wore a wide-brimmed bonnet on her head to shade her eyes from the sun.

Julian did a double take at Melanie's outfit. Seriously? It wasn't that it was surprising she would dress well; he had never seen her do anything but. And she certainly looked amazing. The blues set off her eyes, and the cream complimented her complexion well. A man could just stare at her all day.

All the same, he winced at the thought of those linens and silks getting stained, in all likelihood ruined, by the upcoming weeks or the road. They had to have cost a pretty penny.

Tolburt was not yet mounted. He was busily tying the reins of a sturdy-looking pack horse to the rear of his horse's saddle. And what a horse it was; a dumpy-looking brown mare that had seen better days and that he had clearly purchased at a discount.

"Good of you to join us, Julian," Melanie said wryly.

Julian paused from unhitching his horse and grinned at her. "I live to serve, dear lady." When she rolled her eyes, he chuckled. Some things never changed.

He took one last look over his gear. His saddle bags were full of spare clothing and supplies, his bedroll in place. He was a ready as he was going to be. "You two all set?"

"Obviously," was Melanie's reply.

Tolburt hauled himself up into the saddle of his horse, and nodded.

"Right. So what are we waiting for?" Julian took off his baldric and looped it over his saddle horn, opposite where his quiver hung, then saddled up. He managed a grin that he intentionally didn't make very friendly. "Lead on, Tolburt."

The bearded man's only reply was to nudge his horse into motion to the south, toward Main Street.

The passage out of town occasioned more comment than Julian would have expected. Lydelton was an early-rising town, so plenty of people were out and about. And it seemed every single one of them went out of their way to greet the three of them and wish them well on their journey.

Or really, Tolburt. Oh sure, there were kind words for him and Melanie, but Julian was actually shocked how many people singled Tolburt out.

"Good luck, Jared."

"Save some of that treasure for me."

"Be safe."

That last came from, of all people, Molli Millens, The Oarlock's proprietor and mother of Raedrick's bride. Julian could hardly recall ever seeing Molli outside of The Oarlock's taproom at this hour; there were too many things to do with the breakfast rush. But sure enough, there she was on the side of Main Street in a frilly red dress and apron. She had a wrapped-up bundle in her hands, and stepped out onto the street as they drew near.

"I've brought your first lunch for the road," Molli said.

Tolburt reined in, and she held out the bundle to him. Tolburt looked surprised, but accepted the bundle with a grateful smile.

Molli returned the smile, then looked past him toward Melanie and Julian. "Good luck. Don't go getting yourselves killed over some trinket, here?"

"We'll do our best," Julian said.

She sniffed at that, then nodded. "See that you do."

And then they were off.

The paving stones of Main Street ended at the last row of buildings, becoming packed earth as they proceeded south and east along the shore of Lake Glimmermere. A short while later they arrived at a crossroads; the road to Silver Falls and Calas continuing on ahead of them along the rim of the lake, and the route through the steadily-rising grassy hills leading to Holbart's pass, and Mangin City beyond the mountains, to their left.

As they made the turn, Julian reflected that he had only taken this route once before, three months ago when they chased down Job, Iben, and Farley, the robbers who had stolen a fortune from the Covington Brothers.

A bit more than a year in Glimmer Vale, and he'd hardly set foot out of Lydelton proper. Somehow that didn't seem proper now that he was leaving the Vale completely. Why had he not explored the area more fully? There were probably as many people living in the Vale outside of the bounds of Lydelton as within, on farmsteads mostly. He and Raedrick technically had charge over all of them as much as the actual residents of Lydelton itself.

A pity they'd never taken that opportunity. If only…

He gave himself a little shake. What was this, was he getting homesick for a place he had only recently settled in, and that he hadn't really left yet? Hell, it's not like he was leaving forever.

"Get it together, man,' he said to himself.

But the feeling of impending loss stuck with him.

At one point, he turned around in his saddle and was surprised to see they had already climbed a goodly ways. The entirety of the Vale stretched out behind them. Lake Glimmermere, kidney bean shaped and rippling with the wakes from the fishing men's boats as the night shift returned to Lydelton's docks with their catch. Lydelton itself, spread out along the lake's northeastern shore but looking very small from this vantage point. The rolling grasslands to the south of the lake and the Glamorwood to the north and west. The Eastflow and the Northflow and, far off to the west, the rising mist that marked Silver Falls. And surrounding it all, the peaks of the Saddleback Mountains.

This place truly had become home, something that he would have not imagined possible a year and a half ago. And not just because it was a flyspeck of a village in the middle of nowhere.

"Are you alright, Julian?"

Melanie had reined in beside him. Julian hadn't realized he had stopped his horse, actually.

He rolled his shoulders and straightened in his saddle, flashing her a grin. "Yeah, fine."

She just looked at him for a long moment. Their eyes met, and he could see she was feeling the same things he was.

"Just hope we get back here in one piece."

Melanie nodded agreement.

"What are you two doing? Let's go!" Tolburt was maybe a hundred feet ahead of them on the road. He had stopped as well and was regarding the two of them with ill-concealed impatience.

Julian ground his teeth. But he had to admit Tolburt had a point. Sitting around grousing all day wasn't going to accomplish anything.

"Right. Let's get moving." He kicked his horse back into motion, and they proceeded east, toward Holbart's Pass and out of Glimmer Vale.

✳ 7 ✳

CONCEALMENT

An hour and a half later, Melanie pulled her horse to a stop. "Hold here, gentlemen."

Julian had fallen back so he was bringing up the rear. So when she stopped, he was pretty much forced to do the same.

Tolburt, on the other hand, had continued to lead the way all morning, and Julian was content to let him do so. If Tolburt was in a hurry to get himself into trouble, why should he stop him? Not that Julian really expected trouble here, within the borders of Glimmer Vale. But the principle was sound.

So it took Tolburt about twenty yards before he noticed they had stopped. When he did, he frowned and turned his horse around, then walked back to Julian and Melanie.

"Might want to speak up next time," Julian said, then grinned at Melanie's annoyed glance his way. She had spoken loudly enough. Tolburt had either ignored her or not heard her. Either way, it was foolish.

"What's the problem?" Tolburt asked as he halted his horse next to them.

"No problem," Melanie replied, keeping her expression even. "But I think it's time we start taking some precautions."

Tolburt looked confused.

"There are probably people watching for her, Tolburt," Julian said.

He blinked. "You're on the run too? Is there anyone in Lydelton who isn't in trouble with the law?"

Melanie's look could have shattered boulders. "You know better than that, Jared. I have an agreement with the Magestirium to remain in Glimmer Vale, which I am now breaking in order to make sure you don't get killed on your quest." To his credit, Tolburt held up under her gaze for a full five seconds before looking away in embarrassment. Sniffing, Melanie turned in her saddle and unlaced one of the pouches on her saddle bags. She began rummaging within as she spoke. "We are not yet fully into Holbart's Pass, so I doubt they will have set up any tracers here. But it is all but certain they will be in place further up the road."

She stopped her searching then and, with a satisfied nod, withdrew a fist-sized jar filled with…dirt?…from the saddle bag.

"Dismount please." True to her request, she slipped off her saddle. "And gather close. The effect does not extend very far, not without tremendous effort and expense."

Julian knew this drill. Melanie had cast a concealment spell on him and Raedrick when they first came to town and needed to scout out a lair of brigands. It had required a lot of chanting and throwing of silver powder, but it had worked.

Still, there was a problem.

"Do you have enough of that stuff?" he asked as he dismounted. "Last time it only lasted a few hours."

Melanie looked at him in confusion for a second, then shook her head with a slight chuckle. "Different spell, Julian. We do not need to hide from sight - "

"You can do that?" Tolburt interrupted, sounding surprised.

She stopped. Looked at him. Cleared her throat. Then continued. "Yes. Now as I was saying, the tracer won't be looking for us with eyes. It will sense out our…well really *my* essence. Loran Haversted spent enough time with me while he was here to gather a sufficient sample. So the counterspell just has to mask that essence."

"How long does it work?" Julian asked.

She pursed her lips and made a half-shrug. "A single casting should be good for about twenty-four hours." She hefted the jar. "I have enough of the required components for three dozen castings. It should be sufficient."

Tolburt looked doubtful, and Julian couldn't blame him. "This trip is going to take a lot longer than that. It's a month to Mangin City, and that's just the start."

"True. But I doubt there will be any tracers in place looking for me past there. Loran must presume that I could not make it further than that without being detected."

"That's a bit of a risky assumption," Julian said. "And what about the return trip?"

"I can resupply in Mangin City." She looked between the two of them, annoyance showing through clearly. "Now, if there's nothing more, gather close and hold still so I can do this."

Julian and Tolburt pressed in, standing shoulder to shoulder maybe an arm's length from Melanie. She took a moment to look them over, her lips moving slightly as if she were whispering to herself.

Then she bent over, placed the jar on the ground, and unscrewed its cover. A small measuring spoon lay partly buried in the dirt, or whatever it was, within the jar. She scooped out some of the dirt and carefully leveled it off, so as to not take more than was needed, then straightened.

Closing her eyes, she inhaled deeply and slowly. Then she began a chant. The words were in no language Julian had ever heard, that he could recall anyway. They came out in a clipped rhythm that was almost melodious, rising in tone and volume as she continued the casting until, at the very end, she practically shouted out the final word as she flung the dirt up into the air.

The powder separated as it rose and then, as it reached its zenith, a yellow-white flash emanated from within it for a second. The dirt drifted slowly back down, billowing around the three of them in a cloud of dust and twinkling little flashes.

Melanie breathed out, and opened her eyes. "It is done."

Tolburt frowned, looking from Julian to Melanie to their horses and back. "I don't feel any different, and you don't look any different."

"Well, you wouldn't, would you?" She bent over to retrieve her jar and, replacing the measuring spoon, screwed the top back on. Then she replaced the jar in her saddlebags and re-mounted. It took her a few seconds to arrange her skirts appropriately, and when she looked up from that she seemed surprised to see them still standing there, watching her. "Well, what are you waiting for? Let's go."

Julian and Tolburt shared a chagrined look. After a second, Tolburt shook his head, chuckling in soft amusement, and turned to move back to his horse.

For once, Julian could totally agree with him.

Women.

❧ 8 ❧

HOLBART'S PASS

T he land continued to rise as they rode to the east and north, rolling grassy hills that climbed on the front side more than they fell on the back side and often concealed copses of evergreens in the little valleys between them.

The road stretched ahead more or less in a straight line. It would have been easy to find even if it did not; the earth was packed solid by many years of travelers' feet, hooves, and cart wheels. And if worse came to worst, evenly stacked piles of pale stones rose on the road's edge at regular intervals. That was handy for telling distance as much as for keeping in the right direction.

They stopped for lunch beneath the canopy of a trio of pines that grew atop one particularly steep hill. Once the horses were unsaddled and given to graze, Tolburt eagerly unwrapped the package that Molli gave him.

The odors that wafted forth immediately set Julian's saliva running. If there was one thing Molli excelled at, it was spicy grilled fish. Sure, it was hard to find a bad fish recipe in Lydelton, central to the local economy as the fishing industry was. But Molli's speciality was, well…special.

They ate mostly in a loose circle, and mostly in silence, each to his or her own thoughts. For Julian's part, the meal brought back the feelings he had pushed off earlier. Damned if he wasn't going to miss this place, and not just because of the good cooking.

"What do you think this key is?" Tolburt asked, out of the blue.

Julian paused in the act of spitting out a fish bone to shrug. Hell if he knew.

Melanie, of course, was more eloquent. "The books do not say, Jared, and I already told you my guess."

He waved dismissively. "Yes yes. A magical construct. But what sort, I wonder."

"We'll find out when we get there," Julian said. "One thing at a time, Tolburt."

The younger man frowned slightly, but after a moment nodded. There really was nothing to be gained by speculation, after all.

They set off again shortly after that, Tolburt again taking the lead without having to be asked.

The mountains closed in relentlessly as they continued to climb: sharp craggy peaks, some of them still boasting snowcaps, that mocked the strain of their climb so far with the angle of their slopes. And gradually, the grass became more sparse. Bare rock soon became the predominate feature of the landscape, with the occasional tree, bent against the strong winds that must surely blow through the pass in the winter, the only source of green.

At long last they topped a final rise and beheld a long, narrow valley ahead and below them by about seventy-five feet. Steep slopes from the two mountains to either side of the valley's floor walled it off from the rest of the world, and it continued ahead for maybe a mile and a half before bending to the right, around the flank of the southern peak.

"Here we truly enter Holbart's Pass," Melanie said. And she would know. Of the three of them, only she had made the journey through this country before, on her initial trip into Glimmer Vale from Mangin City, more than a year ago.

"How far to where Isenholf's men set upon your caravan?" Julian asked curiously. He recalled her story easily enough, but he hadn't thought about it for some time. And seeing the lay of the land, it was easy to see why the brigands had been able to set up shop so effectively here.

"Two, maybe three miles ahead," she replied with a deep frown. "It was...difficult...evading them, even with my concealment spell."

Julian nodded his head slowly. Yes, there was not much cover at all down there, at least not in this section of the pass. It must have been a harrowing flight.

He glanced sidelong at Melanie. The frown remained, but her eyes were alight, almost glowing with an inner fire. It was not remembered fear lighting them up; it was anger over what had been done to her and her companions in the caravan. Of that, Julian was certain. He had met few women who could match Melanie for resiliency. Or for a thirst for justice.

Even though Lydelton vanquished the brigand band, he had no doubt she would have liked to have gotten her hands on them again, just to beat them down all over again.

He started to grin, but then another memory reached him: Marshall Leminster's news that Isenholf had escaped. The knowledge that they might have to do just what he had been contemplating a second ago drove mirth from him.

Good old Theobald was out there somewhere, and he would not have forgotten them.

Hell, he could be in Mangin City now, for all they knew. And wasn't that potential trouble that they had not even thought about before now.

No sense dwelling on it, though. "You said they felled a tree to cut you off. There's woods ahead?"

Melanie nodded. "Past the bend ahead a ways."

"Then I suggest that's where we camp for the night." Julian glanced at his companions again. "Unless anyone has a better idea."

A pair of head shakes settled that.

"Right then. Let's head out."

For the better part of two weeks, they traversed Holbart's Pass, and the terrain hardly changed. The days flowed, one into another, with the routine changing as little as the scenery. Up at dawn, pausing only for a bite of breakfast and for Melanie to cast her concealment spell again, and riding all day until very nearly dusk.

And all the time, the mountains on either side substituted one for the other, but they might as well have been the same for all the difference they made on the valley between them. Steep-sloped, with an almost flat area only a few hundred yards wide at the bottom that more often than not was crossed by a stream, or choked with a thicket, or presented some other obstacle. But the road continued on through the valley, weaving around the various obstacles naturally.

At one point, as they forded a stream that turned out to be quite a bit deeper than it appeared, Tolburt inquired as to how the caravans made it up the road, treacherous as it was in places.

"Slowly," Melanie replied, "and with difficulty."

"You might have noticed we don't get many caravans coming through the Vale, Tolburt," Julian added. "That's because the southern passes are easier. Safer too, since the treaty with the baronies down there. Once the raiding stopped..." He shrugged.

Tolburt frowned. "Must be tough on the town."

Julian nodded. "It has been, but we get by. Hell, the infrequent caravans were one of the reasons Raedrick and I came this way." He paused, then shrugged. "You know."

Tolburt nodded. He knew, indeed. He was in the same predicament Julian and Raedrick were; deserters all.

Well, not the *same* predicament. He was also a traitorous rat, while Raedrick and Julian had made something of themselves. Hell, they even had an arrangement with Marshall Leminster: if they kept the peace in Glimmer Vale, he wouldn't push the issue of their status.

No, Julian reminded himself. He and Tolburt were nothing alike.

The way continued to not be easy, and they were going downhill. Julian hated to think of the fact that, before long, they would have to come back through the other way.

It was not going to be fun at all.

But gradually, toward the end of the second week, things began to change. It was almost imperceptible at first, but between breaking fast and their stop for lunch, Julian noted that the central traversable area of the valley had widened, and the peaks on either side were perhaps a bit less tall than the last few had been.

In fact, come to think on it, he hadn't seen a snowcapped peak in two days.

As well, the gradual downward grade that had persisted for all this time decreased, easing the strain on the legs of both horses and people as they descended.

And then finally, they turned left around an outcropping of rock that jutted out from the peak to their north like a stoney tree that had been uprooted in a great windstorm, and emerged from between the peaks fully.

The suddenness of the transition took Julian aback, and he was reminded of Garrett's Gorge on the other side of the Saddleback range. That transition, too, was sudden, but it at least was an actual crevasse. This...

Well, it was like the southern peak decided to give up and not try to follow them anymore, and all of a sudden they were on top of a hill —a big hill—looking down on the whole world to the east.

"Wow," Tolburt breathed.

It was a sight to behold, that was certain. A few hundred feet beneath them, the hillsides were covered in trees, but here it was mostly bushes and bare rock, with a few scraggly trees here and there and patches of grass. But there was nothing to impede their view, and Julian could see, far off in the distance, a river twisting through the woodland, blue water flashing a reflection of the afternoon sun. And...

"Is that Mangin City, way down there?" He pointed off toward a darker patch near the horizon just north of east from their position.

Melanie followed his finger with her eyes and nodded.

"Doesn't look two weeks away," Tolburt said.

She sniffed. "It's not. If we could fly. But the road meanders in the woods, and we don't want to risk cutting straight through."

Tolburt looked as though he were about to contest that preference, but after a few seconds' thought, he nodded. He might be a rat, but he wasn't a complete idiot. Without a way to keep their bearings, it would be very easy to get completely lost in that forest. Best to stick with the road, even if it takes longer.

"At least the end's in sight," Tolburt said, and he nudged his horse into motion again.

Julian watched him go for a second, then exchanged a quick look with Melanie. She looked as bemused as he felt.

End in sight? Hell, they had barely started this journey.

MANGIN CITY

If Julian never saw another oak tree for as long as he lived, it would be too soon.

For the last week and a half, that was the only scenery they had: trees after trees after tress, with barely a clearing to find along the road, let alone a meadow or pasture. It was a good thing they had thought to bring fodder for the horses; two of the bags the packhorse carried was full of the stuff. There was not enough underbrush for the horses to get a decent meal without it, and that would have been ugly.

Oh sure, the woods were pretty enough. And the shade was nice At this lower elevation, the summer heat was more oppressive than it ever was in the Vale even at summer's worst.

But the endless monotony of it came to be grating after a bit.

Julian managed to amuse himself with a couple of evening hunts and succeeded in taking a buck on the fifth night that replenished their stores nicely. But that was all the variety the forest offered the entire time.

So it was almost with a sense of relief that he rode at the head of their little column out from beneath the canopy and into the direct sunlight a couple hundred feet away from the river he had seen from the distance, and a great stone bridge that spanned it.

And on the other side of the river, Mangin City.

It had been a while since he'd been to a proper city, and he found himself gawking for a moment before he caught himself.

Compared with Lydelton, the place was huge. Great stone walls, probably thirty feet tall and capped with crenelations and guard towers every hundred paces or so. A protruding gatehouse on the far side of the bridge complete with a raised iron portcullis and guard posts on either side of the gate itself.

And the noise. Even from this distance, the sounds of thousands of people, and all the arguments, laughter, and commerce that went with them, reached his ears in a mad jumble that raised the hackles on his neck for a moment before making him break out in a big grin.

"It has been a while," he said, reining in to let the others catch up as he just looked at it.

"Indeed," Melanie said as she came to a halt beside him. Glancing aside at her, Julian could not tell if she was excited to be back here or resigned. The two emotions seemed to be at war on her face for a moment, then she smoothed her features and took on an air of calm. "I take it neither of you have been to Mangin City before?"

Julian replied, "No," and on the other side of her Tolburt shook his head.

Melanie nodded. "I know a good Inn a short distance from this gate."

"Why not just continue north now?" Tolburt was sounding impatient again.

"I told you. I need to replenish my components. And we need a map of the area to the north, so we can plan the next leg. Besides," she sniffed sharply, "you both need to bathe. Badly."

Julian chuckled and nudged his horse forward, paying no mind to Tolburt's protests to the contrary.

When they reached the far side of the bridge, they came upon a small line of travelers waiting outside the gate. Waiting for customs, Julian presumed. And sure enough, looking up to the front of the line the guards were taking names and searching bags for contraband.

He frowned, considering that. It was doubtful they would have a deserters list with them, but it was possible. And Loran Haversted, or another of the Magestirium's agents, could have left Melanie's name for the authorities. It was a wrinkle he hadn't thought of before.

As they fell in to the back of the line and dismounted, he could not help but wonder if they were walking into a trap here.

But Melanie either had no such concern or didn't care about it. She simply led her horse past him, ignoring his attempt to stop her to discuss it, and took the lead in line, too close to the people ahead of them to make any discussion of the issue possible without arousing suspicion.

Great.

The line moved faster than he would have thought. Even though only half a dozen individuals were ahead of them, he figured a search would take some time. But before he knew it, Melanie was standing in front of the Sergeant of the guard and giving him their true names.

Julian had to restrain a groan over that. But a second later, with nary a look at the papers his assistant was holding on a writing board, and after a search that could barely be considered lackluster, the Sergeant waved the three of them inside.

And then they were through, past the twenty-foot long kill zone between the outer gate and the inner, thinner gate, and into the city proper.

The first thing that struck Julian was the smell. The noise, he had already come accustomed to. More or less. But the smell...

Body odor, rotting food, sewage, the stench of animals of all kinds, spices, and the smell of cooking meat all reached his nose at the same time. It was almost enough to knock him over.

Lydelton had a population of just slightly over a thousand adults, spread out in tidy dwellings and boarding houses without a wall to impede the town's sprawl. That combined with the breeze coming off the lake and through the passes on either side of the Vale tended to keep the smells down.

On the other hand, Lydelton's entire population could fit into one corner of Mangin City, and the people here were packed in seemingly cheek by jowl in comparison with Lydelton's relaxed spaciousness.

Julian shouldn't have been surprised by the press, and the odors that went with it. He had been in enough large cities before to know the drill.

But he was. Good clean country living had, apparently, made him soft.

He very nearly gagged for a second there.

"This way," Melanie said, and pressed forward into the throng of people without hesitation.

Julian moved to follow, but a line of burly fellows in work coveralls and pushing wheelbarrows pressed between her horse and him. By the time they passed and he was able to move, he almost lost sight of her in the crowd. Only the fact that she was tall for a woman saved him from losing her completely.

He shoved his way forward, ignoring an annoyed oath from a fellow he cut off, and hurried to catch up.

"I'd forgotten about this part of city life," he said when he reached her side, trying to sound cheerful about it despite the rising annoyance the crowd was stirring within him.

"Yes, that is one good thing about home," she said tightly, and he could see the crowd was getting to her a bit as well. "To the right at the next intersection, then a half block down on the left."

After they made the turn, the press of people eased. That street must have been one of the primary thoroughfares in the city. The cross street was much easier, and a short time later they stood before a set of wrought-iron gates leading into what was clearly the stable yard of a prosperous-looking inn.

The Oarlock back in Lydelton could have fit within this place three times over, from the look of it. Four stories tall to The Oarlock's two, and longer and deeper to boot, it clearly saw a lot of business. Its stable yard alone was probably the size of The Oarlock's entire ground floor.

A wooden sign, painted garishly with the image of a fool in motley dancing atop a horse while juggling a half dozen balls, hung next to the gate.

"The Juggling Gypsy," Tolburt read from the top of the sign. "Are they serious?"

"A silly name, true. But I assure you this is one of the finest Inns in the city," Melanie said.

Julian shrugged. "You say so." As long as the beds weren't infested with rats.

"Come on."

The Inn's stablehands were the soul of efficiency. One look at Melanie's demeanor, and her attire, and the supervisor had his hands scurrying about taking charge of their horses almost before they had finished dismounting.

"Checking in, my lady?" the supervisor asked. He had that fakely-greasy tone of obsequiousness that seemed to go with service people who considered themselves just a bit more important than they really were. He bowed meekly enough when she nodded, but his eyes, beneath a peaked hat made from rough blue-dyed wool, were hungry, and just slightly contemptuous. Particularly toward Julian and Tolburt, who he obviously took for Melanie's servants.

"Very good, my lady," he said. "My boys will take charge of your bags. Bring them straight to your rooms, they will."

"Thank you," Melanie said, taking on the aloof tone of a woman of means, maybe even low nobility. Which was to say, not all that far from the tone she normally used around annoying people she had just met.

She handed over her reins to one of the stablehands, then turned away without a second glance and headed toward the Inn's front door.

"Pay the man," she said over her shoulder.

Julian had to force himself not to scowl. She *was* playing the lady and servant routine up, wasn't she?

Beside him, Tolburt chuckled softly, then handed his own reins off to a different hand. "You heard the lady," he said. "Pay him."

Then he followed Melanie to the door, leaving Julian standing there feeling all of a sudden like a complete ass.

It was all he could do not to leap over and throttle Tolburt where he stood.

But he couldn't exactly leave the stablehands unpaid. And it wouldn't do any good to start a fight and cause a bunch of trouble after having been in the city for less than an hour.

So, scowling darkly and thinking of all manner of nasty ways to let Tolburt have it later on, he opened up his belt pouch where he kept his money and handed the supervisor a silver.

Then, not waiting to hear the man's thank you, he hurried to follow his two traveling companions into the Inn.

❧ 10 ❧

THE JUGGLING GYPSY

I f you've seen one tap room, you've seen them all. Or so Julian
would have said a minute ago. But The Juggling Gypsy's was
unique.

While most tap rooms were fairly stuffy and at best dimly lit—
even The Oarlock's, and it was spacious compared with most—the
Gypsy's was bright and airy, with tall vaulted ceilings and oil lamps
hanging at regular intervals just up out of reach. The windows were
large and well-crafted, allowing a clear view of the stable yard on one
side and the street out front on the other.

The tables and benches were clearly of superior workmanship,
carved from mahogany unless Julian missed his guess, and the bar
along the left-hand wall was topped by polished marble. Marble
Opposite the bar along the right-hand wall was a semicircular stage
where, naturally, a juggler plied her trade to the accompaniment of a
flutist and harpist, all dressed in motley in the exact shades as the
fellow on the sign out front.

Pricey-looking tapestries hung from the walls, and the pleasantly
musky odor of high quality incense hung over the room, almost but
not quite suppressing the smell of freshly-baked bread and roasting
meat that wafted out of the kitchens in back.

There was no way they could afford to stay in a place like this.

Melanie and Tolburt were easy to spot, over by the bar. Or Melanie was, anyway. But then, she tended to stand out. She was speaking with a portly man with greying hair and a mustache-less beard wearing a pristinely white apron over a red shirt, who presided behind the bar like a king of the realm.

Julian hurried over to Melanie's side, ready to suggest they go somewhere else. But the innkeeper's words brought him up short.

"...always a pleasure to have you with us, Mistress Klemins. I believe we can work you into your usual suite." His eyes flicked past Melanie to Tolburt, appraising him for a moment. "How long will you be staying?"

"Two, maybe three days. I'll need a separate room for my companions as well."

The Innkeeper caught sight of Julian then and paused to look him over quickly before nodding greeting. "Of course." He extended his hand over the bar. "Oleg Kaversham."

Julian bit back the words of fiscal warning he was about to say and clasped hands with Oleg. "Julian Hinderbrook." He grinned, putting all of the warm friendliness he could muster into it. "Nice place you've got, Oleg."

The innkeeper smiled and inclined his head slightly at the compliment. "We do our best." With that, he turned his attention fully back to Melanie, all business. "Well then, I'll see you to your rooms so you can get settled."

"Thank you, but I recall the way, Oleg. Besides, I think we'll take a spot of lunch first. It smells like Sylvie has outdone herself today."

That caused Oleg to beam a smile in Melanie's direction. "I'll tell her you're here. I'm sure she'd love to see you again." He gestured toward a table in the far corner of the room, near a pair of double doors that led further back into the Inn. "You'll want your usual table, I assume?"

Melanie returned the smile. "Of course."

"Right this way."

Oleg led them past three long tables that were laid out in front of the stage, then to the table in the corner. It was mahogany, naturally, and was more a booth that anything else, with high-backed benches on either side of the table. And was that a draw-curtain across the gap between the two benches?

"Make yourselves comfortable. One of the girls will be by to take care of you in a moment, and I'll have my men go ahead and bring your bags up to your rooms," Oleg said, gesturing for them to seat themselves.

"Thank you, my friend," Melanie said, and took a seat on the rearmost bench, so her back was to the wall and she could see the Inn's entrance.

Julian had noticed she had gotten out of that habit over the last several months in Lydelton; when they all first arrived, you couldn't have made her sit without her back to the wall for any amount of money. It was a testimony to how much she felt at home in the Vale that she had eased up on her cautious ways.

But now, away from Glimmer Vale, it seemed those earlier instincts were back in force.

Not a bad policy, that.

Julian slid into the bench opposite her, and made room for Tolburt to do the same. He waited before Oleg had left before leaning in to speak quietly. "You know how expensive this place probably is?"

Melanie smirked ever so slightly. "I know exactly how expensive it is, Julian. Don't worry."

"Great."

Beside him, Tolburt piped up, "I tend to agree, Melanie. And we definitely don't need to stay here three days."

Julian shot a glare at him, and Tolburt flinched slightly. He had the grace to look a little contrite at least. Still… "Tolburt's right. Let's just get your supplies and get moving. This is expense we don't need, and some of us aren't getting paid for this trip."

Melanie's brow furrowed. "None of us are, Julian." She looked at the expressions on their faces and sighed. "The items I need aren't exactly common. My supplier should have them, but if he needs to restock it may take a day or two. We also need to learn more specifics about where this formation is. There are people in town who may have that information." Her eyes twinkled in the lamplight. "But all that pales in comparison to the need for a good bed and a bath."

Julian opened his mouth to reply, but he thought better of it. Some battles were lost before they were begun, and from the look or Melanie's face, she wasn't about to be budged. Not this afternoon, a- least.

So instead, he peeked around Tolburt's head looking for the

legendary waitress Oleg had promised. "Fine, whatever. I need an ale."

legendary waitress Oleg had promised. "Fine, whatever. I need an ale."

II

HARPS AND ALE

Julian had to admit he felt a whole lot better after a bath.

The Juggling Gypsy had men's and women's bath rooms on each floor, each equipped with a trio of large, cast-brass tubs that were just big enough to submerge one's self without feeling too cramped. He spent the better part of a half hour soaking and scrubbing, and after drying off and putting on fresh clothes he felt like a new man.

So maybe Melanie had a point.

He wasn't going to admit that to her, though.

The other good thing the Gypsy had was a laundry service. All he —and Tolburt, who he was forced to share a room with—had to do was put his grimy road clothes into a supplied bag and leave it just inside his door, and one of the staff would pick it up and see to getting it scrubbed.

That was service Julian had never experienced before, ever.

He tried very hard not to think about how much it was costing. It was the only way to avoid a stomach ache.

Shortly after his bath, he clumped down the stairs from his room on the third floor, across the hall from Melanie's suite—and why was she always getting a suite?—and re-entered the tap room.

It was getting on toward evening, and the place was quite a bit more packed than it had been when they arrived earlier. Men and women in colorful and obviously well-made garments lounged in the booths and on the benches of the taproom, almost to a person giving the small stage their rapt attention.

And well they should. The afternoon's entertainment had left, and in place of the juggling woman in motley, a woman with reddish-blonde hair in a blue skirt and white blouse sat upon a lone stool on the stage. She cradled a harp in the crook of her left arm and strummed out chords with her right while singing a haunting melody that brought Julian to a halt at the corner of the bar.

It was like she was casting a spell, so deeply did the tenor of her voice draw him in. Her tune and words contained a sense of longing, of loss, that brought forth in his mind, all unbidden, thoughts of home. Not Glimmer Vale, but Taris, the city by the sea where he grew up. Where his father worked on the boats and his mother kept him and his brothers clothed and fed even when the two of them obviously despaired of being able to.

He could never go back there. Not after fleeing the Army the way he, Raedrick, and the rest of their fellows did.

It had been a long time since he thought of that fact, but for whatever reason the song sent his thoughts back there. He saw his mother's face, the way she smiled when his father told a joke.

It was enough to break a man down.

Mercifully, the song ended a moment later. There was a long pause, and then the crowd in the taproom clapped heartily, if not exactly uproariously, for the woman on stage. Looking around, Julian saw many a watery eye; obviously she had affected them the same as him.

He sniffed and turned his back on the stage, facing the bar fully, and waved at the barkeep.

It was Oleg, the Innkeeper. As he approached, he gave Julian a knowing look. "Hilda's a wonder," he said, nodding toward the stage.

"Yeah, she's alright, I suppose," Julian replied. He nodded toward the casks that Oleg had set up behind the bar, one and all tapped with shiny brass taps. "Ale."

Oleg raised an eyebrow but didn't say anything more. He just picked up a tankard, turned toward the closest cask, and set to filling it.

"Got something in your eye there, Julian?"

He stiffened and looked to his left, and saw Tolburt, two stools down, leaning on his elbows with his back to the bar and smirking at him knowingly. Like Julian, he had cleaned up, and now wore a light grey shirt tucked into brown pants that were held up by a thick brown leather belt. He must have left his sword upstairs, but a long knife hung at his left hip.

Tolburt's eyes twinkled with amusement as he regarded Julian.

Julian returned the amused smirk with a scowl. "Why don't you go bother someone else?"

Tolburt's half-smile faded and the twinkle of amusement left his eyes, replaced by smoldering anger. He pushed himself off the bar and took a step in Julian's direction. "What's your problem?"

For a second, Julian was so taken aback he couldn't muster a response. What was his problem? Was Tolburt really that stupid that he didn't know?

But then he thought back to what he knew about the man, and the various things he had done, and Julian decided that yes, it was possible he really was that stupid.

Tolburt thrust his jaw out. "Well?"

"Maybe you should think on that for a while, Tolburt. It'll come to you."

Oleg returned then and paused in the middle of setting Julian's tankard down, eyes flicking between the two of them. "No fighting in here, gents," Oleg said, his tone iron-hard. "I won't stand for it."

Julian held Tolburt's gaze with his own glare for another several seconds, then picked up his tankard. "No worries, Oleg," he said, not looking away from the traitor. "I was just leaving." He pulled a coin out of his purse and dropped it onto the bar, then turned away from Tolburt as deliberately as he could and walked over to one of the long tables in front of the stage.

There was a gap between a couple of skinny fellows in flowing yellow and green robes and a swarthy man in more subdued grays and blues.

"Mind if I sit here?" he asked.

No one objected, so he sat down.

He never looked back, but he could feel Tolburt's eyes on his back the entire time.

The hell with it. He resolved to have as good a time as he could, and who cared whether that rat was offended.

The young lady with the harp took a drink from a cup that she had left sitting on the floor next to her stool. As she lowered the cup back down, Julian noticed that she was, in fact, quite striking. The quality of her music had blinded him to that fact earlier. But now, from up close, the rosy tone of her cheeks and the green-blue of her eyes were easy to see, and he found he could not look away.

She could definitely be trouble, if a fellow wasn't careful.

Good trouble.

The singer strummed her harp again, and conversation in the tap room hushed. Then she began another tune, and Julian quickly found himself putting Tolburt and all thoughts of what he lost out of his mind. He just took a swallow of ale and relaxed back on the bench, and enjoyed.

The girl's voice drifted higher as the song drew on, and Julian found his spirits rising along with it, the melancholy of the previous song fading from memory as though it had never existed. By the time she finished, he felt as though he were sitting atop the world, and from a glance around it looked like everyone else in the tap room felt the same.

He joined in the thunderous applause that came at the end of her song, and could not help wondering if she wasn't some sort of pseudo-mage, like Melanie was.

Then she was placing her harp into a carrying case and snapping it shut, her performance done. The applause continued, becoming more wistful somehow as she put her instrument away, and she smiled broadly.

Two hands raised in front of her silenced the crowd, and she said, "Just a few minutes to get a bite of supper and wet my lips, if you will, then I'll be right back."

No one voiced objection; why would they?

And so she descended from the stage and headed to a table sized for two, though only set for one, in the rear left corner of the room. There she sat, facing the appreciative crowd, and a serving girl hurried over to take her order.

"She is something."

Tolburt's voice to Julian's right made him jerk away from his study of the singer and return to more immediate reality. Julian turned toward him, beginning a scowl.

Tolburt held up his hands in front of himself in a disarming gesture. "I'm here to make peace."

Julian snorted, and Tolburt frowned.

"Look, I guess you don't like me - "

"Oh, you've got no idea."

Tolburt paused for a few seconds, then nodded. "Fair enough. But I don't see why you can't let bygones be bygones the way the Corporal has."

Julian just looked at him incredulously. "You're kidding me, right?" He shook his head and took a quick drink from his tankard. "You really are dumb, aren't you?"

"Then what are you doing here, helping me?"

"I'm not here for *you*, Tolburt. I'm here to make sure you don't get Melanie killed."

Tolburt's eyes widened slightly, and then he grinned lasciviously. "So that's how it is. The two of you, huh?" He looked past Julian's shoulder toward the double doors leading back to the kitchens and the stairs to the higher levels. "I would have thought she was out of your league."

Julian's scowl must have been darker than he thought, because when Tolburt looked back at him, his smile faded completely and he swallowed visibly. He tried grinning again after a second, more placatingly this time. "You don't have to worry, you know. Trust me, I'm not going to do anything to her. Besides, she can take care of herself."

Julian snorted again. "That's rich, coming from you."

That smile faded again, and something darker crossed onto Tolburt's face. Guilt?

Well, he should feel guilty, the little weasel.

"Look," Julian said, leaning in a bit closer and meeting Tolburt's gaze fully. "You just do what we say and don't try to think on your own, and we'll get this stupid errand of yours done before you know it. Then you can go the hell away and we won't have to bother with each other anymore. Deal?"

Tolburt looked away. "I...was hoping..." Julian detected a hint of a plaintive tone creeping in there.

"Forget it. Like I said, I'm here to make sure Melanie gets back to the Vale in one piece, that's it." He took another swallow of his ale.

Tolburt pursed his lips slightly, then nodded. "Deal."

"Good."

Julian turned away from him and and went back to looking at the still empty stage.

A few seconds later, Tolburt got up and went away.

Took him long enough.

12

SHOPPING SPREE

The next morning, Julian found Melanie at a table near the front window of the taproom, sipping at a cup of tea. She had on another of her fancy dresses, this one dark red, that he had no idea how she kept from being destroyed on the road.

Yet she managed it, somehow.

"Join you?" he asked as he slid into the chair across the table from her.

She raised an eyebrow. "What would you do if I said no?"

"I guess that depends on whether you decided to spit fire at me again or not." He thrust his chin out impudently, but kept his tone teasing.

Melanie laughed softly and shook her head. Was she actually flushing? "That was…not one of my better moments. But you did deserve it."

The hell he did. But he didn't feel like spoiling the light moment by arguing the matter. "What's on the plan for the day?" he asked, to change the topic.

Melanie sipped at her cup. "I need to resupply some of my components." She arched an eyebrow, and he understood her meaning. She needed the component for the spell hiding her from the Magestirium's tracers. "Also we need to get our bearings for the next leg. Fortunately," she smiled slightly, "both can hopefully be obtained from the same man."

Julian nodded. "Great. Let's go."

"I'd like to finish breakfast, if you please," she said, archly. "Besides, Jared may wish to come as well."

"Doubt that. When I went up, he was well into his cups and going strong with a couple of burly local types. I'll wager he didn't leave the taproom until sun-up."

Melanie's earlier smile turned into a disapproving frown.

"He'd just be in the way anyway."

Julian turned in his chair and waved down the passing serving girl, an almost pretty redhead who needed to eat a few meals herself. She wore a plain blue dress with the white apron that serving girls seemingly could never do without.

The girl stopped and looked at him quizzically.

"We're ready to order."

The streets were maybe slightly less crowded than they had been when Julian, Melanie, and Tolburt first arrived in Mangin City. And it was just him and Melanie on foot, without horses. So Julian would have thought the going would be easier this morning.

No.

Somehow, despite the fewer people and lack of animals, he found himself getting jostled back and forth by passers-by constantly. It was difficult to walk more than five paces in a straight line, and he quickly took to walking with his hand clenched on his belt pouch.

He had no more income for the foreseeable future. It would not do to have his pouch slit this early in their travels.

But for whatever reason, Melanie seemed to walk through the crowd untouched and unbothered. Maybe it was her nearly regal demeanor, or something. But as lovely on the eye as she was, she certainly attracted attention, and Julian would have thought at least some men would try to come make nice with her. But no, everyone stayed away.

What was he missing?

She led him through five or six turns down packed, winding streets until finally they came to a stop before a two-story building made of brick, with a simple wrought-iron business sign announcing

"The Bowl And Quill" above the entrance, a red-painted wooden door with a fancy thumb latch for a door handle.

"This is it. Be polite, and do try not to stare," Melanie said.

"What, does he have two heads?"

"You'll see."

With that, she stepped up to the door, pressed the latch, and stepped within to the accompaniment of a ringing bell that was probably set above the inside of the doorway.

Julian followed, and immediately stopped as he passed the threshold.

He had never seen so many books in his entire life.

The front room of the shop was full of them. Dark wooden shelves that reached all the way to the ceiling, ten feet up, filled cheek by jowl with tomes. Each shelf had this sort of ladder on wheels attached to it, so a buyer could get all the way up to the topmost shelf. The entire place smelled of old paper and dust, and the light from the front windows almost seemed to be soaked up by the dark color of the shelving.

More light came from the back, where Julian could just see, between two of the six rows of shelves in the front, a long counter and at least one oil lamp.

Melanie didn't hesitate; she walked straight back to the counter. After a moment's gaping, Julian followed her.

The counter ran the length of the store, except for a narrow opening at the far left side where a person could squeeze through if he really worked at it. The proprietor sat on a stool behind the counter, and he...

Julian found he was gaping once again.

He had never seen man who was so...pretty.

There was no doubt this was a man. Even if Melanie had not told him, it would be plain from his cheekbones and the relative broadness of his shoulders, and from the wisp of an almost-not-quite tussle of hair that originated at the very center of his chin that nevertheless managed to stretch down a good two inches.

But he was made up. More than a woman. He wore rouge on his cheeks, and his lips were unnaturally red. His eyelids were colored a deep blue to offset the green of his irises, and he wore a flowing cream and blue robe that almost could be called a dress. His hair was the color of straw and wove down his head in languid waves that seemed as though they had been sculpted.

"Mistress Klemins," the man said in a voice that was perhaps a bit too high for his build. He got up off of his stool as Melanie approached and bent over the counter to give her a long, warm hug. "It has been too long."

As he released Melanie from the hug his eyes found Julian and his lips pursed slightly. "And who is your handsome friend?"

Julian, taken aback, could only managed a pathetic-sounding, "Uh…"

Melanie saved him. Of course. "Hans Olbermon, meet Julian Hinderbrook."

Julians stepped forward to the counter, and Hans extended a hand to him. "Charmed, my good man," Hans said, and they clasped hands.

For whatever reason, Julian had been expecting a weak grip, but Hans' could break an anvil. "Nice to meet you," he said, holding back a wince as the man released him from his iron grip.

Hans merely smiled warmly, thought his eyes had a suddenly penetrating look about them, as though he was sizing Julian up completely. Maybe a bit too completely.

Then the moment ended, and Hans looked back at Melanie. Whatever hardness he had reserved for Julian faded into total warmth. "What can I do for you, my dear?"

"You received my pigeon?"

Hans nodded gravely. "I did, and it was very hard to come buy." He tsked softly, then turned away from the counter and to a large chest-of-drawers he had standing on the rightmost wall. "But I managed," he said as he pulled open the center draw. He rustled about inside for a minute or so, then turned back around with a large jar filled with what looked like the substance Melanie used for her masking spell and stoppered with a sizable cork.

He set the jar down on the counter with a dull thud, and smiled at her. "I'm afraid I'll have to charge a bit more than advertised," he said, managing to sound apologetic but firm. "For the extra trouble."

"How much?"

"Five marks."

Julian almost choked, but he managed not to. Five marks!

"Done." Melanie slipped her hand into a pocket that he would never have suspected was there if he hadn't seen her use it, then pulled out a stack of coins. She counted the money out carefully before placing it on the counter next to the jar.

"A pleasure doing business with you," Hans said, and began to move back to his stool.

"One other thing, Hans," Melanie said, and he perked up slightly. "I need a map of the countryside between here and the eastern spur of the Saddleback range. And, if you have one, a detailed map of those mountains."

Hans' eyebrows lifted, and he pursed his lips again. "The first is easy." He waggled a finger toward a shelf behind them and to Julian's left. When Julian turned to follow the finger, he saw that unlike the other shelves, this one was full of hollow wooden tubes, most of which obviously held rolled-up parchments. "Tube twenty-one. But the second," Hans sounded apologetic, "I can't help you. The only map of the eastern spur I had was purchased three weeks ago. And frankly, it was almost fifty years old, so things have probably changed quite a lot."

Melanie frowned. "Any suggestions?"

Hans shrugged. "If you're going that way, I suggest you stop in Woodhaven. Charming little town along a tributary to the river Wendelyn. Lots of trappers and woodsmen stop through there. Everyone who knows the lay of the land anyway."

"Thank you, Hans. I will probably need more of this," she lifted the jar that she had just purchased, "when I come back through."

"And when will that be?"

Melanie paused, and Julian could see the gears turning behind her eyes as she worked the math. "A month. Maybe a month and a half."

Hans inclined his head. "I will have it ready."

***

The door to The Bowl And Quill shut behind them, and Julian let out a whistle. "What in the hell was that?"

Melanie chuckled in amusement. "Hans is a unique character. But don't let him fool you. He knows more than four other men combined, and he can be formidable."

"Yeah, I got that much anyway."

They began forcing their way back through the crowd, Melanie again taking the lead. "While we're out and about, we should resupply our other provisions."

"I was just thinking the same thing. Don't need to spend any longer here than we have to. Your Inn is pricey."

Melanie chuckled again. "We'll leave first thing tomorrow, is that good enough for you?"

"Wonderful."

13

WOODHAVEN

The trip from Mangin City to the village of Woodhaven took just under a week. It was a bit more than a seventy mile trip as the crow flew, but just as in the case of the trek through the forest to Mangin City, the road meandered around obstacles, sometimes going miles out of the way before making any progress toward their destination.

If the obstacles had just been thickets in the wood, that would have been one thing. But they quickly left the forest of oaks and elms behind, emerging into a rolling grassland that became more and more interspersed with flat-topped rocky buttes. They ranged in height from a few tens of feet to several hundred, and in breadth from a few hundred feet to several miles.

On the bright side, it made for a scenic ride.

Still, after four days traversing them and only having covered thirty-five miles toward their destination according to the map Melanie had obtained in Mangin City, Julian was more than looking forward to getting past them.

Less than a day later, he got his wish, as the slowly rising terrain subsumed the buttes until all that remained were gradually increasing hills, and the shadows of the eastern spur of the Saddleback Range beyond them to the north.

Woodhaven lay on the western side of a mountain stream that flowed briskly toward an intersection with the great River Wendelyn, which traveled past Mangin City on its way to the sea far to the south. As Julian's party crossed a small wooden bridge that looked as though it had just been freshly stained a deep reddish-brown, he could see Woodhaven was not even the size of Lydelton. The buildings were low, constructed from felled logs for the most part and topped with thatch, with the exception of the Town Hall and the town's small chapel to the gods. Those two buildings rated slate shingles and walls of actual cut timber, painted in blue and white to match the town's banner, which flapped beneath the kingdom's on a little flagpole that stood in a small patch of green in front of Town Hall.

"Nice place," Julian said. And he meant it. Small though the town may be, it was well kept. The buildings were tidily maintained, the streets well-packed and kept clear of rubbish, the green spaces well trimmed, almost manicured. It was obvious the residents cared about their homes and wanted to present a good appearance to others, and he had been to enough shanty towns that obviously did not share that minimal amount of self-respect that he could appreciate it wherever he found it.

Melanie sniffed softly, then after a few seconds looking around, nodded agreement. "There must be an Inn of some sort. Though I question what sort of accommodations are possible here. Still..."

She trailed off and nudged her mare ahead, gracing the Town Hall, off to their right, with only a peremptory glance.

Julian couldn't help but chuckle. You could take the fancy city girl out of the city, but you couldn't take the city out of her. And never mind that Melanie had actually grown up in a village even smaller than Woodhaven: she was a city girl, through and through.

Beside him, Tolburt looked less amused by her attitude. "A bit uppity, isn't she?" he said, giving Julian a meaningful look, the sort you would normally give to a friend.

Julian just scowled at him, then kicked his horse to follow Melanie in her search.

Some people never learned.

Naturally there was an Inn. And it was small. A single story, and though it sprawled more than most of the structures in the village, it clearly had only a fraction of The Oarlock's capacity. It sat a short way up the main road from the Town Hall and, like the other buildings in town, was constructed of logs stacked atop each other, with a freshly-laid thatch roof and a couple of chimneys near its front.

Sure enough, when they entered after tying their horses to the hitching post out front, they found that the front room was...a taproom. Inns were nothing if not predictable in that regard. But despite that, the place managed a rustic charm that Julian liked immediately.

The furnishings were simple: six carved wood tables flanked by four chairs apiece and a small counter off to the left in front of a trio of ale casks. Everything was plain, unadorned but all the same the furniture's construction shouted that it had been built with care, by a skilled craftsman. A single flagstone fireplace, opposite from the little bar, stood empty but was pristinely clean. The walls were adorned with small woven images of hunting scenes, and the stuffed head of a large elk hung mounted over the fireplace.

The place smelled of woodsmoke, overlaid with a spicy odor that Julian could not place.

Nice place, except it was empty of patrons.

The innkeeper, seated at a desk adjacent to the entrance, was a young man, thin and dressed in plain grey wool, without the white working apron that Julian had grown accustomed to seeing Innkeepers wear.

Although, now that he thought on it, it mostly had been Molli Millens who did the apron.

He chuckled softly to himself as it came home again just how much Lydelton had come to dominate his view of what should be.

The innkeeper eyed them as they entered and nodded greeting, a professional smile coming to his lips. "Morning. Harlon Fingerson. Welcome to the Hidden Gem. You'll be wanting rooms?" His voice held a note of barely-suppressed hope as he said that.

Melanie nodded briskly, sparing a moment to glance around at the taproom's modest furnishing before regarding Harlon fully. "I trust the rooms are clean."

Harlon's lips turned downward into a small frown. "Of course, my lady. Betsy sees to every room each day, whether occupied or not."

"Very well," Melanie said, apparently finding his explanation acceptable. "My men will require their own room."

"No problem." Harlon rose from his desk, pulling open a small drawer to remove two keys. "You'll have the place to yourself." He gave a little shrug and managed a self-deprecating smile. "It's the slow season."

Was there ever a busy season here? Julian thought better than to ask that.

Harlon led them through a doorway at the back of the taproom, then past another doorway on the left that led into the inn's small kitchen and around a corner to the right toward the rear of the building. Their rooms were at the end of the hall, Melanie's on the right, his and Tolburt's on the left.

Harlon handed Melanie her key and smiled, much more warmly this time. "I trust you will enjoy your stay, my lady."

She accepted the key and inclined he head in response. "I'm certain we will, thank you." With that, she turned, unlocked her door, and stepped inside.

The door shut behind her solidly, leaving the three men alone to look at the door with bemusement.

"Guess we'd better get the bags," Tolburt said, resignedly.

"Did you really expect anything else?" Julian couldn't help but chuckle. Shaking his head, he looked back at Harlon and took their key. "Thanks, Harlon."

"Of course."

* * *

"Laying it on a bit thick, weren't you?" Julian said as he lugged Melanie's bag into her room.

It was a modest affair, as far as her taste in lodgings went. Just a single room with a bed sized for a single person, a dressing table with a mirror just a bit larger than a person's head, a four-drawer dresser, and in the rear corner, a narrow cabinet for hanging attire. Everything was competently carved from what Julian presumed was local wood, and stained a pale shade of yellow-brown. The bed's covering was a patchwork quilt of various flowers and other plants, and a little painting of a placid lake beside a forested mountain hung at the head of the bed.

It was homey, comfortable. And well below Melanie's normal taste.

Standing beside the dressing table, she shrugged. "Appearances, Julian. I'm the pompous lady of means and you two are my man-servants."

"Well," he said, plopping the bag down on the bed, "you've got the pompous thing down, anyway." He grinned to show he meant nothing by it, but she just rolled her eyes.

No offense taken.

"I did some asking around," Julian said. "Harlon knows a fellow who knows the back country here like his own face. He usually makes an appearance in the taproom in the afternoon when he's in town."

Melanie nodded. "Let us hope that he chooses to appear quickly." She looked around the room, and sniffed. "We really ought to push on."

Julian could not help laughing at that.

"Sure I know where the Raptor's Ascent is," the old man sad, looking at them through narrow eyes that seemed sunken into their sockets beneath grey-white eyebrows that went past bushy to overgrown. "But I ain't taking you there."

Melanie looked sidelong at Julian, who had to work to keep a frown off his face. He drew a quick breath. "Why not, sir?"

The old man snorted out a laugh. Instead of answering, he took a draw on his tankard. Smacking his (mostly toothless) gums, he set the tankard back down on his table and wiped his mouth on the back of his once-white shirtsleeve. It was more tan now, from all the dirt that had entrained within it. He definitely had the look of a fellow who spent a lot of time out in the wild, between the grimy clothes, outrageous eyebrows and a beard to match, and that little bit of madness in his eyes.

He certainly smelled the part, too.

"Don't call me sir, boy," the old man said in a tone that could either be gruffly amused or angry; it was hard to tell. "Name's Gamlin."

Julian nodded. "All right. Why not, Gamlin?"

"Place is haunted, that's why." His eyebrows rose to accentuate his words. "It's more'n a man's sanity's worth, to go there. 'Specially this time of year."

"I don't..." Julian looked away from Gamlin to Melanie.

She stood next to him in front of the old man's table in the taproom of The Hidden Gem. In the three days they had spent waiting for Gamlin to make his appearance, she had changed clothes. Her normal silks and linens were gone, replaced by blue wool that could have come from any number of small towns. Probably wanted to blend in; the gods knew Woodhaven was far from cosmopolitan. She still managed to look, if not regal, at least impressive.

She was frowning deeply now. "What do you mean haunted? And what's so special about this time of year?"

"Strange noises. Spirits flying around. You know...haunted." Gamlin shrugged. "As to the rest... It always seems to get worse in the summer. Don't know why; don't think anyone does. But it does, and that's all there is to it."

"If it's a matter of money - "

Gamlin held up a roughly-callused hand, cutting Melanie off. "It ain't."

She pursed her lips, pondering for a moment, then returned Julian's gaze with a small shrug as though to say, "Well, that's that."

Julian sighed. "Thanks anyway, Gamlin. Good day."

"You too," the old man said, nodding.

Julian turned to leave, following Melanie, who was already a step away. "There must be someone else who can show us the way," he said to her.

"Let us hope so," she replied. "There is a lot of country to cover."

"Hold on a second."

Julian stopped as the old man's voice carried across the small taproom. It had only taken a few steps to get almost all the way to the front door, and Gamlin hardly had to raise his voice to make himself heard. Still, he shouted.

Julian turned back around and looked inquiringly at the old man, who gestured for him to return.

"You really are determined to go there, aren't you?"

Julian nodded.

"Why?"

He paused. What reason to give? The three of them had decided to keep the true nature of their quest a secret. If word of the treasure got around, some damn fool would probably decide to try for it too and get himself killed. Or, worse, decide to jump them on the way to or from the Falconer's Stairs, and that was trouble they didn't need or want.

Fortunately, Melanie was quicker on the draw than he was. "I have read about the structure and wished to study it. The writings of the geological survey team who documented it are...lacking."

Gamlin snorted. "What are you, a philosopher of rocks?"

She shrugged. "Something like that."

The two of them locked eyes for a moment, then Gamlin returned the shrug. "I won't take you there," he said, but when Melanie opened her mouth to reply he continued quickly, "But I can draw you a map. Save you a bit of time, if you're determined to go."

"That would be very helpful, Gamlin. Thank you."

Another shrug, and then he grinned broadly, showing off those gaps between his teeth. "No skin off my back. Come back for dinner, and I'll have it ready."

"I'm sorry?"

His grin grew even broader. "That's the price, my lady.'

"The map, for dinner."

He nodded.

"With you."

Another nod.

Melanie looked dubiously at Julian. He nodded assent; what could it hurt?

"Very well, Gamlin. We'll return at dusk."

"No, no." He pointed a finger at her. "Just you."

Melanie's eyes widened in shock. "Are you asking me on a date?"

"If you want to call it that." Gamlin leaned back in his chair and stretched his back. "Been a long time since I've had a nice meal with a lady as lovely as yerself."

A two year old could have knocked Julian over with a feather, he was so taken aback. "You're not serious."

The look Gamlin shot him was far from friendly. "Totally." He regarded Julian for a long moment, then sniffed dismissively and looked back at Melanie. "Well?"

Melanie surprised Julian. He would have expected her to take affront, and skewer Gamlin with cold anger. Instead, she smiled very nearly as broadly as he had the moment before. "Very well, I accept." She raised the index finger of her right hand. "On the condition that you bathe between now and then."

Gamlin's eyes about bugged out. "Bathe? Woman, I'll have you know I've not bathed in - "

"At least thirty years, I can tell," she interrupted. "That is *my* condition, Gamlin."

He scowled, but nodded after a second's contemplation.

"Very well." She made a little half-curtsy. "Until this evening, sir."

He snorted, but the scowl was already beginning to fade.

$$\text{\textsectoriented}\quad 14 \quad \text{\textsectoriented}$$

THE RAPTOR'S ASCENT

Tolburt stared intently at Gamlin's map, his eyes squinting nearly shut in the overcast morning's grey light, and muttered darkly under his breath.

They were four days out of Woodhaven, and Julian could understand his annoyance. The map was anything but precise. A few squiggly lines that indicated branches of streams running down from the mountains. A pronounced valley that arced to the northeast, and finally a prominent peak that looked across a narrow vale to the outcropping that formed the Raptor's Ascent. It made the trek seem easy.

Of course, there were not two or three, but a dozen branching streams coming down from the mountains in the vicinity of Woodhaven.

That was not an exaggeration, either. In their first day climbing from the foothills into the eastern branch of the Saddleback Mountains, they passed at least that many flows, and they could not have been the same stream bending back on itself.

And there were plenty of valleys between the peaks, and many of them veered off to the northeast.

And naturally, every peak they made it past revealed another, apparently very prominent, peak beyond.

Their spirits, buoyed by Gamlin's cartography when they rode out of town, had lowered appreciably over the last few days.

"You really couldn't get Gamlin to come with us, Melanie?" Julian quipped, looking to his left toward where she sat, thin-lipped, upon her mare. She had kept on wearing the woolen dresses she had switched to in the village, this one green to match her eyes and trimmed in cream at the bodice.

She rolled her eyes, not even bothering to sniff at him.

Julian had actually been surprised at how well that worked. Or rather, how well Melanie seemed to have enjoyed her evening with Gamlin.

He had tried to talk her out of it, Tolburt as well. The old man was clearly just playing with her, and she didn't need to put herself out over it. Who knows if he'd really been to the Raptor's Ascent anyway? But she insisted on going; in fact she claimed to be looking forward to it.

So Julian had, grudgingly, spent the evening with Tolburt in the little dining area of their Inn, and she went off to entertain Gamlin. And when she came back, two hours later, she was smiling contented, with a self-satisfied look on her face, and holding a piece of parchment the size of that book of history she had shown them in her shop —Gamlin's hand-drawn map.

The old fellow had actually come through after all.

Now, though, Julian was back to wondering if he hadn't managed to take them all, Melanie especially, for a collection of fools.

"Hmm," Tolburt said, looking up from the map. "I think we're almost there."

Julian looked back at him doubtfully. "How do you figure?"

"We've been heading more east than north all morning."

Julian looked up at the overcast sky, visible between a break in the oak trees above them, then down the trees' trunks to ground level. It was all but impossible to tell from the sky, but from the way the moss was growing on the tree's trunk...

He nodded agreement. "Looks that way. So?"

Tolburt nudged his horse a bit closer to Julian's and held the map out for him to see. The younger man pointed at a particular valley that was crossed by two streams. "I think this is the stream we passed after we broke camp," he said, tracing his finger along the valley. "So we ought to hit this one in the next couple of hours."

Julian frowned. "You say so." He looked around at the tree trunks spreading out all around them. "But this looks like every other valley we've passed through so far."

"Almost. But look at this."

On the map, one particular mountain had been drawn wider than the others, like it had been stretched sideways. "I don't..." Then it hit him.

Earlier that morning, shortly after they crossed the stream, Melanie had noted a peak to the northwest that looked as though it had the top of it lopped off by some great woodman's axe. It almost looked like one of the buttes they passed between Mangin City and Woodhaven, except that it was surrounded by other mountains.

Which made it look even more strange.

He hadn't thought anything more of it at the time, just that it was strange. But now, looking at the map again, he saw it.

That stretched-out mountain lay on the northern side of the two-streamed valley Tolburt was pointing at. And that valley led to the one they sought.

From the scale of the map, it couldn't be more than a few miles ahead of them.

"Hot damn, Tolburt. I think you're right."

The younger man grinned then. He folded the map up, then slipped it back into his belt pouch. "Shall we?"

Julian gestured for him to lead the way.

Tolburt's estimate was correct.

Maybe an hour after their navigation break, they emerged from beneath the forest of oaks into a clear area that stretched the width of the valley. Tough mountain grasses fought against white and orange wildflowers for purchase in the rocky soil, with the occasional bush or sapling pushing up here and there. But for the most part, the terrain was clear ahead, except for a briskly-running stream that cut across their path and then down a narrow ravine leading to the south.

Sure enough, looking past the stream, it looked like their valley ended in another one that ran to the northeast. Julian could see copses in the distance over there: oaks, and probably firs or pines, but not the complete growth that they had just come through.

And over there, in the distance along the valley's direction of travel, one particularly large peak dominated the surrounding mountains. Like Tollard's Peak back in Glimmer Vale, it topped the other nearby mountains by half of their own heights, and its upper slopes remained white with packed snow despite the midday heat here at its feet.

Looks like Tolburt had been right.

Julian said as much, and Tolburt nodded, grinning in satisfaction.

"Like I said, trust me."

Julian didn't reply to that. Instead, something else occurred to him. "How come Gamlin didn't make the route more obvious on his map, I wonder?"

Tolburt frowned and took the map back out. They looked at it again, and no, still no recommended routes drawn there. Just Woodhaven, a few streams and valleys, and this one particular valley more prominent than the rest.

It was almost like he wanted them to get lost, now that Julian thought about it. But that was absurd.

"He was reluctant to even make a map," Melanie reminded him. "The place is haunted, remember?" She smirked as she said that, clearly not believing that claim.

Julian wasn't so sure. Not that he believed in ghosts. Not exactly. But he had seen a lot of strange things, and one creature from a different plane of existence. If Out-Dwellers were real, why not something that a person who didn't know any better would take for a ghost?

Regardless, that belief was as good an explanation for the map's inaccuracy as anything. And it really didn't matter. They were here.

Well, almost.

They got moving again. The travel was easier in the open terrain; certainly it felt like they were covering more ground without the forest's canopy blocking their outside reference points.

Even the overhanging clouds began to burn off. By mid afternoon, the sun was clearly visible behind the now thin cloud cover, as well as the occasional complete break in the clouds, on its way down to its bed in the east.

Things were looking up all over.

The tall peak—Julian decided to call it Tollard's Brother since he didn't know the mountain's actual name—grew ever closer until, as the sun began its final descent, Julian realized they were, in fact, riding up its flank.

The valley had been gradually growing more narrow as the day wore on, and they were unable to avoid the copses, pines all, that had been visible earlier. And for a time, the extent of the valley's contraction was not evident. But then they broke out into the clear just as the sky was beginning to turn orange-pink in the east from the approaching sunset, and Julian found he had to shield his eyes.

The snow and ice atop Tollard's Brother had caught the sunlight and was refracting it toward him almost like a beacon.

Julian looked away, and was surprised to find that they were, in fact, riding laterally across a moderate grade, the valley forgotten.

But no matter. The terrain rose easily, trees forgotten and only scrub grass and the occasional bramble offering any obstruction, until they reached the top of a hill that anywhere else would have been a fair-sized ridge. But compared with Tollard's Brother, it was barely noticeable as such.

Julian reined in atop the rise in surprised recognition.

Below them, the ground fell away in a steep slope, descending toward a roughly circular vale, maybe a mile and a half across. The vale was dominated by a lake so still it reflected the peaks on the other side as clearly as a mirror reflects a lady's face. On the north side of the lake, the vale was wooded in what looked like evergreens. The south side was mostly grass and rock.

It was almost like coming home, except for the vale's size.

"Oh my," Melanie said, coming to a halt beside him.

He was going to say something in agreement, but he noticed her eyes were fixed, not on the lake, but on the rising terrain to the lake's south.

He followed her gaze away from that perfect mirror and up the side of the ridge to its summit, and his jaw dropped.

The ridge ended in a double peak, the farther summit from them taller than the nearer, but it was the nearer that demanded his attention. It was craggy, rock strewn, and it seemed to twist and turn as it thrust its way skyward. From this angle, the striations of the rock looked like stairs. And at the top of those winding stairs, the rock bent up and over itself in just the right way that, from this angle, he would have sworn he was looking at a bird spreading its wings and about to take flight.

"The Raptor's Ascent," Tolburt said, satisfaction and eagerness coming through plainly in his tone.

The setting sun bathed the entire area in an orange-red glow, and for a second it appeared the bird's eyes were visible in the rock, a pair of fiery brands that gleamed with malice. And then the effect passed as the shadows lengthened, and it was just rock again. But Julian could not suppress a shiver as a feeling of encroaching dread came over him.

They had arrived, and he had the feeling that might not be a good thing after all.

SHIFTING SHADOWS

"Let's go!" Tolburt said, eagerness plain in his voice and his eyes fixed on the rock structure across the vale from their location. Before Julian could voice a protest, he nudged his horse forward.

The slope was steep, steep enough that riding straight down would have been dangerous, so Tolburt picked a path across the slope and downward to their right, the quickest direction around the vale to the Raptor's Ascent.

"Tolburt, wait." Julian shouted after him, but the other man did not respond, just kept going.

"It would be better not to rush into this," Melanie said, levelly.

"No kidding," Julian replied.

He scowled, but had little other choice than to follow Tolburt, so he kicked his horse's flanks and started after him at a jog.

Tolburt wasn't a complete idiot. He was just walking his horse; he wasn't trying to canter down the hill or anything idiotic like that. Consequently, Julian was able to catch up with him after only a hundred yards or so. By that point, they had already descended a fair distance, however, and the long shadows cast by the last glow of the sun plunged the vale, and its approaches, into premature darkness.

"Seriously, Tolburt. Wait." Julian said again, practically spitting out the words as he all but shouted at the man.

Tolburt glared at him, but slowed his horse, and then stopped altogether.

Julian reined in and frowned at him. "Do you have a plan or were you just going to go charging headlong into the gods only know what sorts of traps?"

"It's growing dark quickly, Jared," Melanie said, more gently, as she drew near. "I'm just as eager as you are to see what awaits us there. But I'd rather do it in the daylight, when we're rested." Her eyes flickered toward the looming rock structure, and Julian thought he saw a hint of apprehension there.

Gamlin's words in the taproom came back into Julian's head. "That place is haunted."

Looking up at the Raptor's Ascent now, the last red of sunset made it seem as though it was bathed in blood. Again that shiver went up his spine, and he swallowed. Hard.

"Let's get down to the woods and set up camp for the night," he said. He had to work to keep his tone calm; the sudden bout of nerves made him unsure of himself right that second.

Tolburt continued to look longingly upward, but after a moment, he nodded acquiescence.

The descent into the woods by the lake went quickly, despite their need to switch back to avoid over balancing. They lost the last of the light before they had gone more than a quarter of the way down, but Melanie solved that easily enough by conjuring one of her magical glowing globes that rose from her hand to hover about six feet over her head, so that it illuminated the area better than a half dozen torches.

Naturally, after she did that, Julian let her take point.

The blue-white light of Melanie's spell drove back the darkness well while they were out in the open. But once they got beneath the canopy of the evergreens, the trunks on either side seemed to loom toward them, pushing against the light as though trying to snuff it. There was an oppressive feel to the place, and Julian found himself nudging his horse closer to his companions without even thinking about it.

They moved, and it seemed the pines moved with them.

That was absurd, of course. It was just the effect of their continual movement causing the tree trunks' shadows to move that created the illusion, nothing more.

Still…

"This place gives me the creeps," Tolburt said.

"Yeah," Julian replied in fervent agreement.

It wouldn't do a lick of good, but he loosened his sword in its scabbard.

From ahead of them, Melanie chuckled. "You two really are something." She glanced back over her shoulder at them and raised a mocking eyebrow. "One old man says a place is haunted, and you start jumping at the slightest thing."

From the tone of her voice, she was neither nervous nor particularly interested in this little stretch of woods.

"Yeah well…it's still creepy," Tolburt said, sounding a bit deflated.

Melanie rolled her eyes and turned back to face front. Julian could have sworn he heard another soft chuckle from her.

The trees thinned as they approached the lake, then parted completely about twenty feet from the shore. As they broke out from beneath the canopy, Julian was struck by the immensity of the night sky above them.

Oh sure, he had seen the stars in all their glory countless times. Though he grew up in a city, he had spent most of his adult life on campaigns in the field with few lights around to drown out the stars' light. And for some reason, in Glimmer Vale the stars seemed a bit more crisp and bright. So it wasn't like he was seeing them for the first time.

But for whatever reason, as the firmament above came fully into view, a waxing gibbous moon starting its rise in the west just to the side of Tollard's Brother, his earlier unease was replaced by a feeling of awe.

Maybe it was the way the still waters of the lake reflected the night sky exactly. Or maybe it was the outline of the Raptor's Ascent, easily visible in the moonlight across the lake from where they halted. Or maybe it was just relief from getting out from under those trees and their seemingly creeping shadows. Whatever it was, he felt almost immediately better, and was glad for it.

They dismounted and set about getting camp squared away.

It was a clear night, only a few puffy clouds visible, and they were far off, and moving farther from the look of them. So there was little worry about rain, and Julian and Tolburt quickly decided not to bother with setting up shelter. Instead, they all unrolled their bedrolls in the grass a few feet from the lake shore.

Then Tolburt hobbled their horses near the edge of the trees while Julian went in search of firewood.

He immediately wished he had not. The shadows closed around him as soon as he stepped beneath the canopy, and that feeling of well-being vanished. Creeping dread returned, a slowly-rising chill going up his spine.

There were eyes in the forest, watching them. He was certain of it.

Julian swallowed and, drawing his sword slowly, backed up.

Something was moving out there. Something he couldn't see, but he felt it clearly.

It was watching. Waiting.

Coldly malevolent, and hungry.

He backpedalled more quickly, and his heel caught on a root. He went down hard onto his backside, and lost his grip on his sword.

At once, a soft hissing sound came from the shadows in front of him, and it seemed the darkness itself was gathering to lash out at him.

Julian pushed himself backwards with his heels and palms, scrambling to move quickly but not willing to take the time to get to his feet.

The hissing grew louder.

It was coming, and there could be no escape.

Mind all but blank with fear, he cried out and pushed himself backwards with all his strength.

All at once, light shone all around him, banishing the encroaching shadows to a distance of about thirty feet.

"Julian, are you alright?"

Melanie's voice, but it hardly registered beneath the pounding of his heart. The shadow was still out there, past the ring of light. Waiting.

They had to get out of here. Right now.

"Julian!"

Something struck his shoulder, and he jerked back to his senses.

He looked up and to the left, and saw Melanie at his side, her globe of light suspended above her. But that was not the only source of illumination. She held her hands in front of herself like a man getting ready for fisticuffs, but no man would want to trade blows with her, not with orange-yellow flames encircling her hands, ready to launch. She looked out into the woods, her eyes narrowed, focused.

To her left and a few feet ahead, Tolburt stood in a ready stance with his sword drawn. He looked far less poised than Melanie, almost as terrified as Julian had felt a moment ago. He flexed his fingers on the grip of his sword, and with his free hand, he wiped his brow before turning to look back at Julian.

"What happened?"

Julian shook his head, trying to clear it. "The shadow... it..." He swallowed hard. "We need to get out of here."

Melanie frowned, at the tremble in his voice as much as at his words, and looked down at him. "What did you see?"

He tried to find the words, and failed. "It was like something blacker than black. Like..." He cast about in his mind for an explanation. Finally, he recalled last summer. "Like when the Out-Dweller attacked."

Melanie's brows rose, and he thought he saw her jaw clench for a moment. "Impossible."

"Well I know what I saw." Slowly, Julian pushed himself to his feet. He wiped his hands on the thighs of his pants, and paused. "Or..." He shook his head. "I didn't actually see it. It was like..."

"Like you could feel it," Tolburt interjected. He looked away from them, back toward the darkness in the trees, and shuddered slightly.

Julian nodded.

Melanie lowered her hands and the flames surrounding them went out. "I sense nothing," she said, sounding perplexed. She was silent for a long moment, then shrugged slightly. "Come back to the camp. I can make us a fire without wood."

Julian nodded eagerly. He really needed to get out of these woods, right now.

He left so quickly, he almost forgot his sword.

Almost.

❧ 16 ❧

A SUBTLE MAGIC

The return to the lake shore lifted Julian's spirits, but not the way it had just a few minutes earlier. His experience in the woods was too fresh, the adrenalin still pumping through him.

And he could swear he heard, as they exited the wood, that hissing sound. Softer, just barely audible. But constant, insistent.

The moon had risen fully above the mountains by the time they reached their bedrolls, and the temperature had dropped noticeably. A thin film of mist had begun to form out in the center of the lake, lending an eery slant to the pristine landscape.

And was that something moving, over on the far side of the lake?

No, he did not feel much better about their situation at all.

Melanie sent her light globe further aloft, so that it hovered a good dozen feet above their heads. Then she looked at Julian levelly.

"Now," she said, crossing her arms over her chest. "Let's go over it again. Describe, precisely, what happened."

He told the tale as best he could. The words came out in a jumble that he wasn't sure made any sense. Melanie pursed her lips thoughtfully as she listened.

He finished, and she was silent for a few seconds, pondering. Finally, she said, "Are you certain you didn't imagine it? The woods at night can - "

"No. Damn it, Melanie, this isn't my first time out in the wild. You

85

know that." Julian turned away, staring back at the evergreens and almost willing the…whatever it was…to show itself, if only to prove he wasn't going crazy. "I'm telling you, there's something out there."

"He's right," Tolburt said. He stood closer to the lake, and he had not sheathed his sword. His eyes darted about in a nervous scan of the area, and there was a quaver in his voice that spoke volumes. "It's watching us."

Melanie looked between the two of them, her frown growing deeper. Probably wondering if they had lost their minds. Then she nodded quickly. "Let's see, shall we?"

Her saddlebags lay next to her bedroll. Squatting down, she opened a side pouch and rifled through it. When she stood back up, she held her spellbook, a small, leather-bound book with many tabbed pages, in her right hand and a bulging pouch in her left. Spell components, unless Julian missed his guess.

Melanie pressed the pouch into Julian's hands, saying, "Hold that please. Be careful not to touch anything." Then she opened her spellbook and flipped to a tabbed page about two thirds of the way back. She scanned the page quickly, then nodded in a quick, businesslike manner.

Setting the spellbook down at her feet, she took the pouch back from Julian and, reaching within, pulled out a small bundle that was wrapped in thin, crackling paper and tied off with a yellow ribbon.

Julian noticed all this in passing; most of his attention was toward the trees still. He fingered the pommel of his sword with his left hand, uncertain. Was he just jumping at shadows? Melanie didn't seem concerned. Then again, Tolburt was right there with him.

Of course, Tolburt wasn't exactly the most reliable person ever. So there was that.

Melanie dropped her pouch to the ground next to her spellbook, then closed her eyes and drew a deep breath. She began a low, rhythmic chant in a language Julian had heard her use before but did not understand, and slowly raised her hands in front of her body, hands cupped together and the bundle she had taken out of her pouch cradled in them. She chanted for several seconds longer, then closed her hands and drew them to her lips. Her voice dropped to a whisper as she spoke two final words.

Then she pushed her hands forward and spread her fingers. A

globe of yellowish light appeared where the bundle had been, then expanded more quickly than Julian could follow, spreading outward in all directions at once until it disappeared from sight, and the surroundings returned to the way they had been the moment before.

Melanie opened her eyes and looked around slowly.

"What was that?" Tolburt asked, his eyes a bit wider now, though he still had that quaver in his voice.

"A detection spell," she said in an absent tone. "If there is enchantment here, the spell will reveal its presence." She turned a slow circle as she spoke, her gaze sweeping over everything in sight. When her circle was complete, she remained standing still in silence for a time.

"Wha - " Tolburt began to say, but he shut his mouth when Melanie held up a silencing hand.

Finally, after several seconds of silence that seemed to take a year, she nodded slowly. "I was right. There is magic at work in this place. But it is faint, diffused." She pursed her lips thoughtfully. "I can't determine what it is intended to do, but I think it's safe to assume it was put in place by Hevergod's sorcerers to keep interlopers from his son's inheritance."

Julian nodded slowly. That made sense, but… "But you didn't see anything."

She shrugged slightly. "I am a practitioner," she said, as though it explained everything.

It didn't, of course.

"You're not saying you're immune to magic," Tolburt said, almost hopefully. He seemed to have gotten a better handle on himself now that they knew it was an enchantment at work and not some real menacing creature, or something.

Melanie chuckled softly. "Of course not. But Timon taught me to be cautious, and I know some personal defense charms." She paused. "Still, this magic is subtle, and my charms are…not. I suspect it could have penetrated them without much difficulty, had it been programmed to." She shook her head. "No, if I were to hazard a guess, I'd say the original sorcerers set the enchantment against mundanes, but not practitioners. Maybe at Hevergod's order, or maybe just as a precaution. They would have wanted to check up on the site, or in the worst case, retrieve Kalem from the Falconer's Stairs, and they wouldn't have wanted to have to fend off their own defenses."

"They couldn't just code it for themselves, personally?" Julian said, because that made far more sense.

"Oh they certainly could have. But they might not have been the ones returning. It could have been one of their fellows, in which case they would have to attune the enchantment for them as well. But you can't do that without the person present. So..." She looked at him and raised a meaningful eyebrow.

Put like that, Julian had to concede she may be right.

Still, it was an academic discussion, and not truly relevant for their current situation. He didn't know about Tolburt, but even knowing what he knew now, he couldn't look at the woods without that feeling of dread creeping back into him. He forced himself to remove his hand from his sword's pommel, and rubbed his palms together. They were sticky with sweat that had nothing to do with the long-since faded warmth of the day.

"Can you get rid of it?"

Melanie got that thoughtful look on her face again. After a moment's consideration, she shook her head. "I don't think so. It's too subtle. There's almost nothing to grab onto. Probably there is someone in the Magestirium who could do it, but not I."

That admission had to sting a bit, but she showed no sign that it had. She stood just as proudly erect as she normally did, and was giving him a direct look as though challenging him to make a big deal of it.

He wasn't that dumb.

"Well, knowing it's not real should help. Maybe. Not sure how much sleep I'll be able to get tonight, though. Tolburt?"

The younger man shook his head, and his eyes flicked back toward the trees.

Julian nodded. "Ok, I guess we'll just keep watch then." He forced a grin. "Just because magic is trying to scare us doesn't mean someone else might not be out there looking to get us. Right?"

"Or we could leave this vale for the night," Melanie offered. She gestured to the west, the closest ascent that did not pass through the woods.

Julian looked up the rise, and the urge to just flee this place came back, strong. Very strong. It was all he could do not to break into a run, now that the potential to leave had been given voice.

He licked his lips, not trusting himself to speak for a moment.

"More trouble than it's worth." The calm resolved in Tolburt's voice surprised Julian. Looking over at him, he obviously was in the grip of the same nameless fear that Julian felt. But his expression was set, firm. And his voice was steady.

Their eyes met, and Tolburt flashed a grin that said, "I got this."

Bloody hell. No way Julian could let Tolburt, of all people, get up on him here. He nodded.

"Yeah, the horses are nice and comfortable, and - "

As though they had been waiting for his words, the horses picked that exact moment to start screaming.

❧ 17 ❧

STAMPEDE

Where Tolburt had hobbled them earlier, the horses now reared and kicked, screaming in panic as if they had been set upon by a pack of wolves. Their tethers strained, and still they struggled, their eyes wide with fright and their screams growing ever stronger, more panicked.

And all the while, there was nothing accosting them. Nothing visible, anyway.

Julian sprinted toward them, but in the space of only a few steps, the closest, Melanie's mare, broke her tether and galloped away, still screaming.

The others were not far behind, unless he could get them calmed.

Of course, he was hardly calm himself, so probably that was not going to be very easy to accomplish.

Tolburt sped past him, his longer legs covering the distance with ease. But even he was not fast enough. The pack horse broke free, and then Julian's. They followed Melanie's mare in her mad dash up the eastern slope of the vale.

That just left Tolburt's animal.

Tolburt slowed as he neared her, making low calming noises, and Julian caught up to him.

The horse bucked and kicked every which way; there was no way to get closer than a dozen feet from her without risking injury unless she calmed down. And it didn't look like that was going to happen any time soon.

From out in the woods, a light appeared. Greenish yellow and diffuse, it seemed to emanate from everywhere at once, back beyond where sight could penetrate beneath the canopy of trees. It pulsed softly, and shifted in tint, and was at the same time entrancing and sickening.

Just viewing it sent Julian's head reeling as though he had spun three quick circles with his eyes closed.

He staggered backwards, pressing his hands to his temples as he attempted to regain his equilibrium. Beside him, Tolburt actually tripped and fell over.

The horse reacted even worse. Julian thought she had been struggling before; now she went absolutely wild. She pulled and strained at her tether until, with a loud snap, the tether broke and she was free.

She did not get very far.

Turning wildly, she launched herself ahead, but she must have been even more affected by the strange light than Julian and Tolburt were, because instead of bolting after her fellows, she veered toward the woods.

The sound of her impacting the first tree was like a punch landing against a man's cheekbone, but amplified tenfold. She screamed and turned, only to run into another tree, then another. Turn though she did, she could not seem to extricate herself from the trees' embrace. She collided again and again, and Julian almost thought the trees must have moved to intercept her, so unerring were the collisions.

But of course, that was impossible.

Finally, the mare tripped over something Julian could not see, and she fell sprawling onto her side. There she lay, screaming in panic and pain, struggling to rise but clearly unable to do so.

And the light vanished, just like that.

Julian had not realized he was on the ground. At some point, he must have stumbled and fallen onto his backside. His head still swimming, he looked around for the others and saw Tolburt laid out completely off to his left. Melanie was just pushing herself to her feet a few feet behind them. She looked a trifle sickened, but otherwise none the worse for wear.

So much for those protective charms of hers.

Julian, suppressing a groan, pushed himself up to his feet. He swayed there for a second, but kept his balance.

"What - " He paused, cleared his throat, then spoke again, more loudly to be heard over the stricken mare's cries. "What in the hell was that?"

Tolburt groaned, but said nothing.

Melanie… Melanie just looked stunned.

"I… I didn't see it coming," she said, utterly taken aback. "There should have been some warning from the spell I put up, but…" She shook her head. "That was something new, more powerful."

"You think?" Julian couldn't keep the sarcasm out of his tone.

That earned him a look from Melanie, but it was not her usual "don't mess with me" stare. She was clearly not up for that. "It came from nowhere, beneath the vision of my spell. I…I don't know what it was."

Well that was great.

Tolburt had pushed himself up onto his elbows, and was staring at his fallen horse with a stricken expression. Julian followed his gaze and sighed, then offered the younger man his hand, to help him up. Tolburt accepted it with a grateful smile, and Julian hauled him to his feet.

They walked over to the still-thrashing horse together, Tolburt surely feeling as much or more trepidation as Julian did. He really did not want to see what had happened to the poor animal.

Yeah, it was bad.

The mare's flanks and shoulders were torn open from her many impacts with the rough bark of the evergreens, the flesh hanging off in bloody strips exposing muscle beneath. But worse than that, her left foreleg was bent almost double in the wrong direction.

What she had stepped into to break her leg so was unclear, because even with Melanie's globe of light trailing them he could not see any deep depressions or the like. But then, they were dealing with magic here. Did there really have to be a visible culprit?

He let that, extremely uncomfortable, thought just ride right on by.

"Lame," Tolburt said, pity in his voice. "And even if she weren't…" He left the rest unsaid.

"You want me to take care of it?"

He shook his head. "No, I got it."

Tolburt drew his dagger and squatted down next to the horse. She was still squirming about, but she clearly was losing strength; her struggles were growing visibly weaker with each second.

Julian turned around—he had no desire to watch as Tolburt put the animal out of her misery—and walked back to Melanie.

She had followed a few paces behind, and from the look on her face she agreed completely with his not wanting to bear witness to this. Their eyes met, and they just looked at each other for a bit.

Behind him, the horse let out one final cry and then was silent.

Tolburt joined them a moment later.

"We're in trouble." Julian gave voice to the thought that had to have come to all of them when the horses bolted. "Took long enough to ride in here. On foot…" He shook his head, inwardly wincing at the notion of walking all the way back to Woodhaven, if not home. They probably had horses in Woodhaven—what place didn't—but would there be any for sale? And would they be worth a damn?

Tolburt's frown spoke volumes. "To say nothing of our supplies…" He looked over to the areas where the horses had been hobbled. When he got them situated for the night, he had removed their bags of supplies from their pack horse and stacked them nearby. And now they were all trampled, their contents crushed, scattered, or both.

"That's why we have bows," Julian replied.

Of course, hunting would take time. A lot of time, considering the few game trails they had seen on their trek into to the vale, time they could be using to get to the bottom of Kalem's birthright, so they could get out of here.

There was not much else to be said. They left the woods and meandered back to their bedrolls, each lost in their thoughts.

Dreary thoughts, Julian was sure.

It wasn't until they were most of the way back to the camp that he realized one positive thing about their situation.

That oppressive sense of dread, the encroaching hunter preparing to jump on them, the terror that he had been forcibly keeping down to prevent himself from turning tail and fleeing the vale right bloody now was gone. Vanished from his mind, as if it had never been.

Then again, maybe that wasn't such a positive thing after all.

He couldn't help feeling something even worse was due to happen any moment now.

18

DAYLIGHT

mazingly enough, the hammer did not drop on them that night.

Julian and Tolburt took turns standing watch; neither thought it proper to impose on Melanie to take a shift, and not just because she was a woman. She might be a mage, but she was not trained in woodcraft, and watchstanding. There were tricks to it that were easy to miss, and a slip-up could have disastrous results for their expedition and health.

More disastrous, really.

And truth to tell, Melanie didn't seem bothered by their planning without her. She simply tucked herself into her bedroll and closed her eyes without comment, like being watched over by them was her due.

It was his idea to do just that, but still, she could have at least offered to take some of the burden. Of course, Julian knew better than to go there.

He had the first watch, and he fully expected to have to rouse the others quickly, and probably often. Instead, the hours passed dully, slowly, and with great effort until it came time to nudge Tolburt awake and then take to his own bedroll.

When Julian awoke in the morning sunlight, he was honestly surprised at how refreshed he felt. Getting more sleep than expected was always good for that.

As he extricated himself from his bedroll, he spied Tolburt and Melanie sitting in the grass near the horses' area, going through the remains of the group's supplies. Julian winced. This was not going to be pretty.

He paused for a moment to stretch his back and left shoulder out. He had a knot beneath his shoulder blade and it took a little while to work it out; must have come across a rock or a root or something during the night.

By the time he got over to where Melanie and Tolburt sat, they had a sizable pile to their left that very clearly consisted of items that were too damaged or soiled to be of any more use. The pile to their right, which contained items that appeared more or less intact, was significantly smaller.

Julian winced. "It's pretty bad, huh?"

Tolburt nodded gravely. "We've probably got enough food for a week or so, but," he gestured toward what had once been a pretty decent pot that now rested atop the pile on their left. It was badly dented in three places. And not just on the side of the pot, either. That would have been easy to overcome. No, these dents were in the bottom of the pot, and where its walls and bottom met; the thing would not sit correctly again, not without spilling its contents. Tolburt finished his thought, "cooking is going to be…awkward."

Julian sighed. "So it's jerky and bread."

Tolburt nodded glumly. "And some cheese is salvageable."

That was less than optimal. But what the hell. "We've eaten worse," he said.

Melanie surprised him by nodding emphatically. "And I may be able to assist with some of the perishables." She set a crushed box down in the pile to their left and took a moment to brush her hands off before rising to her feet. "Regardless, we should have enough to complete our business here." She looked away from him, across the lake toward the Raptor's Ascent.

Julian followed her gaze with his own. "Did you find something else in that book that you didn't tell us about?"

She chuckled. "No, I still have no idea what…what else…lies in wait for us. But logically, I don't believe Hevergod would have made the challenges for his son too long-lasting. He was needed at court, and leading their armies, not traipsing about the mountains for months on end."

She made a valid point. Still… "Well no sense burning daylight, I guess." He looked over at Tolburt. "Ready to go see about this treasure of yours?"

Tolburt grinned up at him. He took a second to grab up a roll the size of his fist and toss it toward Julian. "Absolutely."

Julian caught the roll and took a bite. It was almost rock hard, the recipe having been modified only slightly from the one they used on long-distance sailing ships to keep their stores fresh. They had restocked in Woodhaven, but even this far inland, the recipe for hard tack had been adopted; practicality travels the miles easily.

Despite the roll's hardness it was tasty, and his stomach was growling in his belly. So Julian bore with the difficult chewing experience and did his best to enjoy the morsel.

Good thing there was a lake nearby, to wash the thing down with.

"Quite right, Jared," Melanie said, approvingly. "Breakfast first. Then," she looked back at the Raptor's Ascent, "we see what there is to see."

Tolburt inclined his head to her, still grinning. His spirits were remarkably high, considering their major setback the night before.

Speaking of that. "Shouldn't we try to find the horses?" Julian wondered aloud.

Melanie shrugged. "I can locate Seybyl when I need her," she said, and Julian realized with a start that he had never asked her mare's name before. Quite an oversight, that. "I suspect the others will not wander too far from her. We should have no trouble finding them when the time comes. Besides," she frowned in irritation, "if we bring them back here, there's no telling what will happen to them next."

That was enough to put a substantial downer on Julian's spirits, which had been rising steadily since he first saw the bright daylight when he woke up.

He nodded agreement with Melanie's final words. No use buying themselves more trouble before they really got into the quest.

He forced the last of his roll down and took a long drink from a waterskin that they had placed next to the right-hand pile. Then, taking the waterskin with him, he walked back to the lake to refill it.

On the bright side, his fear from the night before remained absent. That magic had fled. But as he filled the waterskin, he looked up toward the Raptor's Ascent and wondered what was to come. Whatever it was, he would bet good money it was not going to be pleasant.

It was going to be a very interesting day.

19

INTO THE AIR

Julian wiped the sweat from his brow and blew his breath out with as much force as he could muster. Then he drew a long, deep breath. Following that, he exhaled again, more slowly this time as he remembered back to his martial instructor from when he first entered the army.

Sergeant Falston had always counseled that the best way to recover from exertion was to control your breathing and take long, slow breaths in and out. It was the control he emphasized, not the length of the breaths. Control your breathing when you most wanted to gasp and cough, and you learned to control the rest of yourself for later, when it might matter most.

Or at least, that's what Falston said.

Julian had scoffed at the entire notion at first. If that were the case, why would you naturally default to sucking in air as quickly as possible when you exerted yourself?

The explanation Falston gave had been less than satisfactory at the time, and even now, years later, Julian could not take the man's reasoning seriously.

That didn't mean his method did not work, however.

He looked over his shoulder and winced at the glare of sunlight reflecting off the still waters of the lake in the vale below. Raising one hand to block the unexpected brightness, he realized with surprise that they had climbed an appreciable amount. Several hundred feet at least.

Sure, they had been walking for a couple hours, and lately more climbing than walking. But the southern slopes of the vale had not looked nearly that high from their earlier vantage point at the lake shore. He panned his head around, and noted that the slope they had meandered down the previous afternoon was already beneath their current position, though Tollard's Brother itself still dwarfed everything else in the immediate vicinity.

Turning back to the path before him, Julian looked up at the mostly bare rock and earth that lay ahead, and sighed.

They had obviously left the tress far behind, but he hadn't really noticed the sparseness of the grass on the flanks of the Raptor's Ascent until he looked back into the relatively lush vale behind them and below. Even the gentle breeze flowing past brought only the odor of dirt to his nostrils.

At least it wasn't too terribly hot. The climb was difficult enough without that extra bit weighing them down. His mail and pack were burdens enough. Stifling heat... He shuddered to think on that, and silently thanked the gods for little mercies.

"What happened to those stairs?" Tolburt quipped, from his position about fifteen feet above Julian and to his right. He was in the process of hauling himself up a short ascent that was very nearly vertical, and looked to be having the time of his life, from the way he grinned down at Julian.

Julian recalled Tolburt had always enjoyed scurrying up trees, back in their army days. That had endeared him to the rest of the squad, because he was so good at it, and it allowed them to get a better idea of what lay ahead of them when they had scout duty.

He still had it, looked like. But then, he wasn't wearing armor, so it was easier for him to be a mountain goat.

"Just an illusion," Melanie replied, from over to Julian's left and down a few feet, "caused by our distance from the formation. Little features become lost as our eyes integrate the..." She stopped and leaned forward, placing her hand on the rock beside her to steady herself. "Oh my," she said, more quietly.

Julian hurried to her side, pulling off the water skin he had looped over his right shoulder and handing it to her. "You alright?"

She accepted the skin with a grateful smile and drank, then nodded. "Yes." She handed it back to him, flushing slightly. "I suppose I've let myself get out of shape."

"I don't know about that," Julian said, slinging the skin back over his shoulder. "Do you need to stop, or - ?"

She narrowed her eyes at him, then pushed herself off the rock and resolutely started back up the rise.

Julian watched her go, half expecting her to stumble. But after a few steps, she seemed as spry as ever, so he shrugged and followed.

Above them both, Tolburt looked back down in their direction. His eyes met Julian's, and he smirked in a manner that was probably meant to be playful.

Showoff.

Finally, after a small eternity, the slope they had been clambering up reduced and then, in the space of a few paces, leveled off completely. The peak had been narrowing as they climbed, and now as it leveled off it was maybe a hundred feet around. They had, in the process of finding the easiest way up, rotated halfway around the formation. From this angle, the rock structure that topped the rise resembled nothing aside from a jumble of rocks.

"Doesn't look like much, does it?" Tolburt said as he came to a halt and bent over, placing his hands on his knees to help him catch his breath.

At least the strain of the climb had finally begun to show for him. Julian had barely been able to put one foot in front of the next for the last half hour, so badly did his thighs burn.

"If you've led us all this way and there ends up being nothing here, we are going to have some words, Tolburt," Julian said with as much sternness as he could manage. After all, he did not really think they wouldn't find anything; not after the magical shenanigans down in the vale.

Melanie wiped her face on a kerchief that she produced from her belt pouch and rolled her eyes at them, but said nothing. Instead, she walked—a bit gingerly—around the summit.

"Do you notice anything odd about this place?" she asked from a quarter of the way around.

Julian looked from her back toward rock pile in the center of the leveled-off area. He frowned. It really did just look like a bunch of rock. A bunch of rock that grew wider the higher up he looked; the formations that looked like wings from afar stretched probably a hundred feet beyond where they stood on either side. But they knew that's how it looked before they came up here. He looked around the summit again. He didn't...

And then he saw it, and his jaw dropped open.

"Is it a perfect circle?"

Melanie looked back at him and nodded. "It does appear that way, yes. We would have to measure to be certain but it does look as though someone or something leveled out this area quite precisely."

Tolburt frowned. "Kalem's father?"

She shook her head. "Remember, he referred to this place by name in your letter. So Kalem would have known about it, or it would have been common-enough knowledge that he could find it easily. I'm all but certain this structure predates Hevergod and his son by some time."

Julian moved to join Melanie in her circuit; she was now almost on the other side of the structure and she was going to pass out of sight soon. Probably better to keep in view of each other up here. It was a long tumble back down into the vale. Sure, the grade was not steep enough that sliding down would kill someone. But it still wouldn't be pleasant.

And then there was the climb back up.

"If someone built this place intentionally, why make it so only one side looked like anything? That seems a bit..." He waved his hand vaguely. "Odd," was all he could say to describe it. But that didn't really do the job.

Melanie shrugged slightly, but nodded. "There may be some mystical significance. People have always had a variety of beliefs on that subject."

"Yeah I guess, but that still doesn't sound right."

Tolburt spoke up, "Does it matter?"

Melanie looked as though she was going to snap at him for a second, but just as quickly, her expression mollified and she nodded.

"You are correct, Jared. We are here for a different purpose. Besides, we could only speculate at this point, anyway."

Tolburt grinned.

They had fully circled back to the side of the structure that faced the vale, and they stopped to look up at it from this new angle.

Even from up close, it really did look like a bird of prey getting ready to take off. The wings extending out majestically to either side. The taloned feet. The vicious beak on the head, that was stretched to look off toward the western horizon. It all fit; if just not as precisely as it did from afar.

"Well, this is definitely it," Julian said. "Now what?"

Melanie looked at him, then over at Tolburt. Their eyes met, and both shrugged.

It seemed that was, indeed, the question.

Finally, Melanie started forward toward the clutching talons that were the base of the rock structure above them. She reached the rock and stood there, motionless, for what felt like a long while. Then she spoke up.

"This is interesting."

Tolburt and Julian exchanged glances, then they walked up to stand on either side of her. Looking at the rock face, Julian saw immediately what she was talking about.

The rock was reddish-brown and well-weathered, smoothed by the passage of time and the elements. Yet here, about five feet above the base of the rock, there were lines engraved in the rock. The edges of the carving were sharp, fresh, as though they had been made within the last few weeks. They certainly could not have been five hundred years old, to look at them.

And yet, amidst the sharp angles and meaningless symbols, Julian could, after a few second's examination, see a single word carved there.

Kalem.

⚜   20   ⚜

THE FALCONER'S STAIRS

"You've got to be kidding me," Julian said, earning a shrug from Melanie. She didn't bother with any other response.

Julian reached out and ran his fingertips along the surface of the rock. Though smooth, it had a gritty feel, like sandstone, and a film of dirt rubbed off as his fingers traced over it. The rock beneath was more grey, and glinted in places.

His fingers reached the edge of one of the cuts and he pulled his hand back with a yelp. The cussed thing was sharp! Looking down, he saw a small line of red welling up from his fingertips.

"Bloody hell," he said, and he turned his hand so the others could see.

Melanie raised an eyebrow. "Interesting." She stepped closer and leaned in to examine the rock where Julian had cleared off the dirt. "This is not granite."

Julian sucked on his fingers to stop the bleeding, and snorted softly. Whatever kind of rock it was, it should not have been that sharp, even if those lines had been carved recently. Removing his fingers from his mouth, he said as much.

"Perhaps," Melanie replied. "Remember that Hevergod's men were powerful sorcerers. It would not have been terribly difficult for them to preserve this place."

"For five hundred years?" Julian couldn't keep the incredulity from his voice.

Tolburt seemed to agree with him. "Yeah, the rest of the thing looks pretty weathered."

She looked back at them. "So someone else carved this here then? Why? How? No one else could have known Kalem was supposed to come here." There was a moment of silence while Julian was unable to come up with a way to refute that. She nodded in a brisk, businesslike manner. "No, this is it." She turned back to the rock face. "Take a step back. I'm going to try something."

Tolburt swallowed visibly and complied. Julian did as well, and crossed his arms over his chest, curious.

This could be interesting.

Melanie pulled out her spell book and flipped open to one of her tabbed pages. She traced a finger down the page, mouthing words silently as she read them. Then, after a minute, she nodded and clapped the book shut. She pulled something out of the bag she wore over her shoulder and began to chant softly.

It sounded very similar to the chant from last night. At first, Julian thought it was the same chant. But it didn't last nearly so long this time, and instead of making a flinging gesture with her spell components, she crushed them together between her palms, and twisted.

A flash of light sprang out from the crevice between her two hands for an instant.

And then nothing.

Melanie drew a deep breath, her shoulders rising and falling easily, but aside from that remained still.

Julian was just about to ask what the spell was supposed to have done when the stone in front of them began to glimmer.

It was faint at first, but gradually it grew in brilliance until he was sure his eyes were not playing tricks on him. A blue-white radiance seems to flow through the cracks as though seeping out of the rock itself and running at random through the carved design.

It was actually quite lovely.

"Whoa," Tolburt said, brilliantly. Glancing aside at him, Julian saw an amazed expression on the man's face.

Seriously, he hadn't been with their unit that long before everything went to hell, but he had seen the mages assigned to their division doing their work. And he had been around Melanie for a while now. Another bit of magical shiny should not have amazed him this much.

Julian shook his head in a mixture of annoyance and bemusement at Tolburt's reaction.

He recalled a conversation he and Raedrick had with Melanie a few months earlier. "Is that the spell you worked out to detect magical constructs?"

Melanie looked back and nodded. "You remembered." She smiled, looking pleased, though she sounded surprised.

He rolled his eyes. She never gave him any credit.

He must have reacted more than he thought he had, because her smile faltered a bit and she flushed. He thought she was going to apologize, of all things, but instead she squared her shoulders and nodded. "Yes, this," she turned back to the rock face and gestured at the glowing designs within it, "is definitely magical. I don't sense any wardings or the like, so I don't think it's dangerous." She frowned, tapping her lips thoughtfully with the index finger of her right hand.

"Any idea what it is supposed to do?"

Melanie sighed, shaking her head. "It's powerful. Very powerful." She drew a quick breath. "Maybe I can - "

Tolburt interrupted, "I don't think so."

Melanie and Julian both turned to look at him. She looked curious, which was big of her.

Tolburt noted their stares and responded with a challenging glare of his own. After a couple seconds, his expression changed to one of incredulity. "Seriously?" He shook his head and stepped forward to Melanie's side. "Look. Kalem wasn't a sorcerer, he was just an excellent fighter and a leader." He raised an eyebrow at Melanie. "You told us that, remember? So if this is his quest, whatever this is supposed to do won't require magic. Otherwise he would have been doomed to fail from the start. His father doesn't sound like the most gracious of men, but he wouldn't want to leave his son with no hope of success. Right?"

Melanie blinked. Then after a brief moment, she nodded, chuckling softly. "You're right, Jared."

Tolburt nodded quickly, a self-satisfied grin appearing on his face.

"So do you have an idea of how to make this work then?" Julian asked.

Another nod. "Aye, I do. Stand back."

Melanie obliged, coming back to stand next to Julian with a look of curiosity on her face. She didn't seem at all put out by Tolburt's pushing her aside.

But then, why should she? This was his quest, after all.

Tolburt ran his fingers lightly over the rock, being careful to lift them up when they came near the carvings. He had learned from Julian's misadventure there. After a good minute or two of doing that, he took a half-step back and nodded to himself.

"Don't seem to be any latches or buttons."

"You think it's a door?" Julian hadn't considered that.

"Or a safe of some kind. Hevergod said the inheritance was at the Falconer's Stairs. That says strongbox, at least, to me." He drew his knife and tested the edge with his fingertip for a second. "I once saw Stefan do a thing…" He trailed off, and winced.

Stefan, Tolburt's erstwhile friend, had played him for a fool. Talked him into bringing him along on his trek into the mountains near Glimmer Vale looking for a cave that supposedly contained a great treasure. In reality, the cave, when Raedrick and Julian finally found it, only held Kalem's note inside a deadly magical trap. On top of that, Stefan had betrayed him, faking an injury to get rid of him and turning the map to the cave over to his real friend, the bandit Geoff.

That had been the misadventure that cost Povol his fingers and almost ended in Julian and Raedrick's death up on the flanks of Tollard's Peak.

Julian hadn't realized how much what happened had bothered Tolburt. Stefan's betrayal anyway, if not the rest of it. Looking at him now, Tolburt obviously found the memory of his false friend hurtful.

Served him right.

Tolburt shook off his memories and stepped back up to the rock. Moving to the left, where the first letter of Kalem's name was carved, he inserted the tip of his knife into the crack of the carving. He ran the knife down the crack as though he was writing the letter with the blade, tracing every inch of the crack.

Immediately, the carved letter began to glow.

Or rather, it started glowing in a different way than it had been at Melanie's enchantment.

The new emanation was red-orange, and cropped up immediately behind the knife as it travelled in the crack. When Tolburt finished with the letter, its entire length was aglow, and remained that way when he withdrew his knife.

Tolburt looked back at them with an excited grin, then moved on to the next letter. And then the next, repeating the process with increasing quickness each time.

All of the remaining letters in Kalem's name reacted in the exact same way. For a second as Tolburt stepped back to join Melanie and Julian, they just sat there, glowing red-orange and looking faintly ominous, actually.

Then a deep cracking sound issued from the rock in front of them. A new line in the rock appeared, splitting Kalem's name exactly in two along the length of the L. Two more lines appeared, at the top and bottom of the new line and parallel with the ground they stood on.

The rock face opened up, the two halves of Kalem's name swinging outward as though on hinges.

Grey mist poured out from inside the now open portal, covering the three of them for a few seconds and obscuring their vision. It was cold, clammy, and had a semisweet odor. It seemed somehow… unclean as it wafted around them. Normally, Julian would have welcomed the coolness in the face of the day's growing warmth. But something about that mist made his skin crawl, and he had to force himself to stand fast and not wipe it from his skin, futile though that effort would have been.

Fortunately, the mist spread out and dissipated quickly, and they regained their vision, if not their sense of well-being; Julian could tell from their expressions the other two had liked the mist no more than he had, but like himself they were working to keep their cool.

Tolburt recovered first. "By the gods."

Julian turned his eyes back to front, and he did a double take.

The stone doors stood wide open, and beyond them lay blackness. Blackness so deep it seemed as though no light had, or ever could, penetrate it.

Except that light did. White-blue light that had no discernible source cast a pale illumination onto a staircase, wide enough for two people to walk abreast comfortably, that started from just inside the door and ascended into infinity. Or if not infinity, it went as far as Julian could make out.

Mist crept down the stairs in a continuous stream and flowed out of the door, but now that it had a place to flow, it only extended a couple inches above the ground; it didn't even come to the top of Julian's feet.

The white-blue light made the mist glow an unearthly hue as it flowed. But neither that glow nor the light from above did anything to make the blackness all around any less deep.

The entire scene was eery. It was beautiful.

It was the single most terrifying thing Julian could recall seeing, even above the Out-Dweller that the mad mage Telurian had brought to Lydelton a year ago. At least that beast had form, and could be fought. The blackness surrounding the stairs was... Well, it was just empty, a formless void that drew him in deeper the longer he looked at it, and remained completely devoid of...anything.

It made some deep part of Julian's mind shriek in denial.

Nothing could be that dark. That empty.

He took an involuntary step backward and swallowed hard.

"The Falconer's Stairs, I presume," Melanie said.

❧ 21 ❧

RIFTS

Melanie's voice was cool, contemplative. But when Julian looked aside at her, he noticed that her hands were clenched into fists at her sides and her brow was furrowed. She was working hard to remain calm in the face of that insane void, the same as he.

"This guy Hevergod really did not like his son, did he?" Tolburt said. He, too, looked decidedly uncomfortable.

"What was your first clue?" Julian replied. "The entire idea of this sort of inheritance treasure hunt is twisted." He looked back into the rock door, at the misty stairs ascending beyond sight. He tried not to peer into the blackness surrounding them, and mostly succeeded. It made his head swim, and he looked away quickly. "Is it just me or do those stairs go higher than the rest of the mountain?"

"Hmm." Melanie still sounded contemplative. "I believe you may be correct. Fascinating."

Tolburt snorted. Loudly. "Fascinating?"

"You don't find it so?"

Julian looked back at them in time to see Tolburt's mouth twist in distaste. He flung a hand toward the open rock face. "That...is more disturbing than fascinating, you ask me."

Melanie actually laughed, and it seemed the stress she had been holding left her in time with her sounds of amusement. "Perhaps that is what is so intriguing about it." She raised an eyebrow at him, then stepped deliberately toward the opening in the rock face.

Julian had to restrain the urge to spring forward and drag her away, but he managed it. If anyone had the wherewithal to evaluate this…whatever it was, it was she, after all.

Melanie tapped at her lips thoughtfully for a moment before making a little nod of her head. "I suspect this is another trans-planar rift."

Julian blinked, surprised. "You mean like where Isenholf's brigands set up their headquarters in that ravine in the hills?"

She nodded. "If you recall, Raedrick and Selam reported the place was filled with an odd mist. And the passage rose much higher than the ravine could have allowed before reaching the place where the brigands made their encampment." She looked back at him and Tolburt, her expression deadly serious. "If I am right, this is going to be extraordinarily dangerous."

Now it was Julian's turn to snort. "We already knew that, Melanie."

"But not the depth of the danger." Her lips turned downward into a dark frown. "I do not wish to even speculate on what the result of falling off these stairs might be. Where you might end up." As if feeling the need to restate the incredibly obvious, she added a heartbeat later, "We must be cautious."

No kidding, Julian didn't say.

Instead, he nodded agreement. He drew a breath and rolled his shoulders, and the feel of his mail settling more naturally on his torso made him feel a bit more comfortable.

A bit.

"Well," Tolburt spoke up, "We didn't come all this way just to back down when the going got tough."

That was…surprising, considering the source. Julian looked Tolburt's way and found him wearing a determined scowl and standing proudly erect, his shoulders thrown back as he looked directly into the maw of the rock and did not flinch.

Except for the nervous tapping of his fingertips on the pommel of his sword, he looked the epitome of confident determination.

Julian found he was actually impressed. He nodded agreement. "Yeah. Let's get to it."

Melanie's lips turned upward slightly. "Very well," she said.

Then she turned and, stepping out, placed the toe of her left shoe onto the first stair. After a quick breath, she visibly steeled herself, then stepped fully onto the staircase.

Julian moved to follow her, and Tolburt came along at his side.

❦   22   ❦

EVER UPWARD

They had ascended half a dozen steps when the door behind them shut.

Julian had proceeded as quickly as he could while still being careful to verify his footing on the next step before committing to it. He kept his eyes firmly locked onto the stairs ahead of him, and Melanie's back two stairs above him. He didn't dare look aside into that horrible black void surrounding the staircase.

And besides, Melanie's backside made for a nice view.

He had just decided that maybe this ascent would be doable when the sound of cracking behind them caused him to turn around.

He very nearly lost his balance as the void seemed to grab his eyes and keep them locked in place while his body turned. But he managed to rip them away from that emptiness.

Just in time to see the last sliver of daylight from the world they had left wink out as the rock face closed with a thud so firm he could feel it in his bones.

Tolburt breathed out a vile curse and bounded down the few stairs they had covered. Reaching the rock, he pounded on it with the flat of his fist.

And the rock simply vanished.

Tolburt's oath turned into a bellow of surprise mixed with terror as the force of his swing caused him to overbalance. Arms pinwheeling for a second, he teetered at the edge of the stair he stood on, only black void ahead of and below him.

Julian acted without thought. He took the stairs two at a time and grabbed Tolburt's pack with both of his hands.

For a second he thought they were both going to go over. Then he heaved backwards with all his might, and the pair of them collapsed onto the stairs behind and above them.

They lay there for a long while, Tolburt breathing in quick gasps as his body came down from its panic-driven surge of adrenalin, while Julian just worked very hard to not think about the fate they had narrowly avoided.

"Thanks," Tolburt said, his voice trembling and his earlier poise gone in the face of his obvious relief.

"Don't say I never did anything for you."

Julian worked his way clear of the other man and pushed himself to his feet. Then he turned to begin the ascent again.

He heard Tolburt rise behind him. "No, really. Thanks."

Julian looked back at him, and he could see that the younger man was truly shaken, and also truly grateful. That was the last thing he needed, Tolburt thinking he owed Julian some sort of debt. Then he'd never be rid of the man. "Don't worry about it."

Above them, Melanie was frowning, but if she was concerned—or more concerned than she had been—she didn't show it any other way. "We now have only one path available to us," she said.

"Looks that way," Julian said, because it was obvious. "I just hope they left some sort of exit for Kalem at the end, and that we can use it."

"If they did not, that would defeat the purpose of the test, would it not?"

Julian shrugged. That all depended on whether the test was genuine or not. But that was a problem they could deal with when they came to it.

He gestured for Melanie to continue upwards.

The stairs went on forever.

At first, it wasn't so bad. The angle of ascent wasn't all that steep, and the stairs were spaced comfortably so that going from one to the next did not involve too much effort. But before long, Julian's thighs began to burn from the exertion of the continual climb, and he began dripping sweat, despite the pleasantly cool temperature of the air in the place.

Since he was the only one in armor, the others took longer to show signs of exertion, but soon they all walked hunched forward, feet trembling with each new step and breath coming rapidly. For his part, Julian's heartbeat thumped in his ears and his chest was on fire.

But if that were the extent of the discomfort, it would not have been—that—bad.

The bigger problem was the place itself.

It was completely silent, aside from the sounds of their footsteps and breathing, and the occasional exchanged words, though those were few and far between to conserve energy and breath. But at the same time, it seemed as though something was talking to them, just below the level of hearing. Something bent on their failure if not their outright destruction. Several times, Julian could have sworn he almost heard something, but then just as quickly the feeling faded.

Except for the unease that second of hearing-but-not-hearing imposed on him.

He found himself having to fight a growing dejection. The stairs had no ending. They were going to die here, gasping out their last breaths through parched throats as they tried in vain to get to a place that did not exist.

Better to just lay down the burden, save death the trouble.

Step off the edge.

It would be so much easier, so much less painful.

Julian hadn't even realized he had veered toward the side of the staircase until Melanie's voice, whipping into his consciousness with a sharp call of his name, brought him up short.

He came back to himself and found that he had his left foot raised and about ready to land on…nothing.

He could not hurry enough in putting his foot back down on the solid stairs and backing away from the edge.

"What are you doing?" Melanie's tone carried rebuke, concern, and confusion. All at once.

"I…" He stopped. How to explain what he had just experienced? He shook his head.

Beside him on the stair, Tolburt wet his lips, his eyes darting about nervously. "I know what you mean," he said, locking eyes with Julian. "It's like…" He spread his hands helplessly. "Like in the woods. But different." Tolburt lowered his gaze, abashed. "That doesn't make any sense."

Melanie's eyebrows shot up, and she shook her head. "No, it makes perfect sense. And I should have thought of it before. More manipulation; part of the traps the sorcerers laid here."

"You don't feel it at all?" Julian asked her, and she shook her head again. He sighed. "Just like before." Turning to Tolburt, he asked, "Did you bring any rope?"

Tolburt nodded and unlimbered his pack. Setting it down on the stairs next to him, he untied the clasp on the pack's main compartment and dug around for a few seconds. When he straightened, he held a strand of narrow rope in his hands.

Tolburt raised an eyebrow at him. "Buddy belay?"

Julian nodded. "That way if one of us loses his footing or - "

"The others can pull him back," Tolburt finished. He nodded briskly. "Good idea."

It took a minute to arrange, tying the three of them together at the waist with about six or seven feet between each other. When the job was done, Julian felt a bit more confident, if not comfortable, with their situation.

A bit.

Still, as they continued upward, each step feeling heavier than the last and the muscles of his legs protesting continuously against any further climbing, Julian silently cursed himself for a fool to come along on this quest.

Finally, after a small eternity of ever slower climbing, he ventured a look upward, away from the thing that had captured his entire attention for more time than he wanted to think about: the next couple of stairs.

At first, what he saw did not fully register. He had to blink twice, and rub his eyes with the back of his hands, before he could bring himself to believe. "Is that…a door up ahead?"

His companions both looked up; not one of them had the energy to do anything but stare a few feet ahead of themselves, and hadn't for a while now. After a few seconds, a broad grin appeared on Tolburt's face.

"It is. Hot damn!"

"About time," Melanie said, sounding completely spent and extremely relieved.

Their acknowledgements confirmed it. Standing there, perhaps a hundred feet ahead and thirty feet above them, sat a set of double doors. They looked to be wooden, with brass pull-handles on each half of the door.

A way out of here.

Julian's spirits, sunk down beneath the foot of the mountain a moment before, buoyed. He surged forward toward the door with renewed energy, practically tasting the anticipated fresh air on his tongue as he thought about getting out of this place and back to the normal world.

Melanie and Tolburt pushed with equal zeal, and very shortly they all stood in front of the door, breathing heavily and soaked in sweat but with a brightness in their eyes that spoke to hope. Or at least gratitude for an end to the monotony of their interminable climb.

The doors were far larger than they looked from a distance. Twelve to fifteen feet tall, made of solid hardwood, bound in blackened iron strips, they looked strong enough to hold off a battering ram for a good long time. Plenty of time for folks above to douse the rammers with boiling oil a dozen times or more before the doors gave way.

And didn't that bring up pleasant memories from the few sieges Julian was lucky enough to take part in, back in his army days.

The brass pull-handles were each as long as Julian's arm, and thick around as three of his fingers pressed together.

"Who was this made for, a giant?" Tolburt asked. His tone was lighthearted. Well, as lighthearted as possible in this place. But glancing aside at him, his serious expression said he did not rule out that possibility.

Melanie snorted. "There are no giants." Reaching out, she laid the palm of her left hand lightly on the wood of the door and closed her eyes. She murmured something quietly, just loudly enough to hear but not loudly enough to understand.

A few seconds later, she lowered her hand and opened her eyes, shrugging softly. "I can't find any new magics here. It seems to just be...a door."

Right. As if anything was completely what it seemed in this rift, or whatever it was. Just because it was not magically trapped did not mean there weren't more tangible dangers here.

Hevergod had built this place with both physical and magical security, after all. Or so Melanie's book said.

Julian peered intently at the area around the pull handles. "I don't see a keyhole, or a lock."

"Well then, that makes it easy," Tolburt said.

He reached out and took hold of the two brass pull handles, one with each hand.

"No Jared - " Melanie started.

"Tolburt - " Julian said at the same instant.

But Tolburt didn't hear, or didn't heed. Flexing his shoulders, he pulled on the humongous doors.

And they swung open silently, on hinges that were apparently as smooth now as they had been when this place was first made.

Julian took a reflexive step back, in anticipation of disaster when something nasty did something horrible to Tolburt. When that did not happen, he blinked, then belted out a quick half-laugh.

"Well," Tolburt said, grinning broadly. "That worked."

Julian laughed more loudly this time, and with more genuine mirth. Leave it to Tolburt to do something hair-brained, and have it work out.

Golden light poured out of the open doorway, engulfing the three of them and banishing the ever-hungry void that surrounded the stairs in waves of warmth and an overwhelming sensation of well-being. Of welcome, even.

Julian breathed in deeply, and smelled a faint hint of honey. It brought back memories of the bakery a block down from the flat where he had grown up with his parents. Mother always made a point to scrimp and save in order to get them honey cakes on the holy days.

His mouth watered at the memory, and he could not help smiling broadly, all of his cares vanishing in the all encompassing sense of wellness that the light brought.

His eyes were adjusting to the increased glare now, and he began to make out features in the glow. A large circular room, with a statue of some kind in the center. And were those other doors in the walls, leading off in every direction?

Without thinking, he stepped forward, drawn by the invitation of that light. Beside him, Melanie and Tolburt did the same.

He really should not have been surprised when the door slammed shut behind them as soon as they passed through.

But he was.

23

THE LORD MAGUS

The golden glow faded as soon as the door shut until it lit the room about as well as a series of oil lamps on the walls would have.

The smell of honey lingered, though. There was that, at least.

The room was probably thirty feet across and perfectly round. The wall was stone, the ceiling rising in a high dome that contained, at its peak directly above the statue, clear crystal through which he could see...red sky and pink clouds.

It made a stark contrast with the golden light within the room.

The smell of honey lessened, fading slowly away and leaving the air smelling stale, dusty. But the room was spotless, as though a platoon of maids had just come through and dusted the place in preparation for their arrival.

Julian blinked, some of that feeling of well being fading.

Where in the hell were they?

"Melanie," he said, not taking his eyes from the top of the dome.

"I see it," she replied. "Interesting."

"Isn't everything," Tolburt said softly. Not softly enough.

"If one has the wit to see it that way, yes," Melanie said tightly in reply.

Julian opened his mouth to tell them both to knock it off, but a flicker of movement in the center of the room drew his attention toward the statue.

It sat atop a circular dais, and was a life-sized figure of an elderly man in flowing grey and blue robes sitting on a chair that was almost a throne. His forearms lay limply on the arms of his chair, and his head hung forward as though he had nodded off to sleep. His hair was grey, long and flowing, as was his beard, though it was well manicured. A long wooden staff with a black ball at its top leaned from between his feet onto the arm of his chair adjacent to his left hand.

It took a minute of looking closely at the statue before Julian realized that…it was not.

In fact, the man's chest was moving, as though he was taking long, slow breaths.

This could be bad.

" - may not have gone to some fancy school, but I - " Tolburt was in the middle of saying, his tone belligerent, annoyed.

Julian cleared his throat loudly. "Shut it!"

His two companions looked at him, Melanie quizzically, Tolburt as though ready to throw down.

Julian gestured toward the man on the dais. "Look."

As though on cue, the man lifted his head, and his eyes flicked open. They were deep blue, and seemed to glimmer with cold intensity that called to mind winter's deepest depth.

Those eyes moved to regard first Julian, then Tolburt, then Melanie in turn. Then the man's lips moved, ever so slowly as though the effort of moving them was a thing he was unused to, into a frown.

"You…are not Kalem." His voice cracked, and its timbre called to mind the sound of a honing stone scraping against steel. But it also held a note of confidence, even power, that made Julian draw himself erect into a position of attention before he realized what he was doing.

A long, uncomfortable silence loomed for several seconds, as Julian struggled to decide what to do next. He had envisioned a lot of possibilities for what they would find here. But a living man addressing them was not one of them.

It seemed neither Melanie nor Tolburt had been expecting this either, because they hesitated as well.

The man on the dais rolled his shoulders, and the joints made audible popping sounds. Then, taking hold of his staff with his left hand, he pushed himself up onto his feet. More popping, from his knees this time, but the man's face showed no discomfort from the process.

He regarded them balefully, his frown deepening. "Well? Speak up! Who are you to disturb me?" His voice had recovered a bit. It did not crackle the way it had when he first spoke. It was deeper, more commanding.

Julian cleared his throat. Better answer the guy before he became annoyed. "Ah," he said, then paused when the man's gaze landed on him fully. It was like those eyes were peering straight through him and could see every inner recess of his being, down to his bone marrow.

Julian licked his lips and lowered his gaze slightly, so he would not have to fully meet the man's eyes. Not that he was scared, of course. It just seemed prudent, is all.

"I'm Julian Hinderbrook," he said, then gestured toward his companions. "This is Melanie Klemins and Jared Tolburt."

The man nodded slowly. "Are you servants of the Lord Magus as well?"

"Ah…Lord Magus?"

Melanie interjected, "He means Hevergod," softly. Then she spoke more loudly, to the man on the dais. "No. He is five hundred years dead, as is his son Kalem."

The man on the dais blinked, his frown diminishing as surprise flashed across his face for an instant.

"Five hundred years," he said, slowly, as though tasting the words. He shook his head. "Time runs differently here, but I didn't realize… Has it been so long?" Then he gave himself a little shake and the momentary look of introspection left him. His eyes narrowed as he looked closely at Melanie. "You have proof of this?"

Melanie blinked in surprise. "I have a book of history, but it is - "

"Show me."

"I cannot," Melanie replied cooly. "It is in my bag at our campsite at the foot of the mountain. And," she added, a hard edge coming to her voice, "it is in disrepair, thanks to what you did to our horses."

The man's lips turned upward into a small, mysterious grin. "Do I detect a rebuke, girl?" He chuckled softly. "How droll." After the briefest of pauses, he shook his head briskly. "I cannot accept your claim. It is entirely improbable that Kalem would have failed at the previous four tasks." His eyes narrowed dangerously. "You are thieves."

The black ball atop the man's staff began to flicker with flashes of white and red light. Julian sensed a growing pressure in the air, a buildup of potential like in the moments before a thunderstorm breaks, when the clouds are heavy and dark and the air is moist and warm, and it seems the air is so laden with humidity that it must burst.

The last time he had felt something like that, he had been standing between Melanie and Loran Haversted, when they almost killed each other the night they all faced down the Out-Dweller.

Oh, this was not good at all.

He stepped forward, raising his hands, palms open and facing the man. "Wait."

Those frosty eyes turned on him again, and Julian swallowed. Hard.

"We're not thieves. We, or rather he," he gestured toward Tolburt, "found a map that led us to the cave that held your freezing trap."

"A favorite of mine," the man said, and Julian thought he saw a twinkle in the man's eye. He turned toward Tolburt. "Show me."

Tolburt cast a withering glance Julian's way, but wasted no time in taking off his pack and undoing the ties that held it close. A moment's digging later, he held out a piece of paper, unfolded so that man on the dais could see its contents.

The bearded man pursed his lips, then gave a little nod. "That is my map." His eyes narrowed. "Where did you get it?"

Tolburt shrugged slightly and bent to replace the map into his pack. "Won it in a game of dice. Man I won it from said it lead to a cache of treasure."

Dice. Seriously, dice?

"Dice!" While Julian found that notion amusing, the man on the dais sounded as though Tolburt had just cursed his mother as a two-penny harlot. His eyes flashed, and his face twisted into an enraged scowl. "The path to birthright of the Lord Magus' son was passed to you over dice?" That flashing was moving faster in the orb atop the man's staff.

Tolburt froze where he stood and looked fully back at the man, then he nodded.

"Unacceptable."

"What is unacceptable," Melanie said, taking a half-step forward and crossing her arms beneath her breasts as she looked at the old man levelly, "is that you question us without even doing us the courtesy of giving us your name."

The old man's eyes swept back to her, but some of the wind seemed to have gone from his sails. The flashing from his staff slowed and his scowl, while not fading completely, lessened somewhat.

"I am the chief servant of the Lord Magus, girl. That is all you need know."

Melanie pursed her lips in thought for a moment, then her eyebrows lifted. "High Sorcerer Lucius Feirhard?"

The old man cocked his head to the side, clearly surprised. He did not reply, but Julian could tell Melanie had hit the nail on its head.

For her part, Melanie looked confused. "But...the histories said you stayed by Hevergod's - "

"The Lord Magus!"

Feirhard's tone, almost vicious in its insistence, gave Melanie pause. A moment later, she nodded. "You stayed by the Lord Magus' side and remained his servant until his death and the fall of his kingdom."

Feirhard's scowl departed completely, replaced by a slight, ironic smile. "As you can see, that is the truth." He spread his hands out to his sides, a gesture that took in the room, and really the entire building. "I serve him still. And for that reason," his eyes flashed again, "his son's inheritance will remain safe from those who would usurp it."

"Usurp? We found this place fair and square," Tolburt said, anger plainly showing through in his voice. "We - "

"So you admit you have come here for Kalem's birthright." Feirhard shook his head slowly. "You shall not have it."

"But - "

"You have no claim on it!" The power of the old man's voice was almost like a physical blow. He glared at Tolburt. Hard. Then turned that same look on Melanie and Julian. His little smile became broader, almost anticipatory.

"Kalem is dead," Melanie said, reasonably.

"And if you persist, you will join him."

The certainty in the old man's voice seemed to drop the temperature in the room to the freezing point.

Julian moved to his left to put distance between himself and his companions, his hand finding the grip of his sword.

Across from Melanie, Tolburt moved similarly; he retained some of his Army training at least.

Feirhard obviously noted their movements and, if anything, his expression grew amused. "Shall we begin then?"

Melanie stood still, eyes locked onto Feirhard's and her expression determined. "Don't be foolish." Though she didn't look away from him, she gave the clear impression the words were for Julian and Tolburt, not the sorcerer. "We didn't come here to fight."

"Pity."

Feirhard gave no outward sign of attack: no movement, no chanted spell, nothing at all. Between one moment and the next, a rainbow of misty tendrils erupted from the black ball atop his staff and whipped toward Melanie.

Her eyes widened and she started to move her lips, recoiling and raising her left hand in a warding gesture. But in the heartbeat it took to do that, the tendrils surrounded and enveloped her. On and on the glowing mist wrapped, encasing her from head to toe until, when the attack stopped as quickly as it began, she was left encased, statue-like, in a shroud of luminous, multi-hued strands.

The rope that had connected her to Julian, and on the other side to Tolburt, fell to the floor, severed, landing with a semi-audible pat that seemed, in that awful instant, to echo with the force of a thousand kettle drums.

Julian did not know what curse he shouted. He never gave thought to his advance. He simply ripped his sword from his scabbard and leaped at Feirhard, razor-honed steel streaking toward the man's neck.

The old man's eyes moved toward him, and, in mid-leap, Julian's muscles locked up entirely. He fell, landing awkwardly on his right hip and then rolling onto his back, his sword arm locked in mid-swing.

The golden light in the room glinted off the tip of his blade in the air above him, a stark counterpoint against the red of the sky atop the room.

Powerless to do anything but wait for the sorcerer's death stroke, Julian fumed in impotent fury.

He only had to wait for a few seconds.

Somewhere to his left, he heard Tolburt cry out, a mixture of pain and helpless anger.

And then all was silent, except for the swish of Feirhard's robes and the soft pressure of his shoes on the paving stones.

The sorcerer's face appeared in Julian's vision, eclipsing the dome in the ceiling with his mocking smile.

"My master may be dead," he said, and placed special emphasis on the word may, "but my duty remains. The Lord Magus' inheritance was Kalem's, but only if he proved himself worthy." An eyebrow rose slightly. "Mayhap you will prove worthy in Kalem's absence, and save your sorceress' life."

Then the old man vanished.

24

RAISED STAKES

The invisible bands that had been holding Julian's body loosened, and he half rolled more fully onto his back. His arms dropped to his sides, his sword clattering against the stones at his side as his fingers relaxed. He lay there, stunned, for a few seconds, his mind willing himself to move, to see to Melanie—and Tolburt, he supposed—but he couldn't force his limbs to move.

A groan from off to his left told him that at least Tolburt was conscious. That was something, at least.

It took a supreme act of will to make his body respond to his desires, but finally Julian rolled himself onto his belly, then rose up onto his hands and knees.

Lifting his head, he finally took in the scene.

Tolburt lay on his back, one forearm thrown over his face as though to ward off a blow or a very bright light. His chest rose and fell quickly, but he did not look hurt.

Melanie...

Julian's breath caught in his chest, and a lance of cold raced down his spine, turning his guts to water when he saw her.

She stood just as she had when Feirhard made his move, left hand outstretched, mouth agape. The tendrils of magic, or whatever, were gone, but she remained perfectly still. No blinking, no shaking. No hair waving from the normal small movements of her body.

No breathing.

"Gods, no." Julian vaulted to his feet and across the space between them, every fiber of his being screaming a denial as he reached out to her.

Two feet away from her, his outstretched hands ran smack into an invisible, but very solid barrier, and he came to an abrupt halt.

"What the - " He stepped to the right and tried again. The barrier remained.

Again he tried, and again, until he had circled Melanie's inert body completely. The barrier surrounded her on all sides, and stretched from the floor to as high as Julian could reach. It had some give, but that was like a thing layer of fat above a strong man's belly: something that would give you a bruise instead of a handful of broken bones if you punched him.

"Damn it!" He slammed the heels of his fists into the barrier, impotently. Then he did it again.

It hurt. It hurt a lot. But the pain was nothing before the sight of Melanie, lifeless. And unreachable.

"Oh hell." Tolburt had regained his feet, but he both looked and sounded poleaxed.

"You've got that right," Julian snarled, turning on the man and advancing, fists clenched. "Are you happy now, Tolburt? Proud of yourself?"

The younger man flinched, but did not retreat. Julian reached him and grabbed him by the collar with his left hand, drawing back his right fist.

"You stupid bastard! She's dead, and it's your fault!" Julian heard his voice break when he said the words. His vision blurred for some reason, and his entire body trembled.

Tolburt did not resist. He didn't even look at Julian, just kept his eyes of Melanie. "I'm sorry," he said simply.

The words brought Julian up short. His fist trembled in the air next to his face; all he wanted to do was throw it. Knock Tolburt to the ground, then hit him again. And again. And then...

"What?"

Tolburt finally looked Julian in the eye, and he could see clearly the veil of guilt in the younger man's gaze. "I'm sorry. I didn't want something like this to happen. I - " He looked away, his eyes lowering. In shame? Certainly not.

A pair of heartbeats passed.

"Go on, do it if it'll make you feel better."

Did it sound like Tolburt actually wanted to be hit?

Julian tensed his shoulder for the blow. Vengeance.

But Tolburt hadn't really been the one to cause Melanie's demise, had he? Beating the snot out of him might be satisfying, but…

No it wouldn't. It wouldn't at all.

Julian released Tolburt's collar and stepped back from him. He lowered his fist, and turned away.

He realized he was sniffling, and his vision was still blurry. He rubbed at his eyes and…was he tearing up?

Probably some dust in the air, kicked up by the scuffle with Feirhard.

"I don't think she's dead."

Julian wiped his eyes and looked back at Tolburt, who was back to studying Melanie, where she stood encased in her invisible prison.

Tolburt must have felt the incredulous look Julian was directing his way; he looked over at Julian and raised an eyebrow. "Feirhard said if we proved worthy we'd save her life, right?" He shook his head. "Hard to do that if she's dead already."

Julian blinked. Considered.

And cursed himself for a blasted fool. Feirhard had said that, hadn't he? But one look at Melanie in this state, and he had forgotten…

He turned his gaze back onto Melanie, and the earlier despair of his impotency in the face of her state returned. She was his friend, and he couldn't see a way to help her.

A voice in his head asked whether she really was just his friend. No, she was more than that. But…

But he did not have time to waste pondering that right now.

He drew a deep breath and tried to force himself to calm. Tolburt was right. She was not lost; not yet. But they would have to pass whatever tests Feirhard had waiting for Kalem if they wanted to save her.

Calm eluded him though. The best he could manage was a cold anger as he thought about that damned sorcerer.

Slowly, deliberately, Julian went bent over and picked up his sword from where he dropped it. Sheathing it, he managed a grim smile.

He would play Feirhard's game, and save Melanie from whatever it was the old man had done to her.

Then he would take it out of the bastard's hide.

25

DOORS WITHIN DOORS

Julian looked around the room, at the ring of doors surrounding the dais where Feirhard had sat. Slept. Whatever. For five hundred years.

A terrible thought came to him as he considered that. "How long have we been in here, do you think?"

Tolburt looked at him askance. "An hour, maybe two, I suppose." The question in his tone was plain.

Julian gestured at the now empty chair. "He said time runs differently here. He certainly couldn't have really been five hundred years old."

Tolburt's eyebrows rose, and he swallowed hard as realization came over him. "We'd better hurry."

Julian nodded agreement. "Or we might come back and find everyone we know long dead."

That thought sent a shiver up his spine. Sure, it would be interesting to see the development of the world in a couple hundred years. But he wasn't ready to lose his family, his friends. Not for a stupid quest like this.

Resolutely, and quickly, he turned his back on the dais and examined the doors. All were identical except for the one they had come through from the stairs; that one stood twice as tall as the others, and twice as wide.

"Do you have a preference?" He couldn't see anything that would make him select one door over another, but maybe Tolburt had an idea.

Tolburt just shrugged. "Not the one across from the way we came in." He nodded toward that particular door, directly across the circular room from the giant door. "That's too obvious."

Julian was inclined to agree. "Ok then."

He turned left and marched to the room's wall, and the door there. It was a quarter of the way around the circle from their entrance.

"This ought to be as good as any," he said, and then he took hold of the door's simple iron knob.

Beyond was a narrow hallway, just barely wider than the door itself and certainly without room for more than one man to walk through at a time. Despite the lack of lamps on the walls, the hallway was well-lit. It ran straight for about fifteen or twenty feet, then ended at another door, seemingly identical to the one Julian had just opened.

After exchanging a quick glance with Tolburt, who gestured for him to lead the way, Julian shrugged and stepped into the hallway.

Nothing happened.

So he moved quickly toward the next door. He heard Tolburt shut the door behind him and then rush to catch up, and stopped himself before he dressed the other man down. Yes, it was probably prudent to not leave a certain indication of where they had gone; that would slow any pursuit. But seriously, who would be following them here, of all places?

On the other hand, he could foresee any number of reasons to leave the door open.

Ah well, done was done, and he really didn't feel like arguing with Tolburt again. So, instead, Julian just pressed his ear to the new door and listened for a few seconds.

Nothing.

Straightening, he told Tolburt as much, then, when the younger man voiced no objections, he took ahold of the doorknob and twisted.

The knob turned freely, and the door swung away from him on hinges that ran so smoothly, without even a hint of a squeak, that Julian would have presumed they were brand new.

Subdued golden white light on the other side of the door illuminated...the room they had just left.

"Son of a bitch," Julian breathed as he stepped through the door opposite of the one he had opened just a few moments earlier. The dais and Feirhard's throne stood just where it had been, as did Melanie, trapped in her invisible prison.

They had done a loop.

Tolburt closed the door behind them and moved to the next door, immediately to its right. "Think they all do the same thing?"

"Only one way to find out." Julian nodded at him.

Tolburt returned the nod and opened the next door. Beyond was an identical corridor to the one they had just walked through.

Frowning, Julian loosened his sword in his scabbard then stepped into the hallway. "Wait here. And leave the door open this time," he said over his shoulder.

He waisted no time in the corridor, he just went straight to the end and through the door open.

And emerged on the other side of the room, looking at the open doorway opposite him, and at Tolburt's back.

Turning around, he could see the corridor, Tolburt standing in the doorway, and beyond him the dais…Julian saw his own back.

He got a crawling feeling along his spine, and was unable to suppress a shudder for a second there.

"I guess that answers that," Tolburt said, frowning.

"Yeah." Julian rubbed at his chin, thinking hard. He glanced around the room at the other doors in the walls. They couldn't all be the same way…could they? "Let's check the other doors. Just open them all up."

Tolburt blinked, surprised, then nodded as he understood what Julian meant. He went left while Julian went right.

Half a minute later, all of the room's doors were open wide, even the huge doors they had entered through initially. Every single one of them led to identical corridors that led to their counterpart on the other side of the room. Even the large entrance doors opened into that same narrow passage, and how that shift in size worked Julian could not imagine.

Not that it was easy to imagine how the room could loop back on itself like this. And yet, somehow, it did.

"Bugger me," Julian muttered to himself.

Tolburt was more demonstrative. "There's no way out!" He shook his head, eyes wide as he looked, futilely, from one door to the next.

His voice broke a bit as he went on, "No way out. We'll starve to death in here."

Julian snorted. "Doubt it." When Tolburt looked as though he was about to object, vigorously, Julian raised an eyebrow at him. "This place is a test, remember? Not much good if there's no way to pass it. This," he gestured toward the oddly looping doors, "is just the next step."

Tolburt took a deep breath and visibly worked to get himself under control. He mostly succeeded, though that tightness about the eyes that reveals deep stress or fear remained. Still, his voice was under control when he spoke again. "Ok, so we just have to figure out the key to the puzzle." His peered about, stopping as his eyes came to rest on the only other object in the room: Feirhard's throne.

Tolburt bounded up the dais and squatted down next to the throne. He looked closely at it as he ran his hands lightly along its parts, probing. "Maybe there's a catch, or lever, or something. You know, to open a hidden door."

That was actually not a bad idea, but Julian let Tolburt investigate on his own. The throne wasn't all that large, and he wouldn't need the help.

And besides, Julian had another idea. He turned his eyes upward toward the domed ceiling and the glass enclosure at its peak. And the strange, red world beyond the glass. Could be the way out was up there. Even if it required breaking the glass, if they could figure a way to climb up, it could work.

Except that Julian couldn't for the life of him see a way to boost themselves up that high. Even if they ripped every single door off their hinges and somehow used them all to construct a scaffolding of some sort—and that would be a neat trick without tools and fasteners—he still couldn't be sure it would reach high enough.

So much for that idea. Hopefully Tolburt -

"I think I've found something!"

Wondering at the fortuitous timing, Julian turned away from his pondering of the dome and joined Tolburt atop the dais next to the throne.

"Look here," the younger man said, pointing eagerly at the chair's arm that was closest to him.

Julian had to squint to see it.

The chair was intricately carved and inlaid with numerous depictions of men in uniform and armor engaged in combat, of mages casting spells and generally looking aloof from the bloodshed nearby. The engravings flowed upward along the arm and then up the side of the throne until finally, near where Feirhard's head had rested, they ended at a carved image of the sun peaking out over distant mountains.

All that was impressive enough, but what really drew Julian's eye after a few seconds was a secondary design, on the periphery of the armored men. The design consisted of five doors, all closed against entry but engraved with small letters near their top, just barely visible: K-A-L-E-M.

Tolburt looked up from his study of the throne's arm and grinned as his eyes met Julian's. "The doors are close enough to reach with all five fingers at once." He held his hand out to demonstrate; the tips of each finger could easily fall on the letter at the top of each door together. "Clever, that." Tolburt licked his lips and his shoulder tensed; he was preparing to apply force to the doors.

"Hold," Julian said, and Tolburt gave him a questioning look. "Did you check the other arm?"

Tolburt blinked, then shook his head.

Julian went around to the other side of the throne and, sure enough, the opposite arm had a similar design. In fact, looking at it more closely and then comparing it with the distance across the throne, he figured a single man of average size could easily activate all ten finger pads, if indeed the throne's designers had intended them to function that way.

It would be tricky, but a man could do it.

Julian gestured toward the engravings on his arm and stepped back. "Your duty."

Tolburt looked toward where Julian pointed and, seeing it, smirked slightly, but nodded. He rose and maneuvered around to stand in front of the chair, facing it. Then, leaning forward, he extended his hands until his fingertips hovered above each of the little engraved doors.

"Here goes nothing," he said.

Then he took a deep breath and pressed his fingertips onto the carved letters in each door.

26

DESCENT

For a second or two, nothing happened. Then a sharp click echoed throughout the room, emanating from the chair itself. The sound of rock scraping against rock followed, and the chair began to move backward.

Julian took a reflexive step backward. Tolburt jerked as though wanting to do the same, but he remained still. Probably didn't want to risk halting the chair's movement by releasing the carved doors.

And good that he did not.

As the chair moved, it took the rock it had been resting on with it, opening the top of the dais like a great maw spreading wide to swallow some prey whole. The opening beneath was black. Not the sort of completely empty, all-consuming black that had surrounded the stairs leading to this room, but the more normal black of a cavern that doesn't have access to light. Beyond the first few feet, the dimmed light of the throne room simply could not illuminate it further

But that light was sufficient to reveal flagstone steps leading downward, almost the mirror image of the stairs that ascended the dais itself, except that this new passage was more steep and clearly extended a long way down.

A puff of wind billowed forth from inside the downward passage, carrying with it the smell of damp decay, like one encounters at the edge of a hot, stagnant pool in summertime down south, where everything is swamps and biting flies.

Not the sort of place Julian was apt to remember kindly. Except for the way the women preferred to dress there, anyway.

The scraping sound ended with a solid thunk, and the throne came to a halt. After a few more seconds, Tolburt released the arms and hopped off the chair, over to the right side where the ground was still solid. Wiping his hands on sides of his pants legs, he came back around to join Julian at the opening and looked down into the new passage.

"Well, that did the trick," Tolburt said, sounding extremely satisfied, all trace of his earlier near-panic gone now that the path forward was plain to see.

Julian pushed down the impulse to say something snide in return; Tolburt had found the key to opening the thing, after all. Instead, he allowed a, "Good job, Tolburt," to escape his lips, and even managed to make it not sound forced.

It was good work, after all.

No matter how he hated to admit it.

Tolburt flashed him a grin that faded a second later. "Don't suppose you thought to bring any torches?"

So much for feeling better about their situation. Julian sighed bitterly, and shook his head.

"Crap."

That about summed it up.

There was nothing for it but to go down. They couldn't remain in that room; there was nothing there except no food and Melanie, trapped in her apparently timeless cage.

Her—their—only hope lay forward. And forward was down.

Fortunately, they still had the remnants of the rope they had used to tie each other together on the stairs. It only took a moment to untie the strand from around Julian's waist and then retie himself to Tolburt with what remained of his end of the strand that had connected him with Melanie.

That left a fair amount of flax-twine.

Julian managed, by scraping his knife along the stones making up the dais, to strike a few sparks into the untwined end of the rope. A few breaths later, the rope was burning.

It didn't shed a terribly lot of light, and it wouldn't last all that long, but it was better than nothing.

They hurried down the newly-revealed stairs, Julian leading the way and holding the burning end of the rope above his head, feeding the strand through his fingers as the flame approached to avoid burning himself and hoping they would reach some other source of light before the rope burned away to nothing.

The descent was straight as an arrow, the stairs grey flagstone and the walls on either side the same, so at least there was not the threat of an easy fall into eternal darkness that had threatened earlier. Still, it was not a comfortable descent.

As they went, the air became more and more damp, and the odor of mildew and decay grow stronger. Condensation began accumulating on the walls on either side, and moss began to grow on them, and on the stairs themselves, making the footing slippery and reducing their pace rapidly.

By the time the rope had burned halfway down, they were reduced to timid, tentative steps, testing each lower footfall carefully before shifting their weight downwards lest they slip and fall the gods only knew how far until they reach the bottom of the stairs.

Assuming there was a bottom.

That was a thought Julian could not allow himself. Of course there was a bottom. This place was made to test Kalem, not kill him outright. Sure, kill him it might, if he failed to outwit Feirhard's constructs; Julian had no doubt it was Feirhard who was behind the place's devious puzzles. But the Lord Magus would not have wanted his son summarily snuffed out.

Or at least, Julian hoped he hadn't.

The thought did cross his mind that the wicked old mage-king may have wanted to get rid of a troublesome heir, and fed him a line of hooey specifically to lure him into a place designed to be his doom.

That seemed like an awful lot of effort to go through when an assassin's knife would do the job just as well, though. Especially when the assassination could be blamed on a rival.

So he continued on, one hand holding the burning rope aloft, one pressed against the slime coating the ever more damp wall to his left in order to lend himself a little extra balance as he took his next step. And he tried not to think about what sort of puzzle might await them below.

"Probably big toads down there," Tolburt said, from the stair above and behind him. "I hate toads."

So much for not thinking about it.

"Toads? Really?" Julian lowered his foot down to the next step and slowly shifted his weight.

"Yeah. You ever really look at those things?" Tolburt's shudder was practically audible.

"Whatever you say, Tolburt."

Julian descended another step, trying his best to tune his companion out.

Just put one foot in front of the next. Take the next step. Worry about toads, or whatever, later.

Of course, that didn't help. He could not help but think, with each step lower, that any minute now he was going to come face to face with a frog—toad, whatever—with a mouth as big as his head, just sitting on a big rock and ready to pounce on him.

Naturally it would be him, not Tolburt. It would be just his luck, and besides, why torment Tolburt with death by his least-favorite animal?

Of course, that led Julian to thoughts of what he would look like with a great big frog clamped by its mouth to the top of his head, and he could not help but laugh at the absurdity of it.

First, it was a small chuckle. Then, as the image firmed up in his mind, it turned into a full-on belly laugh that forced him to stop mid-step onto the next stair.

He stood there, laughing, for what felt like a long time, until Tolburt's loudly clearing throat turned his attention to the stairs above, where Tolburt stood looking at him with a confused, and disapproving, expression on his face.

"Keep it down!" The younger man's eyes flicked past Julian, further down the staircase toward whatever lay below. He swallowed, then added, "What's so funny?"

Julian thought to try to explain it, but even doing that much made the laughter bubble up all the more vigorously. He couldn't stop it;

the guffaws just kept coming for a while.

Of course, Tolburt was right. His laughing was making a heck of a racket, and would alert anyone below that they were coming.

Then again, was there any chance creatures that lived down there didn't know already, between the light from their burning rope and Feirhard's all-too-probable alerting?

Still, after a few more moments, Julian managed to get himself back under control. Finally, taking a deep breath to suppress the last of his chuckles, he smiled ruefully at Tolburt. "It was nothing."

Tolburt looked exceedingly doubtful.

Julian rolled his eyes. "I'll tell you later, ok? Let's get moving before we lose our light." He turned back toward the darkness below them and shifted his weight onto his left foot, resting on the stair below him. Then he proceeded on to the next stair below that.

And below that.

And below that.

Through it all, he worked his damnedest to clear his mind of any and every thought except for safely getting down one more stair. As long as he did that, they had a shot, and that was a far sight better than the alternative.

And so, he completely missed the fact that the tunnel below them was gradually becoming brighter until twenty or thirty stairs had passed and he paused to take a drink from the water skin he had slung over his shoulder.

"Um…" he said, pausing as he lowered the waterskin to really take a look around.

"Yeah," Tolburt said. "I think we're getting near the bottom. He paused. "I hope."

Yes, the stairwell was definitely brightening. The shadows were less, the moss on the walls and stairs more clearly green than greenish-black as it was exposed to proper light. The ceiling was actually visible now, twice as high as Julian was tall above them.

Problem was, Julian could not find any source to the light anywhere. Not that he was going to complain about it; the rope was not going to last much longer. All the same, it was creepy.

Still, it was a positive development. Plus, it seemed as though the steps were getting wider ahead, the angle of their descent lowering ever so slowly as they continued down. That spoke to a landing in their near future.

Julian felt a surge of eager energy flow through him at that; he was well past done with this staircase. He grinned. "Let's move."

Picking up the pace was at first difficult, because the stairs remained slick. But after a few dozen stairs, the slow widening had lowered their descent angle enough that a slip no longer carried the prospect of a long and painful tumble down too may steps to count, so before long they were back to making good progress.

The light continued to brighten as well, and after a short while Julian snuffed out the burning rope, the better to preserve what remained of it, just in case. With the light came a growing warmth. Above, the room and stairwell had been just a tad colder than comfortable. Now, as they continued their descent, it became quite pleasantly warm.

Or it would have been, if it wasn't so damp. And the dampness just kept getting greater, becoming positively oppressive and turning the place into a smothering sweathouse.

Julian paused, wiping his brow with the back of his hand—for all the good it would do—and took another drink. His waterskin was half empty; if conditions continued on like this, that could be trouble.

Tolburt came to a stop on the stair next to him. He was dripping sweat and his shirt was plastered to his body like a second skin.

At least he was smart enough to not be wearing any mail.

"Not much further," Tolburt said.

"That's what you said fifteen minutes ago," Julian said as he continued downward.

But he was right. The stairwell widened noticeably below them, both in width of the passage and in width between the individual steps. And the ceiling continued to rise as well. After only a few more minutes of descent, they could no longer touch the walls without untying the rope that connected them to each other, and the distance between steps was a good three feet or more.

And then there were no more stairs. Just a level, featureless stone floor that seemed to stretch on forever and moss-covered walls that moved farther and farther away from them as the floor progressed and a ceiling that was now lost from view high above them. It was all lit by the strange, sourceless light. From somewhere in the distance came the sound of water dripping, but there was no sign of the source anywhere.

For that matter, there was no sign of anything at all.

"There's nothing here," Tolburt said, sounding at the same time awed, confused, and unnerved by the empty expanse that stretched out before them.

"Well," Julian said, turning to give Tolburt a punch in the shoulder that was maybe a bit harder than it should have been. "At least there's no toads."

Tolburt winced at the punch, and shot a dark scowl Julian's way. Then, after a second, the scowl turned into a half-hearted almost grin. "Yeah, I suppose there is that."

"No place to go but forward," Julian said. He made a sweeping gesture with his right hand that ended up pointing ahead in the general direction of that dripping noise.

Tolburt nodded, and, pausing only to untie the rope that connected them to each other, they headed out.

27

BARE SPACE

D rip.
  Drip.
  Drip Drip.
Drip

...

Drip Drip Drip

...

Drip

Aside from the strangely muffled sound of their footfalls and that of their breathing, the sound of falling water was the only noise in this vast, completely empty place.

And empty it was. Within a hundred paces, the walls on either side had retracted so far that they were lost to Julian's sight. Not long after that, they began to fade from view behind the walking men. Though there did not appear to be any when looking around up close, there must have been a thin mist in the air, to obscure the walls so quickly.

And all the while, the uncomfortably warm dampness, with its accompanying odor of decay, drenched their clothing and made breathing difficult, the air seemed so thick. Julian almost stopped to take his mail off, it became so uncomfortable.

Almost.

It was Tolburt who noticed the walls behind them beginning to fade. He cried out in alarm, and Julian turned to look, his hand finding the grip of his sword reflexively.

When he saw what had roused Tolburt's alarm, Julian released the weapon, but he did not relax. "That's not good."

Tolburt shook his head. "There's nothing to use to tell our direction. We might not be able to find our way back, once - "

Julian snorted. "What good would going back do us?"

The younger man blinked, then after a moment shrugged in concession to the point. "Still, I don't like not knowing where we're going." Pursing his lips, he pondered for a few moments. Then he unlimbered his pack and opened it up. Digging around within for a few seconds, he withdrew a lump of charcoal, then bent over and drew an arrow pointing back the way they came onto the stone floor. "At least this way we can have a reference."

Julian chuckled softly, but refrained from objecting. It was probably pointless; they were caught in Feirhard's trap and they weren't getting out until the trap was done with them or until they were dead. But if it made Tolburt feel better about things…

He blinked, surprised at his own thoughts. Since when did he give a damn how Tolburt felt about things? For that matter, why should he?

Scowling, he turned away from fading walls and toward the dripping sound.

They pushed on, Tolburt stopping every few dozen paces to mark another arrow on the floor. For a long time, nothing changed. If it were not for the marks behind them, stretching off into the blank distance, it would have been impossible to tell they were really moving at all.

Time dragged on. Was it still daylight outside, or had night fallen? It was impossible to tell, and not just because of the distorted nature of time in this place. Still, during another brief stop to drain the last of the water from his skin, Julian had to force back a yawn and he realized he was more than just tired from the day's long exertions: he was downright sleepy.

"We're probably going to have to camp sooner or later," he said, and that did not please him one bit.

Tolburt chuckled. "I was just thinking that. Well," he swept his arms out wide to encompass the entire area around them, "at least there's no way to sneak up on us. We'll see anything coming from a good long ways - "

And just like that, the light went out.

28

BLIND FIGHTING

Julian immediately drew his sword and fell back into a ready stance, balanced easily on the balls of his feet with his body turned to present a minimal target area behind his blade.

"Tolburt! Back to Back!"

From his left and behind him, Tolburt replied, "Aye."

Footsteps in the darkness from Tolburt's direction, and Julian risked lowering his weapon to tap the tip against the stones before his right foot.

A second tap, and he felt a hand on his left shoulder. He grunted a wordless reply, and a second later the pressure of Tolburt's back coming up against his own lifted some of the anxiety from his mind.

At least nothing could get him from behind. Not without warning anyway.

A pressure against his right side, and Julian turned to his left to follow Tolburt's movement. He raised his blade back up to a blocking position and focused his attention on listening to his surroundings as they circled together.

Water dripping from somewhere in the distance.

The soft thuds of their boots touching the stone as they moved.

A creaking from his belt as the leather adjusted itself against the new pressure of a body against it as Julian moved.

His heart pounding in his ears.

And, faintly, just barely above register, a dragging or slithering sound, from the opposite direction as the water.

Julian froze, and the pressure of Tolburt's intended circling intensified for a moment, then let up as Tolburt realized Julian was not going to move.

"Hear that?" Julian let the whisper escape his lips with the smallest force he could muster. No one who was not directly up against him, as Tolburt was, could possibly hear it.

The softest of grunts indicated that Tolburt did.

Julian waited, listening.

The dripping water continued, behind him and to his right now that their circling had stopped.

The slithering, off to his left, got louder, going from a subtle intrusion onto his consciousness to a full-on noise that demanded his attention.

Julian blinked away sweat that was dripping down into his eyes, a product of his newly-triggered nerves as much as the ever-present damp warmth of this place. His every instinct screamed out for him to run away from that noise. Go toward the water. Whatever it was, wherever it was, it at least was not something that would kill him in the darkness without warning.

And yet...

"Can we make the water?" Tolburt's whisper was faint in Julian's ears, and sounded doubtful.

And well he should have doubts. They had been following that echo, and their own thirst, for hours, and so far seen no sign of any water anywhere. Just more stone floor advancing endlessly in front of them, and no way to mark their time besides Tolburt's markings and the urges of their bodies.

No, there was no reason to believe a mad dash in pitch blackness would get them to the water before the...whatever it was...set upon them.

Julian shook his head firmly, pressing back against Tolburt to ensure he felt it and understood.

A tension went out of Tolburt's shoulders, and Julian felt him nod. "Didn't think so," came barely to Julian's ears. "We doing this?"

Julian flexed the fingers of his sword-hand on the grip of his weapon and smiled grimly to himself. He would much rather run, but he didn't see much choice, in all honesty. "Yes," he whispered.

Then he drew a deep breath and held it for a second before bellowing, "Over here!"

The silence that followed Julian's shout was deafening. It even drowned out the sound of his own heartbeat for a moment.

And then the slithering changed from a tentative, probing sound into something rubbing deliberately and rapidly across the stone floor. It was coming, coming straight at them.

"My left," Julian said, and half-turned that way to place his sword between himself and the approaching creature.

Tolburt followed his turn, keeping his back pressed up against Julian's until he stopped moving. Then the pressure of the younger man against Julian's body let up, and Tolburt stepped away. Only a pair of fingertips on Julian's right shoulder connected them.

The slithering grew louder, and a new odor assaulted Julian's nostrils. Sweet, but not the sickly-sweet smell of decay that had become so familiar he didn't even register it anymore. This was more like sugar-cookies out of a well-tended oven. Mouthwatering.

Julian pushed thoughts of food from his mind and focused on the incoming threat.

Closer now, the slithering covered an arc in front of him instead of just a single point. The creature, whatever it was, must be big.

"Over here!" he bellowed again, and punctuated the yell with another, sharp, rap of his sword onto the stone at his feet.

There came a sound that was almost a growl, and then the slithering redoubled in its speedy approach.

It now stretched from straight in front of him to halfway around his normal field of view to his left and right. And it just kept getting louder.

Air moved against his face, the slimmest of over-pressure, and Julian knew it was upon him. He dropped to the floor to his left, taking his weight onto his shoulder painfully as he struck the stone. He ignored the injury, focusing instead on the cut he made as he fell, back to his right toward where he was just standing.

The instant he moved, he felt as much as heard Tolburt advance from his own position, closing on the point a couple feet ahead of where Julian had been. The whistle of Tolburt's blade reached Julian's ears at the same time as he felt the impact of his own blade cutting into…something…as he dove to the side.

A heartbeat later, Tolburt's blade made a wet sound as it, too, struck home.

Then a shrill, unearthly scream rang forth, so loud it sent Julian reeling, both hands reflexively cupping his ears to block out the sound, and to hell with holding onto his sword. It went on for a short eternity, and Julian had to clench his teeth to avoid screaming himself, at the agony of that great sound.

And then, between one instant and the next, it was over.

Julian lay there, stunned, for a long time, unable to even register that the sound had stopped. But finally he came to his senses. He lowered his hands from his ears of drew a deep breath then placed his palms on the ground on either side of himself—at some point he had rolled onto his belly—and pushed himself up onto his hands and knees.

He blinked several times to remove dirt from his eyes before it registered that there was light, and he could see.

Julian sprang to his feet—a trifle unsteadily, but he managed—and looked around, wildly.

Tolburt was just getting up onto one knee about ten feet to his right, looking bedraggled and beaten up, but with a determined look in his eyes that said he wasn't ready to give in just yet.

Their two swords lay between them, on packed earth that was bare of any vegetation. Neither weapon had blood on its blade, or showed any sign of having recently been used at all.

Past Tolburt, the bare ground fell away in a moderate slope that ran about a half mile before leveling at the shore of a sapphire-blue lake that rippled softly before a gentle, cool breeze that was divinely refreshing after the oppressive warmth they had lived through the last several hours. The lake was almond-shaped and probably a mile across, without any vegetation visible anywhere along its shores.

But still, a semisweet fragrance, like comes from wildflowers in bloom, reached Julian's nostrils easily, filling him with a sense of restful well-being and tempting him to inhale deeply.

He did so, and only then noticed that the sky above them was clear blue, with a few puffy, white clouds floating along on the breeze.

The sun shone down brightly upon them from its noon-day zenith, adding to the pristine feeling of the entire scene.

"What the - " Tolburt began, then stopped, shaking his head as he got fully to his feet. "Where are we? Are we out?"

Julian frowned as he considered the younger man's words, and looked around again, this time with an eye toward the more distant.

What he saw gave him pause.

The terrain continued rising away from the lake in all directions, apparently ending its ascent well above their current level. It was difficult to tell exactly how much higher though, nor were there any peaks or other features visible beyond the rise. For that matter, the rise itself seemed to be almost completely circular, and when had there ever been a natural feature like that?

Julian shook his head. "No, we're still inside the Rift." He gestured up-slope.

Tolburt followed Julian's gesture with his eyes, and after a moment nodded agreement. "I guess we chose right." He bent down and picked up his sword then, after wiping the blade off on the trailing edge of his shirt, sheathed it.

Julian considered that for a few seconds and was forced to nod agreement. "I don't want to think what would have happened if we'd run toward the water instead of standing our ground." He licked his lips and found he was barely able to wet them, dry as his mouth was. "Speaking of which..." He nodded toward the lake.

Tolburt nodded emphatic agreement.

❊ 29 ❊

LAKESIDE

The lake water looked crisp and clean.

It was so clear Julian could see clearly all the way down to the bottom, even far out from the shoreline. But unlike other such pools he had seen in the real world, in this place there was not even a hint of vegetation, fish, or other life to be seen.

The bare dirt ran right up to the water's edge, becoming mud that sucked on the soles of Julian's boots and made squishing sounds as he approached. Despite that annoyance, the lake beckoned, promising an end to thirst and a reprieve from worry.

Which was why he suddenly found himself very worried, indeed.

Julian came to a halt a pace from the water, and reached out his left hand to stop Tolburt from advancing as well.

Tolburt stopped without resistance, but he turned to regard Julian with a raised eyebrow. "What?"

Julian nodded toward the lake. "Raedrick and me found that note in a pool of water. Almost turned Rae into a block of ice."

Tolburt's lips turned downward. "He told me about that." He looked back at the lake, inhaling deeply as though trying to scent danger. After a few seconds, he said, "This is a bit different though. The test, or whatever, has been draining us for hours, and we made the right decision. This," he stretched out his hand toward the water, "is our reward, and the way we can continue onward."

"That's sort of a flimsy assumption, Tolburt."

He shrugged. "They didn't want Kalem killed outright. They wanted him to be able to earn his inheritance, right?"

Julian frowned, but after a bit of thought he could not deny the logic of Tolburt's assertion. A dead heir is no good to anyone; Feirhard and his cronies would not have made the challenges insurmountable, and they would have had to schedule in periods of refreshment.

He nodded acquiescence. "Ok, but one of us goes at a time, and the other watches him carefully."

"Agreed." Tolburt shook Julian's hand off and, grinning back at him, knelt at the lake's edge. "Me first."

Tolburt dipped his hands into the lake water, and Julian tensed, ready to pull him back at the first sign of anything untoward.

But all that happened was Tolburt raised his cupped hands to his lips and drank heartily. When he lowered his hands, he smacked his lips and his grin practically stretched from ear to ear. "Tastes great."

A second drink was all the prompting Julian needed. He hurried forward next to Tolburt at the water's edge.

Several minutes later, bellies luxuriously full of the sweetest, purest water Julian had ever encountered and water skins filled with the same, the two men stepped back onto dry ground and sat, a day's worth of fatigue dragging them both down toward the tempting embrace of sleep.

It was all Julian could do to clamp his jaws shut against encroaching yawns. If he didn't know better, he would have thought that the refreshing water had been tainted to -

Oh hell.

"Tolburt, don't go to sleep," he rasped out through a throat that felt like it was clenching in an involuntary effort to cut off speech.

But it was too late. At his side, Tolburt's head had already lolled forward, his eyelids drooping shut without resistance. A second later, he slumped over onto his right side, and began snoring loudly.

Julian tried to force himself to his feet; walking had always been a good tool to ward off sleep. But his legs felt rubbery, his muscles bereft of strength.

Cursing his lack of caution, he made to draw his knife. A few nicks ought to do it to keep himself awake.

But even as he did that, his fingers lost their dexterity, and the knife fell out of his grasp onto the dirt next to him.

No! They could not go out like this. There had to…

Had to…

He could not stop a deep yawn, and he reflexively rubbed at eyes that felt gritty with sleep.

Had…

His eyelids weighed a ton each, and he could not stop them from lowering, no matter how he fought against it.

Ha -

Darkness enclosed him then, shutting off his last thought of protest mid-word.

30

IN THE CHAMBER

Vague noises, almost insubstantial in their subtlety, invaded the black silence that had engulfed him. A murmur. A hint of a word. Just barely enough to register, but not enough to be convinced it was real.

A tingling sensation ran through him, a reminder that there was a body out there somewhere, and that body had senses that were just starting to come back online. The tingling intensified, becoming almost painful, and the murmurs increased as well until they were incoherent shouts.

Dull red invaded the black, and eyes that seemed like rocks forced themselves open a crack. Brilliant light forced them shut again, but the damage had been done. Whatever last remnants of sleep had been within him fled that glare, and Julian roused himself fully.

His muscles ached, and there was a bitter taste in his dry mouth. He was stretched out, arms flung out wide. Something hard and damp was pressed up against his back, and cold metal wrapped around his wrists and ankles. The smells of woodsmoke, sweat, and blood dominated his nostrils.

This couldn't be good.

The redness of light coming through his eyelids faded a bit and he tried opening his eyes again.

He really wished he had not.

The room was moderately sized, maybe twenty feet across, and circular. Iron restraints hung from the walls at intervals. Tolburt, head still drooping in sleep and stripped down to his smallclothes, was strung up spread-eagle directly across from Julian, in the same manner that he himself was. His torso was crisscrossed in long, white-pink scars that were clearly visible in the light of a pair of flickering torches that hung on either side of the room's sole door, a monstrously thick-looking contrivance of oak and iron that would take a man with a heavy axe a while to get through. Opposite the door, to Julian's left, a great stone fireplace, almost a blacksmith's forge, was sunk into the wall. A few embers still glowed within, but it had clearly been some time since the fire had last been stoked.

All that was bad enough. The apparatus in the center of the room just made it worse.

It was a sadist's wet dream, all pinchers and knife edges. There were clearly multiple places where a victim would be strapped down, and then any number of horrible things done to him. The thing's wood was stained red-brown everywhere, the evidence of its gruesome earlier use.

From the ceiling above the terrible machine dangled more implements of pain: hooks and brands, long knives and small, at an easy height for the machine's operator to reach if he had desire.

The only bright side was a lack of torturer. But that couldn't last.

They had to get out of here.

"Tolburt!" The word came out in a croak that Julian could barely understand himself. He worked his jaw, spreading what little saliva he could muster and wetting his lips, then tried again.

"Tolburt!"

This time the word carried better. Against the far wall, Tolburt's head moved slightly and a low moan issued from his lips, but he did not stir fully.

Muttering to himself, Julian looked at his bonds.

His feet were held fast by iron rings locked directly into the wall a bit more than shoulder-width apart. That was not so with his hands. The shackles holding his arms apart had about six inches of chain linking them to a mounting plate in the wall, so he had a little play to work with. Maybe he could...

But no, a few moments' twisting and turning showed the chains to be fully as strong as they looked, and though he had some play it was not enough to really get leverage to make a good attempt.

Crap.

Turning his eyes to the ceiling above him did not give him much more hope for escape. Aside from those hanging implements there was nothing that even potentially looked helpful.

"Where - " Tolburt's voice cracked, and he coughed to clear his throat before trying again. "Where are we?"

Tolburt looked like hell, but then Julian supposed he did as well. His eyes were ringed with dark circles of fatigue despite his recent sleep. As he finished voicing the question, he finished looking around the room and fully took in the apparatus in its center. His eyes widened and he visibly paled.

"Oh no," Tolburt said. Then, just barely loud enough for Julian to make it out, he added, "Not again."

"Oh no is right," Julian said. "Can you see a way to get your chains loose?"

Tolburt jerked his eyes away from the apparatus and focused on Julian for a second before he shook his head. "No they're solid."

"Wonderful."

"Yeah." Tolburt looked around again and barked out a bitter laugh. "Guess drinking that water wasn't the best idea was it?" He shook his head. "We're totally screwed. No way we're getting out of this without magic or something."

Julian found it hard to argue with the emotional truth of that statement. But the logic didn't hold. He shook his head vigorously. "No, this was a test for Kalem. He was a warrior, not a sorcerer, so he wouldn't have magic to draw on." He looked about again, searching for some clue—any clue—of a way out. "There must be a way out that he could use if he just put two and two together."

Tolburt frowned, then went back to scanning the room. "I hope you're right."

"Of course I'm right. I - "

A heavy thud from beyond the door to his right brought Julian up short. He froze, icy fear running down his spine and turning his limbs to jelly. They were running out of time.

Tolburt paled even further and tried his chains again, but they did not give. He cast about desperately, looking to and fro. "There has to be something. There has to be something!" he said.

Julian tried to regain his calm, but instead the panic that was beginning to grip Tolburt also filled him.

There was no way out. They were doomed here.

Another heavy thud, and then the door's latch rattled. The metallic sound penetrated Julian's consciousness like an arrow through a hay bale, and his eyes locked onto the portal.

A couple of seconds passed, and Julian dared to hope that perhaps he had imagined the sounds beyond the door. Then the latch moved and the heavy door swung ponderously open, its wrought iron hinges issuing low creaks of protest against the motion.

The door opened fully, coming to rest against the inner wall to Tolburt's left. Reddish light shone into the room from outside, outlining a massive figure who stood just on the other side of the doorway. The figure stood still for several seconds, and it seemed the tension in the room doubled with every beat of Julian's heart while he waited.

Then, with slow, ponderous footsteps, the torturer entered the chamber.

31

TORMENT

Huge didn't begin to describe him.

The torturer was easily eight feet tall. His arms were thicker around than Julian's thighs, and his shoulders were wide enough that Julian could almost lie down and go to sleep across them. His muscles bulged, stretching his deeply-tanned skin so that it seemed it must rip apart at any moment, and yet his belly had a layer of fat that jiggled like a bowl of jam as he walked. He wore short, brown leather breeches that ended before the knee and a sort of leather harness around his chest and back. His head was completely bald, his eyes squinty as though used to long hours staring into a bright flame, and his nose crooked as though broken in a score of brawls. He wore a frown that had become so chiseled into the creases of his face that it looked as though he could not put on a different expression if he wanted to. The heavy boots on his feet made ominous, deep thuds as he trudged into the room, like bass drums rolling out the cadence of a death march.

The very sight of him made Julian shrink back against the wall where he was bound before he realized he was doing it.

The strong scent of long-simmering sweat that came from the man made him nearly gag.

The torturer stopped before the infernal machine in the center of the room and drew a long, deep breath. Then, without moving his head, he looked first at Julian then at Tolburt.

Tolburt shook his head briskly in denial, his wide eyes portraying his sudden terror clearly. He opened his mouth to speak, but all that came out was a low moan.

The torturer sniffed, a sound so loud it easily drowned out Tolburt's whimpers. Then he moved, slowly and ponderously, toward the fireplace.

A bellows was built into the fireplace on Tolburt's side of the room, a contraption Julian had noted but disregarded in his initial assessment of the room. The torturer stopped in front of the bellow, and taking hold of its handles, began to use it to billow the coals in the fireplace with, long, slow strokes.

The coals accepted the additional air and sparked, then burst fully aflame. The torturer worked the bellows for another four puffs, then turned and trudged back toward the door.

He was gone for a seemingly long time, though the analytical part of Julian's mind registered that it could not have been more than a minute. But in that time, the chamber went from comfortably cool to decidedly warm. When he returned, the torturer had an especially large faggot in his arms. He crossed the room just as slowly and deliberately as he had before, then dumped the bundle of sticks and logs atop the burning coals.

The wood caught fire almost immediately—it must have been drying for a good long time—and very quickly the chamber went from merely warm to excessively hot. Julian blinked away sweat that dripped down into his eyes, but he could not divert it all and very soon the salt caused his eyes to sting incessantly. He shook his head, but to no avail. And it was only going to get worse.

The torturer crossed his arms over his chest and turned away from the fireplace. In his slow, deliberate manner, he looked between the two prisoners again.

Julian met his gaze as best he could, but the stinging in his eyes forced him to lower his head.

Across the room, Tolburt's eyes, already wider than normal, seemed to grow so large they eclipsed the rest of his head. He thrashed against his chains, a low bestial sound coming from his mouth, interspersed with a frantic, "No. No. No," as though giving voice to the denial would stop what would happen next.

The torturer let out another sniff, then he reached up and pulled down a brand, shaped like a six-pointed star, and, not bothering to turn around to face the fireplace, shoved it into the burning coals. Then he picked out another implement, one with a long, curved, and very sharp-looking edge. He trudged forward until he was even with the contraption in the center of the room, and, very gently, placed the implement down alongside the place where the apparatus' victim would be strapped.

The torturer stood still for a time, looking down at the cutting tool and inhaling, the long, slow breaths of a man gathering his will.

Then he turned to look fully at Julian, and his lips turned upward into a sadistic perversion of a smile.

32

THE MACHINE

The slow and ponderous movements the torturer had used earlier vanished. Between one heartbeat and the next, he went from standing next to the torture apparatus to looming over Julian where he stood chained to the wall. The beastly man's chest swelled outward as he breathed in, and his knuckles cracked so loudly that for a moment Julian thought there must also be a drummer in the room.

Then he leaned forward.

"Hey now," Julian managed to say, "let's talk about this. I - "

A huge hammer struck the side of his face and he reeled, seeing stars. Pain followed, the entire left side of his face crying out in injury as a flood of blood filled his mouth.

Julian spat the salty liquid out and shook his head, trying in vain to get his bearings.

Then his feet were free, and he sensed—more feeling than anything else as his vision was still a blur—the torturer's hands rising to his wrists.

He kicked upward as hard as he could, and felt the toe of his right boot sinking into something soft where he presumed the mammoth man's crotch to be.

The torturer let out a deep grunt, and for a second Julian thought he had a chance.

Then another hammer struck him in the abdomen.

Julian doubled forward, or would have if his wrists were not restrained, and the remains of his last meal came up, expelled from his body by the force of the blow.

He finished retching and tried to breath, but the air had completely left his lungs and he seemed unable to fill them.

His right wrist came free, then his left, but he didn't care.

Breathe.

Have to breathe.

He felt himself being lifted off the ground at the same moment he managed, after a seeming eternity, to take in air. Then he shuddered in convulsions as a fit of uncontrollable coughing came over him.

He coughed so hard he lost all vision. Even the stars that had flashed before his eyes following the torturer's punch faded to black, but still he heaved out the coughs, until finally his back struck something hard and grainy. The shock of impact seemed to bring his body back into equilibrium, and he managed a long, full breath.

Bindings tightened around his wrists, upper arms, and ankles once more, but he barely noticed as he exulted in the simple joy of breathing again.

Somewhere in the process, he realized he had shut his eyes. So he opened them.

And immediately wished he had not.

Julian lay strapped down in the apparatus. The torturer stood before him, all muscle, fat, and malice, with a look of almost lustful anticipation on his face and a cruel light burning in his eyes.

Though that could have just been the reflected firelight from the forge, right then Julian wasn't going to give odds either way.

The torturer had been busy. All around Julian, embedded in the apparatus' many moving parts and mounting points, were all manner of pinchers, pokers, blades, and other things that Julian could not put names to but appeared custom-made for the business of inflicting pain. The huge man held the long, curved blade that he had taken down from the ceiling earlier in his left hand, and he held it up for Julian to see.

The orange firelight glinted off the blade. For a second, Julian could see his own reflection in the metal; a vision of horrified terror. Then the torturer touched the tip of his right index finger against the blade's edge, so delicate-looking a touch that Julian wondered if the man hadn't been a clock maker in some previous life.

When he pulled the finger back and turned it so Julian could see, a line of red, so thin it was almost invisible, stood out against the torturer's fire-tanned skin.

That was one hell of an edge.

The torturer leaned forward, and his mouth opened a crack. His breath billowed out, pouring over Julian relentlessly and carrying the putrid smell of long-rotten meat. Between that and the metallic taste of blood in his mouth, Julian found himself gagging. He thrashed against his bonds, willing himself not to retch again but knowing he would be unable to stop it.

Finally, at the last second, he turned his head to the side.

Bile came up and little else, but it at least relieved the nausea that the man's breath had caused.

Julian inhaled and turned to look back up at his captor, pointedly ignoring the wetness of his vomit as it followed the slight angle of the apparatus' construction and spread slowly between his shoulder blades and down his back.

The torturer smiled again, revealing yellow-brown teeth.

He wasn't sure how, but Julian smiled back.

The torturer blinked, sadistic pleasure giving way to confusion for a second. He reached up with his free hand and scratched at the side of his face as he considered Julian. Then he shrugged and stepped forward to stand at Julian's left side.

Julian could have killed the mammoth fellow easily, as close as he was. If only he was not bound.

The thought provided little comfort as the torturer shifted the long razor into his right hand. He bent over Julian, nostrils flaring as his eyes widened in anticipation of the delights to come.

The blade approached the exposed flesh of Julian's collar bone.

A wet thud seemed to echo throughout the chamber.

The torturer stiffened, the razor-edge of his blade halting its movement, and his eyes rolled in their sockets as though trying to look directly through the back of his skull.

Another thud, and the torturer gave a spasmodic jerk.

The he collapsed forward, engulfing Julian in his bulk as a long, gurgling, final breath escaped his lips.

"You ok?" Tolburt still held onto the axe that was sunk into the dead torturer's back as though it were a tree limb in boiling rapids, and the only thing keeping him from drowning. But his voice was steady, his expression business-like.

"Yeah," Julian managed, surprise and relief battling for the center of his psyche and all but robbing him of the power of speech from their struggle. He drew a deep breath. "Took you long enough."

Tolburt shrugged, then grinned broadly.

❧ 33 ❦

LOOSED BONDS

Tolburt had to pull the torturer's body off of Julian before he could remove the bonds that held Julian onto the apparatus, and it took a lot of huffing and puffing over the span of a short eternity before he managed it. Finally, though, the weight lifted off Julian's chest as the torturer fell limply to the floor with the most solid thud Julian had ever heard from a body, and he breathed in a long, grateful few breaths.

A few seconds later, Julian was free. He hopped down from the apparatus and immediately found himself swaying. He caught himself with his left hand on the edge of the infernal machine and raised his other to his forehead as a wave of nauseating dizziness swept over him. And with the dizziness, renewed pain from where the thug had walloped him.

Julian swallowed forcefully, willing himself to keep his bile down, and breathed out forcefully.

"You ok?" Tolburt seemed to be asking that a lot lately.

Julian nodded. "Just dizzy. It'll pass in a second."

"Well you took a heck of a hit there." Tolburt patted him on the back, then began to work on getting his axe out of the torturer's back.

Julian had to look away from him as he worked that task, queasy as he was. Instead, he looked over at the wall where the chains that used to hold Tolburt hung empty. He frowned. "How did you get out?"

177

"Bloody - " Tolburt breathed under his breath, then broke off with a satisfied-sounding grunt that accompanied a wet sucking sound overlaying a softer grating. The axe must have come free. Julian tried not to think about what it must have been stuck in.

Tolburt stepped into his field of view, wiping the axe's blade off with a scrap of cloth that he must have gotten fro the torturer somewhere. He nodded at the shackles hanging from the wall. "There's a latch on the inside of the plate that holds the shackles to the wall," he said. "I saw where it was when he took yours off. The chains were just loose enough that I could reach one of them. After that," he shrugged. "The ankle rings had a release switch built into the wall between them."

Julian's frown did not lessen. As he pondered Tolburt's words, it grew deeper. "So this place was designed to allow escape," he said slowly, feeling out the thoughts as he spoke them, "but only if there is another prisoner in the room, so he," he gestured behind himself, toward the dead behemoth, "could show you how."

Tolburt nodded, and his eyebrows rose. He saw it too. "If somebody were to come into this test alone, he would never make it. He'd..." He left off, his expression growing sickly.

"Yup." Julian could not completely stop himself from shrugging. Death by torture...and probably long, slow torture at that.

That did not bear thinking on very deeply.

"We'd better get moving," he said, pushing himself upright now that his dizziness and nausea was fading. He looked around again. "Any sign of our stuff?"

Tolburt shook his head. "Probably in another room."

"Right." Julian turned back to look at the implements mounted to the apparatus. They were cruel, but not...

Ah, there it was. On the floor next to the torturer's body. Curved, longer than a dagger but shorter than a full sword, but better than nothing. Especially with that edge it had.

The blade that had almost flayed him alive.

Julian bent down and picked up the blade. It was lighter than it looked, and the handle seemed to mold itself to the palm of his hand. Though it looked to be made of wood, it was almost sticky in the way he was able to get a firm grip on it, and he felt certain it would not twist in his hand no matter how hard he tried to make it.

Straightening, he whistled softly. "This thing is pretty nice."

Tolburt grunted, turning toward the door.

Julian took one last look around the room; nothing else jumped out at him that would be useful to take. So he joined Tolburt in the doorway.

The reddish light that had shown into the chamber when the torturer opened the door continued to shine, but it was not from lanterns or fires as Julian expected it to be.

Beyond the doorway was open ground. Dry, dusty, with rolling clay hills and a warm wind that blew across his line of sight, kicking off little dust devils here and there. The sky overhead was pinkish, the sun, high in the sky near its zenith, a deep, blood red.

No question what caused that tinted light.

Julian licked his lips, suddenly feeling parched as he examined the dry, dusty landscape ahead of them. "That looks inviting." He poked his head out the door and look to and fro, seeing just more of the same. "No sign of our gear either."

Tolburt grunted again, and turned his head to look back at the chamber. "I don't really feel like staying here."

"True enough." Julian took a deep breath, then stepped out the door.

The ground was dry and warm almost to the point of being uncomfortable beneath his bare feet. The sun, unblocked by the chamber's ceiling, felt cool compared to the heat of the chamber's furnace, but the air was still a bit above pleasantly warm. The smell of dust and, further down almost to the limit of his nostrils' register, decay carried on the breeze.

The landscape was the same in every direction; all low dry hills, and only broken by the small, low building that had housed the torture chamber.

"Kind of an odd place to put a place like that," Tolburt said as he joined Julian outside.

Julian shrugged. "It's all part of the test." He looked around one last time for any indication of where they should go and found none. Finally, with a deep sigh, he pointed straight ahead with his new weapon. "Got any objection to straight?"

Tolburt shook his head.

There was nothing for it but to head out. So that was what they did.

34

DESERT SANDS

The walking never stopped in this strange test of worthiness. Julian supposed there must be a reason for the interminable hikes that seemed to be required here. To show persistence and determination, perhaps. But he would give even money that Feirhard and his guys could have designed the thing to get the effects they wanted without the walking, so it probably was the old sorcerer just being bloody-minded.

Bastard.

Julian stopped atop the fourth hill they had climbed since leaving the torture chamber. His ankles had begun to smart from the lack of boots, and the soles of his feet were beginning to feel rubbed raw. He took a moment to stretch out his calves, but that didn't do much good.

At least the bleeding inside his mouth had stopped. For a while there, he had to spit out a mouthful of red every couple of minutes. Now it just hurt, was all.

Small blessings.

"How you holding up?" Tolburt asked. He looked at Julian with what appeared to be genuine concern.

Julian shrugged. "Felt better. You?"

Tolburt gestured toward his feet, which were covered in dust and grime, and looked as though they hurt a ton from the way he was moving. He didn't voice a complaint, though. Just looked back in the direction they came.

"No sign of anyone following us."

Julian snorted. "You expecting someone?"

"Sooner or later, yes. Still," Tolburt said, "we're in the clear for now."

Tolburt moved to continue forward, down the slope of the hill ahead of them.

"Hold, Tolburt."

The younger man stopped and looked back at Julian, an eyebrow climbing questioningly.

Julian cleared his throat. "I didn't actually thank you for..." He left the rest unsaid, just gestured back in the direction of the torture chamber.

Tolburt shrugged. "You'd have done the same for me."

Julian wasn't sure how to answer that one. A week ago, he probably would not have. But then, leaving another man, any man, to slow death by torture...

"Yeah, well. You could have just slipped out while that guy was focused on me. So, thanks."

Tolburt just stared at him for a long second or two. Then he said, softly, "I learn from my mistakes."

With that, Tolburt turned his back to Julian and re-commenced walking.

Another half hour's walking, near as Julian could figure it, brought an end to the dusty monotony of the parched landscape.

From one hilltop to the next, a smudge appeared on the horizon ahead of them. Just a dark blur at first glance, but as Julian paused to examine it more closely, it resolved a bit, appearing to be a structure of some sort. And was that a flash of light from near the building's base? Like something reflecting the sun...

He moved slightly, and the light faded, leaving just the dark shape, several hills away.

"See that?"

Beside him, Tolburt nodded. He rolled his shoulders and took his axe in both hands, squeezing the grip until his knuckles whitened. "No way we'll be alone much longer." He sounded resigned, but determined at the same time.

Julian could relate. He had had about enough of this place. If it weren't for Melanie's predicament, he'd have said to hell with it a while ago.

Of course, they couldn't just walk out of there anyway. So it didn't matter that Melanie was…

He found himself grinding his teeth. Looking down, he noted that his own knuckles were white on the grip of his short sword.

Oh, it mattered. It mattered a lot.

"Let's go say hello."

He didn't wait for Tolburt's nod of assent before setting off at a trot.

It was not one building but three, set up at the points of an invisible triangle, with their entrances facing a columned courtyard in the center of the space between them. The buildings were all identically rectangular, made of sandstone or something that looked just like it, about fifteen feet tall, twice as many wide, and thrice as long. From Julian and Tolburt's angle of approach, Julian could see the black maw of an open doorway, wide enough to admit the two of them side by side and half again as tall as he was, on the face of the building farthest from them. The other two entrances were not visible, but he presumed they were the same as that one.

The source of the earlier reflected light was plain to see: a raised half-dome of glass or crystal, about four or five feet tall, placed in the center of the courtyard, with what looked like benches ringing it.

He and Tolburt lay on their bellies just below the curve of the hill where the buildings lay, low enough that anyone who might have been in the courtyard, or hiding within that darkened doorway, would be unlikely to see them.

That said, he and Tolburt had been lying there and watching for about ten minutes and there was no sign of any living thing anywhere in the vicinity.

"What do you think?" Tolburt asked.

Julian drew a breath and pondered. He wanted to rush in; the place was clear. But something nagged at the back of his mind.

It was too simple. Too obviously a trap.

He shook his head. "I don't like it."

Tolburt snorted. "Me neither. But we can't just lie here forever."

Thing was, Tolburt was right. There was nothing to be gained by lying there, getting slowly sunburned, and watching nothing happen around a trio of empty buildings because they were too jumpy. If this were any other place, Julian would just run right up. But here…

He sighed. "All right. We go in." He pointed at the closest building. "Split up, hug the wall."

Tolburt frowned slightly, but nodded.

Julian took a grip on his short sword then stood and, moving in a crouch, hurried to the rear of the closest building. He turned to stop with his back against the rear wall and edged his way to the corner; Tolburt did the same on the other side.

Peeking around the corner, Julian saw that nothing had changed. He looked back at Tolburt.

He gave a quick nod; all clear.

Julian made a jabbing gestured toward the courtyard between the buildings then, not waiting for Tolburt's acknowledgement, rounded his corner.

He moved quickly, his back to the wall as he sidestepped toward the courtyard, eyes darting every which way for the threat that he thought sure was going to jump out at him from somewhere. But by the time he reached the far corner of the building, the stillness of the area remained unbroken.

He paused at the corner, heart pounding in his ears as he strained to listen.

Nothing. And yet the feeling of impending attack remained; he could not shake it.

"Nothing for it but to continue," he muttered to himself, then, tensed for action, he rounded the corner to the building's front.

Just as the other buildings across the courtyard, Julian's building had a wide-open, dark entrance in the center of this wall. Aside from that, the wall was featureless; no writing, no designs or engravings. Not even seams between the stones that made it.

That gave Julian pause. What could have put these buildings together without leaving any seams or gaps?

Magic, of course. That much was obvious. But for some reason, seeing this feat of precision impressed him more than the earlier, more flamboyant displays Feirhard had done. It was like -

Tolburt came into view, rounding the opposite corner of the building and scanning the area quickly. Their eyes met, and Tolburt gave a shake of his head. No sign of any enemy.

That didn't relieve any of the tension, though.

Time to ponder construction techniques later. Julian nodded toward the building's entrance, and Tolburt gave a quick nod in return.

Moving in unison, the two men closed on the entrance, then ducked inside.

The room within was thirty feet square, windowless, and adequately illuminated by the sunlight streaming in through the doorway. The walls and ceiling were the same stone as the outside of the building, devoid of decoration or feature, and seemingly solid.

The place was completely empty.

"Weird," Tolburt said. He stepped further into the room, peering about with a curious frown on his face. "There's nothing here."

"You don't miss anything, do you?" Julian moved to the left along the inner wall, dragging the tips of his left hand along the stone. Every couple of steps he stopped and pressed firmly into the stone, but it was firm, smooth, and unmoving. Quickly, he reached the opposite wall from the entrance and stopped, shaking his head. "I don't get it."

"There must be something past that wall," Tolburt said. "The building's too long."

"Yeah, but there's no way through it." Julian backed away from the wall until he reached Tolburt's side. He squinted in the dim light and looked up at the ceilings and the corners, but nothing stood out. Finally he sighed and shook his head. "Let's check the other buildings."

Tolburt nodded agreement.

Five minutes of searching led to the same discovery: each and every one of the four buildings were arranged as the first one had been, and each was just as devoid of clues.

Julian and Tolburt stopped between the two pillars fronting the building opposite the first they had examined and looked around the courtyard. Confusion battled with annoyance to dominate Julian's mind, and annoyance was winning. He was hot, hurting, thirsty; his feet hurt from running around through the sand and rock without boots, and he was developing a wicked sunburn.

He squinted up at the sun, which seemed to not have moved a wit in the time they had been here. "How long til sundown, do you think?" Then he snorted. "Who am I kidding? Damn thing's probably never going down."

Tolburt sniffed. "Sorcerers." He lowered the head of his axe to the ground and rested his hands on the end of its haft. "I don't know. Should we keep going? This is the first sign of any civilization since the chamber, and I don't want to go back there."

Julian suppressed a shudder. He didn't either. "There's got to be more here. We're just missing it."

He looked away from Tolburt and toward the center of the little square between the buildings, where an aspect of the crystalline dome reflected the light from the overhead sun in a small swath of color. Wincing, Julian turned his head a bit further, and the brightness of the reflection passed away from his eyes. He let his gaze linger on the rest of the dome, though.

"I wonder how we get in there," he said, and he walked slowly toward the bench set between him and the dome. "It must have some purpose, don't you think?"

He reached the bench and stepped around it, then leaned forward, pressing his hands onto the glass as he peered into the dome.

"Oh crap," he breathed. Then, more loudly, "Tolburt, get over here."

Soft shuffling announced the other man's approach. "What?"

Julian pointed downward. "All we've done is make a circle."

"Huh?" Tolburt stepped up to Julian's side and looked down, then breathed out a resigned, "Crap."

Below the dome was a round room with open doors in every wall and a dais in the center. A stone throne sat atop the dais, slid back on its base to reveal a stone staircase leading downward into darkness. It was the room they had started in, seemingly so long ago. Except...

"Julian, where is Melanie?"

Julian blinked. Then he blinked again, and pressed his face to the glass.

How had he not noticed the first time? How had he missed it? But sure enough, where Melanie should have been standing frozen in her invisible prison before the throne, there was only empty stone, unmarked at all, as though no one and nothing had ever been there.

"Son of a bitch!" Julian slammed edge of his left fist against the glass. "No!" He pushed himself off of the dome and stumbled backwards a half step. "Where did she go?" he demanded, then he raised his head to the pinkish sky and its unmoving sun. Thrusting his short sword toward that hatefully hot, insistently burning globe, he shouted at the top of his lungs, "Where did you take her?"

As if in answer, the sound of stone scraping against stone began to emanate from all three of the buildings surrounding the dome. Loud, louder than it should have been from having to travel out of the buildings and then to the two men, it went on for several seconds.

And then, silence.

Tolburt moved away from the dome to Julian's side. "I've got a bad feeling about - "

Deep, hoarse voices erupted from the inside of the three buildings, a trio of what could only be battle cries, interrupting Tolburt in mid-word.

And then the horde came forth to do battle.

35

MELEE

They were big. They were muscle-bound. They were stripped to the waist, and wore tight leather leggings over sandals. They were ugly, or at least wore ugly masks showing faces distorted by unnatural growths of horns or multiple noses and eyes, and grimacing in expressions of exquisite agony. They carried long, curved swords of black steel that nevertheless shimmered along the length of their honed edges. They came in pairs, two out of each building surrounding the square.

And they all charged straight toward Julian and Tolburt.

"Crap!" Julian said again, at the exact same time as Tolburt did. He wasted no time, having judged the situation in a glance: if they let their attackers join forces, they were dead.

So he charged forward to meet the two closest fellows head-on.

From the corner of his eye, Julian saw that Tolburt had done the same, meeting him step for step, and he felt a moment's relief that the man hadn't lost all of his battle reflexes.

And then the attackers were on them.

The one on the left, slightly taller than his companion, which placed him a full head above Julian, with a mask of a fellow who had his tongue torn halfway out his mouth, moved toward Julian's direction, while his partner moved for Tolburt.

Tongueless' sword descended quickly, but it was a straightforward swing and Julian avoided it easily, stepping behind the fellow's swing and lunging to cut at his belly with the pilfered short sword.

The man went down in a heap, and Julian stopped for a second in surprise. That was too easy.

Looking to his right, Tolburt stood over the body of his attacker. The man's head was nearly split in two from a blow of Tolburt's axe.

The two of them met each others' eyes, and Tolburt gave a little shrug.

Shouts from the other four men rushing at them interrupted the moment, and Julian spun around.

The pair from the building across the courtyard had reached the benches and had begun circling the dome to the left. The other two were maybe fifteen feet away and charging fast.

"Back to the building," Julian shouted, and backpedalled toward the building the two fallen warriors had come from.

Tolburt followed suit, moving as quickly as he could. But neither of them could match the taller fellows' speed, especially going in reverse, and the second pair, one with a mask of a man that looked half bird and the other of a man with an eye where his nose should have been and two horns growing out of his eye sockets, closed the distance quickly.

Again they split up to face Julian and Tolburt singly.

And again they fell without difficulty at all.

Julian stopped as his assailant fell into a quivering heap, and shook his head. "This is way too easy," he said, eyeing the final pair as they finished rounding the dome and moved toward him and Tolburt. If they showed any sign of dismay over their fallen comrades, they didn't show it.

Julian glanced to the side and met Tolburt's eyes. The other man shrugged, then flashed a grin and raised his axe.

Together they charged the last pair.

A few seconds later, that pair joined the first two in death.

Julian wiped his brow with his free hand and looked down at the corpses. "It doesn't make any sense."

"No kidding," Tolburt replied. He moved over to the first fellow he struck down and squatted next to him. After a few seconds looking the man over, he shook his head. "I dunno. But at least we can upgrade our weapons." He reached down to pick up the fallen man's sword. "These swords look - "

The nearly-decapitated man's arm darted out, catching Tolburt by the wrist and twisting. His words ceased, going from coherence into a sudden squeak of pain as the not-corpse forced his arm in an unnatural direction with one hand.

The other darted across the ground to the grip of his sword.

Julian shouted something and charged. Tolburt tried to raise his axe to ward off the incoming blow, but it was obvious from the awkward angle of his body that there would be no strength behind it even if he could get it up fast enough.

The sword came up, and Julian threw himself headlong at the not-corpse, short sword leading the way in a desperate downward cut.

Julian's shoulder met the not-corpse's at the same time his weapon struck the guard of its sword, then he tumbled off to the side, stunned for a moment by the impact. He forced himself to roll with the fall and rose back up onto one knee, then looked back at Tolburt and not-corpse.

The force of Julian's impact must have knocked Tolburt out of the wrist lock, because not-corpse's sword hand was off at the wrist, and Tolburt was raising his axe to remove the other one.

Julian was just about to grin, but he stopped when he looked past Tolburt to the other five attackers.

They were all beginning to rise again. Awkwardly because of their various wounds. More slowly than before. But implacably.

And, one and all, they were turning toward Tolburt, who was closer to them than Julian right that second.

"Tolburt!" Julian put all the force of warning he could into his voice, and pushed himself up onto his feet, pausing only to pick up his short sword from where he had dropped it.

Tolburt looked back at Julian questioningly, and then reeled back as not-corpse struck him in the side of the head with the stump of his right arm. Julian's comrade stumbled and fell backwards, landing heavily on his backside while he reflexively raised his free hand to wipe off the fountain of blood that had sprayed in his face with the blow.

Not-corpse advanced, bending over and reaching out with his good hand for the fallen Tolburt.

Biting back a curse, Julian sprang forward. He was only a couple paces away, but it seemed an enormous distance right then.

Tolburt blinked away the blood and looked up at the looming not-corpse, and blanched visibly. His bare feet worked against the paving stones of the courtyard, pushing him away from his assailant but leaving red streaks behind. But not-corpse was too quick, and he grabbed Tolburt by the throat.

Tolburt's eyes bulged as not-corpse squeezed, his mouth opening wide in a vain effort to suck in air that suddenly would not come.

And then not-corpse straightened himself, and lifted Tolburt fully off the ground by his neck.

Julian didn't lead with his shoulder this time. He ducked around the flailing Tolburt to not-corpse's left side and plunged his short sword into the impossibly-not-dead man's armpit.

The big man's arm fell limply, and Tolburt fell with it, landing on his backside again as his axe clattered to the stones beside him. The force of the arm's fall brought it down on Julian's shoulder, and he lost his grip on the short sword as he stumbled away.

Not-corpse turned on Julian, and even with the cloven mask hiding most of the man's face, Julian could feel the burning hate in his stare.

Even worse, he could see the other five re-animated warriors beyond him, one and all brandishing their weapons and closing. Rapidly. Tongueless, the first man Julian had slain, was less than ten feet away now.

Crap.

The handless not-corpse stepped toward Julian, and then promptly fell with an inarticulate gurgle that almost but not quite resembled a groan.

Tolburt bounded to his feet and wrenched his axe free from not-corpse's right knee, where he had cloven the man when he turned his attention on Julian. Then he brought it down in a vicious backhanded chop to the back of not-corpse's neck.

Sharpened steel ground through bone—Julian could practically hear it—and not-corpse's head dropped free from his body, which immediately went limp.

If seeing his comrade felled so thoroughly gave Tongueless pause, he showed no sign. He stepped forward with very nearly the grace he had before Julian spilled his guts and swung his sword toward Tolburt. But Julian's comrade saw the attack coming, and he hopped backwards beyond the reach of tongueless' sword.

"Beheading does the trick," Julian said as he glanced around for a weapon. His short sword was still buried in not-corpse's armpit, and it would take too long to dig it out. The man's sword was around here somewhere, though...

Ah-ha!

Julian bounded to the left, passing behind Tolburt as he parried a second attack with the haft of his axe.

"Looks like," Tolburt said, with deadpan calm. He backed away again, drawing Tongueless toward him and away from Julian.

That was all the opening he needed. Bending over quickly, he picked up not-corpse's sword. It was heavier than it looked and the balance was quite a bit different than the straight blade he was used to wielding. It actually looked and felt a bit like the Tyrashi sword that Raedrick had inherited from Selam, a late comrade-at-arms of theirs during their defense of Lydelton, back when they first came to Glimmer Vale.

That sword was plenty fancy, and its curvature and balance made for great, swift cuts and slashes. But Julian had only tried it a few times over the last year. Not nearly enough to get proficient with it.

Looking at the four other not-dead warriors, who by now were very nearly atop he and Tolburt, Julian considered that this was one hell of a time to have to learn.

The sound of steel ringing against steel from behind him brought Julian out of his quick pondering, and he turned to assist Tolburt.

Tongueless' back was to Julian, and he was just raising his blade to attack Tolburt again. The bearded man looked a trifle harried.

So Julian thrust his newly-acquired weapon through Tongueless' left kidney.

The sword was not especially made for stabbing, bit its tip was sharp and Tongueless wasn't wearing a shirt, let alone armor. So the blade sunk into his flesh easily enough. He bellowed and crumpled, collapsing to his left as his free hand went reflexively to the wound.

The sword hand dropped as well, and that was all the opening

Tolburt needed. He hopped forward and swept his axe across Tongueless' throat. More blood sprayed, and the big fellow fell for a second time, his head lolling to the side grotesquely as he landed. Tolburt's cut had gone deep. Hopefully deep enough.

There wasn't time to look in detail, though. Julian turned to face the other four, bringing his sword up to guard in front of himself.

And immediately staggered backward as eye-horn's sword slammed into Julian's.

Julian hadn't meant that as a parry. He hadn't even known the attack was coming. Thanking every single one of the gods for their protection of fools, he backed away to give himself room to properly get set.

The stones were slick with Tongueless' blood, and Julian's bare feet slipped beneath him. He skidded backwards until his calves stuck something soft, and he went down, eye-horn's curved sword whistling through the air above him as he fell.

Twice in less than half a minute, sheer dumb luck had been all that saved Julian. He glanced to the right, and realized it had been tongue-less' limp leg that he had tripped over.

Giving his head a quick shake of amazement mixed with disgust, he looked back up again in time to see eye-horn raising his sword for another attack.

That was quite enough of that. Julian growled and whipped his own weapon forward. He was rewarded by the soft resistance of steel cutting through flesh, and then more blood poured out as eye-horn's thighs opened behind his cut.

Eye-horn stumbled, his attack forgotten as his legs lost their strength beneath him. The big man fell to his left, impacting the ground next to Tongueless, where he squirmed about, howling a mix of pain and frustration.

The others were almost upon Julian; no time to relish the respite.

He pushed himself backwards to get clearance from the two sprawled bodies, and felt hands pulling him upright.

"We have to get out of here," Tolburt said into his ear as he reached his feet.

Julian eyed the three approaching not-dead men and was about to object. Then tongueless began moving again, pushing himself up onto his knees. The axe cut to his throat had clearly not been sufficient to put him down.

Julian swallowed, forcing the ice that suddenly had appeared where his stomach used to be out of his consciousness, then nodded. "To the building."

Tolburt's nod of agreement was immediate.

They wasted no more time, but turned and ran.

❧ 36 ☙

FLIGHT

They ran hard, oblivious to the courtyard's paving stones biting into the soles of their feet, heedful only of the sounds of their pursuing attackers. The closest of the three buildings surrounding the dome lay behind and to the left of the fallen Eyehorn and Tongueless, and Julian and Tolburt veered directly toward its gaping, dark doorway.

Julian hazarded a glance back over his shoulder as they drew near the door. They had opened some space from the walking dead men; their wounds, and their awkward formation behind their two fallen fellows, had slowed them down.

But that wouldn't last.

Tolburt stopped before the doorway and squinted, peering into the gloom within. After a second, he nodded and glanced at Julian. "Looks clear."

"Doesn't really matter, does it?" Julian didn't wait for a response, he just ran inside.

The room was completely different than it had been when they searched the buildings earlier. A second doorway, just as lightless as the main entrance had looked from outside, lay open in the rear wall, just wide enough for one man to pass through at a time. As well, two metal cages, doors flung wide open, now stood in the rear corners of the room. The cages were topped by solid stone; clearly they had risen up from the floor, and had housed Julian and Tolburt's attackers.

Julian suppressed a shudder as the thought of what it must have been like, being entombed in those cages for five hundred years raced through his mind.

No wonder those guys were filled with blood lust.

"We can maybe hold them at the doorway, but - "

Julian interrupted Tolburt, nodding at the shaft leading back into darkness. "We can hold them better from in there."

Tolburt stepped up next to him and frowned. "We don't know where that - "

A guttural sound that was a mixture of a language Julian had never heard and a feral growl made both of them turn around.

Half-bird, blood flowing freely from an axe cut that should have gone straight through a lung and into his heart, seemed to fill the building's entrance with his bulk. His chest heaved, sending blood fountaining out, and he raised his sword to point it at Julian and Tolburt.

Tongueless, his head flopping forward and to the right grotesquely, stepped into the doorway next to his comrade.

They paused there for a second, long enough for the other three to gather up behind them, then they advanced.

"Doesn't matter." Tolburt echoed Julian's words from a few seconds before, then he retreated into the rear doorway.

Julian couldn't fault Tolburt's judgment there. He followed suit, backpedalling quickly while raising his sword to a guard between himself and the advancing dead men.

He bumped into something soft, but firm. He glanced back and saw the back of Tolburt's head. He had slowed enough so they could be back to back.

Good call.

"I can't see much back here," Tolburt said. "But it goes on for a while."

Half-bird twisted his bulk slightly, and his companion entered the corridor after them. "Wish I could say the same." Julian stopped backpedalling. "Hold; I'll let you know if I need a relief." How exactly that relief was to be accomplished he didn't bother to ponder. No point.

Tongueless lurched forward, his bulk blocking out the sunlight that streamed through the doorway. In the narrow confines of the passageway, the smell of sweat mixed with blood assaulted Julian's nostrils as readily as the not-dead man's weapon could have. Julian swallowed an uprising of bile and flexed his fingers on the grip of his borrowed sword, waiting for the inevitable attack.

He almost didn't see it coming, so deeply in shadow were they. A subtle shifting of Tongueless' shoulder was the only tell; it could have come from any number of movements.

But there was only one possible interpretation here.

Gambling that the multiply-injured man would be straightforward in his assault, as he and his comrades had been so far, Julian dropped into a crouch, ducking his head and shoulders beneath the larger man's swing, and was rewarded with a whistling just above his head, and slight breeze that made his hair flutter as Tongueless' sword passed above him.

Then he surged upward, cutting with all his might.

His blade met soft resistance that quickly turned solid as he cut through the meat of Tongueless' upper arm and ground against bone.

Julian's sword could not get through the bone, but he continued the cut anyway, dragging the steel up and to the left, letting every inch of his weapon scrape a quickly-deepening notch until the tip pulled free.

Tongueless made a gurgling half-bellow which only really succeeded in coughing out spasms of blood from the great wound on his neck, and Julian could feel as much as see the big man's sword arm fall limply.

He surged forward, bellowing out a great cry of determined anger —anger at the predicament, the stupidity of their being here, of worry over Melanie's fate, and at a dozen other things that he could not name—and brought his sword back downward as hard as he could.

Tolburt's axe-cut had mostly done for Tongueless' neck. Julian's sword did the rest.

The shock of impact ran up Julian's arm for a second, and then the blade carried on through, and Tongueless' body and head dropped, separately.

Another bulky form filled the passageway beyond the corpse. The glare of the sun juxtaposed with the darkness of the space made it impossible to tell which one, but did it matter?

Julian backed up until he felt Tolburt's back again. "That'll slow them down a little," he said quickly, between heaving breaths.

"Wonderful."

"Hey, there's only four left. We've got this." Julian tried to inject a bit of levity into his tone, but even to his own ears the attempt fell flat.

And no wonder why. The new attacker slowed to step carefully over Tongueless' body, and his bulk seemed all the greater in the glare behind him. Four more just like him, and only one possible mortal wound…

Well, there was nothing for it but to push on. And it certainly didn't make any sense to let this new guy get his feet solidly under him so he could attack in comfort.

So Julian charged.

He came straight on, lowering his shoulder as he surged ahead and hoping against hope that the speed of his attack would bring him within the man's sword range before he could run Julian through. The instant froze into a short eternity, and then Julian was rewarded with a grunt as his shoulder struck the middle of the man's belly.

The big man stumbled backwards, the force of Julian's blow knocking him off-balance. He teetered for a moment as his feet landed awkwardly on Tongueless' body, and then he fell backwards, his arms flailing wide as he reflexively tried to grab out for something to stop his fall.

"Gotcha," Julian growled, and leapt forward, landing on the man's belly and stabbing downward with his sword as soon as he landed.

The curved tip of the blade slipped beneath the man's mask and thrust upward through the flesh beneath his jaw, then stopped as it ground against the bone of his skull.

The man tried to let out a scream, but all he could manage with Julian's blade through his jaw was a pathetic half-gurgle, half-whine. He moved his left hand to grab at Julian's shoulder, and his right lifted his sword, no doubt intending to cut Julian in two. And he would have no trouble doing it, if he got his hands on him.

Desperately, Julian threw himself forward, putting his entire weight into his sword and willing it to drive fully home.

For a second, nothing happened, and he felt the man's free hand grip his shoulder. The sword arm began to come down.

And then came a muffled crack, and Julian's sword ran home another few inches.

The man beneath him grunted, and his limbs jerked. The hand that had been gripping Julian tightened painfully for a heartbeat, then went limp and dropped to the ground. The sword arm did the same, and his weapon clattered onto the stones beside his body.

Julian lay there propped up on his sword hilt for several seconds, just sucking in air. Relief poured through him, and it seemed the strength had left his body.

He should be dead, yet somehow he was not. The gods smiled on fools, it seemed.

"Julian!"

Tolburt's voice brought Julian back around to his situation. He looked up, and blanched.

The next of the men had entered the corridor and was approaching. The sunlight reflected off the honed edge of his blade, illuminating his mask for a moment. It seemed in that second as though his eyes were on fire.

"Oh crap," Julian murmured. He shoved himself backward, pushing off the grip of a sword he knew would not come free. But he didn't go far; his feet tangled up in the two intertwined bodies beneath him. He landed on his backside and slid a half-foot until his shoulder impacted with the wall.

But he hadn't gone far enough. The fire in the approaching man's eyes seemed to flare brighter, and in a motion that was almost too quick to see, he raised his sword, then brought its razor edge down at Julian.

He could only raise an empty hand in a useless attempt at defense, cringe away, and await the end.

37

STANDOFF

The sword came down, and Julian reflexively clenched his eyes shut as he prepared for the pain.

It never came. Instead, the sharp ring of steel striking steel rang out above him, followed almost immediately by a scraping that made him cringe even further. Then came a squishy-thud, and a muffled grunt of pain, and wetness flowed onto Julian's legs.

Julian opened his eyes and looked up.

The wall less than an inch above him was visibly scored where his attacker's sword had struck. The weapon had impacted so forcefully that it had bent; the last inch or so was still embedded in the wall.

Julian moved his gaze up the cold steel toward the hand clenching the weapon, and he felt his eyes widen.

The hand was not attached to an arm.

A flurry of movement above him and to his left drew Julian's eyes higher.

The man who had tried to kill him recoiled, blood fountaining from the stump of his right arm and spraying all over the front of Tolburt as Julian's comrade advanced. His axe, dripping fluid from the blow that had taken the man's hand, rose and fell again. Then again. And again.

The man raised the stump in self-defense, but that proved as effective as Julian's attempt would have been. Tolburt's axe bit into his shoulder, then his other arm at the bicep as he tried to raise it. The axe clove through his left collar bone, then his right, and both arms flopped to his side, useless.

A final blow drove through the man's mask, nearly splitting his head in half, and the man dropped like a stone.

Tolburt bent over, breathing heavily. He placed his palms onto his knees to help regain his breath and looked back at Julian. "You ok?"

Julian nodded, then realized Tolburt probably couldn't see the gesture in the deeper gloom where he lay. "Yeah," he said, and cringed inwardly as he heard the quaver in his voice. That had been close. Too close. Julian swallowed. "Thanks. Again."

Tolburt shrugged. "Don't mention it." He drew a long breath, then straightened and, grasping the haft of his axe, yanked it free of the dead man's skull.

He was clearly visible in the sunlight streaming in through the doorway. Julian frowned when he realized there was nothing, or rather no one, blocking that light. "Where are our friends?"

Tolburt shook his head. "No idea. Three of them here, another one out in the square…that leaves two more."

"Probably they're thinking better of coming at us one by one in here," Julian said. He pushed himself back from the stuck sword and hewn-off hand, then carefully got to his feet.

"Can't say I blame them." Tolburt shook his head. "Probably they're on either side of the hallway out there, just waiting to hack us to bits when we come out."

Hard to argue with that assumption. Julian looked over his shoulder back into the gloom of the hallway. As far as he could tell, it continued on past where the walls faded completely into shadow, but it couldn't run all that far. The building wasn't all that big, after all. Unless there were stairs, or…

"Were you able to tell anything else about what's back there?"

"Not yet. I wouldn't want to try without some kind of light, though."

Julian nodded to himself in agreement. There were too many ways for that to go horribly. "Not much choice but to spring their trap then."

The reluctance in Tolburt's tone as he said, "Seems like it," was plain, and mirrored Julian's own. If the men, whoever they were, *were* waiting in ambush, they would have the advantage. Especially since he and Tolburt could only come out of the hallway one at a time.

All the same, it wasn't like they could just remain here forever.

Julian sighed. "All right. Let's get it done."

Clambering over three dead bodies in the gloom, especially when two of them were lying practically atop each other, was a slow, cumbersome process. Not to mention disgusting. Julian did not think he would ever get the stink of blood, and other fluids he did not want to consider, out of his nostrils. But soon enough, the task was done. Julian only paused long enough to pick up one of the dead men's swords before nudging Tolburt forward.

They approached the opening leading back into the front room cautiously, Tolburt sliding against the left-hand wall and Julian against the right. Moving that way meant they could both just barely fit through the hallway, but it would also mean neither of them would be able to immediately take defensive action. Julian figured it was worth it to get a chance at viewing the waiting attackers before they sprung the ambush.

But as they neared the opening and he leaned to his right, getting as much a view around the corner to the left as he could without sticking his head out into the open, he saw no one there at all.

He glanced over at Tolburt, raising a questioning eyebrow. Tolburt responded with a confused frown and a quick shake of his head.

Julian returned the frown and pondered for a moment. Where had the last two gone? Maybe they were simply farther back from the hallway entrance than they could see from this angle? He made a quick decision. Holding up his left hand with three fingers raised, he caught Tolburt's eye and then slowly lowered his fingers one at a time.

As soon as the last curled back into his fist, Julian surged forward out of the hallway. He ducked his head as he ran, in anticipation of the decapitating strike he could practically feel coming, then spun to his right, sword raised to a guarding position.

And saw an empty room.

Behind him, he heard Tolburt maneuver as he had, then the other man's confused, "What the hell?"

Julian looked behind himself and saw that the room on Tolburt's side was just as empty as his was. The men had simply left. In fact…

"Wait a minute," Julian said. "What happened to the cages?"

Tolburt's mouth dropped open, and he shook his head silently.

The cages, where Julian had presumed the men who attacked them had been lying in wait, were gone, as though they had never been. Moving over to the corners and looking more closely at the floor, there was not even a crack to indicate where the block that had been atop the cages' bars would seat with the remainder of the floor.

It was like they had never existed at all.

"You don't suppose those guys just got back into the cages and..." Tolburt trailed off, making a vague gesture toward the floor to finish the thought.

Julian shook his head in disbelief. "I wouldn't have. Would you?"

Tolburt snorted. "I wouldn't just attack some random people who were just standing around here either. So who knows what those guys would or would not do."

Which was a valid point, though Julian had to restrain himself from pointing out that Tolburt had essentially done that very thing last winter. Or at least, his friends Geoff and Stefan had, and that was close enough.

It didn't take all *that* much effort to restrain himself, though. And that surprised him.

"Well," Tolburt said, interrupting Julian's thoughts. "What now? Should we...?" He gestured questioningly toward the doorway leading back outside.

Julian hesitated. It could be the men had set up their ambush in the open, where they would have more room to maneuver. But that didn't seem like a good play. In closer quarters, they could more probably use their greater strength to their advantage. In the open, Julian and Tolburt could more easily elude them. So if they had set up out there, they must have something else up their sleeve. Maybe reinforcements?

But just like in the hallway, remaining in place out of fear of what might be lurking outside wasn't really an option. If nothing else, should reinforcements be coming, swift movement now might allow Julian and Tolburt to escape before they arrived. Assuming they hadn't already.

More importantly, he had no idea how much longer Melanie had.

Surely she couldn't survive encased like that forever. The more time they spent quibbling over what to do…

A shiver ran up Julian's spine and he felt a creeping dread, but he refused to allow himself to finish that thought. They would be successful, and she would get through this.

Either that, or Feirhard's final days would be a torment of the sort legends are made of.

Julian's sword hand began to hurt, and he looked down at it. His knuckles were white, he was gripping the weapon so hard. That drew him back to the present, and he took in a long, deep breath to calm himself. Time enough for vengeance later; for now, he needed to be cool.

Looking back at Tolburt, he gave a quick nod. "Be ready."

Tolburt returned the nod and raised his axe. Then, together, they turned and advanced through the doorway and out into the open.

And promptly stopped short in shocked disbelief.

38

COOL WATERS

Where before there was a courtyard of stone, surrounded by three stone buildings, and centered on a crystalline glass dome in the midst of a desert that stretched as far as the eye could see, now there were rolling hills topped by copses of elms and oaks, green grass with the occasional clump of colorful wildflowers covering the areas between the copses, and a crystal-blue pool directly in front of the doorway, lined with polished stepping stones and flanked by a pair of closed, iron-reinforced oak chests. The sun, the normal white-yellow sun, shone down from above and puffy white clouds floated on the breeze against a pure blue sky. Songbirds chirped from the limbs of the closest copse, maybe twenty yards away, and butterflies coasted on the breeze, going between the clumps of flowers seemingly without a care in the world.

Where before the air was dry and stifling, the temperature uncomfortably hot and the sun's radiance brilliant enough to burn a man's skin, now it was pleasantly cool, just shy of warm. The air bore the sweet scent of Spring, and was moist enough to maintain the wetness on a man's tongue without either adding to it or sucking it away.

In short, they had stepped into a veritable paradise.

Julian looked around, dumbfounded, and dropped his sword arm to his side without even thinking about it. "What the - ?" he began, then stopped, unable to complete the thought as his eyes locked onto the inviting blue pool and the toll that the last several hours without water had exerted on him fully came into his consciousness.

He had been able to force the discomfort back beneath the needs of the moment. But now, with relief seemingly so close at hand…

He found he had taken three steps toward the pool before he realized what he had done. Only the most supreme effort forced his feet from plowing on ahead toward the water's relief. But he recalled what had happened the last time he and Tolburt had drunk from water that this place had offered them.

"Jared," he croaked out, trying to voice the warning he felt in his heart. Even to his own ears, his voice was guttural, almost unrecognizable.

Nonetheless, he saw Tolburt out of the corner of his eye, not moving toward the pool despite the obvious desire in his eyes to do so.

"I know," Tolburt replied, and the strain was plain in his voice.

"Look around for the last two. This has to be a trap." Even as he said it, the lion's share of Julian's psyche screamed out against the notion. Couldn't he see? The water was right there. Rest was right there. It was no trap. Just reach out and take it. Restore yourself before you collapse!

But he could not bring himself to believe that voice; it had betrayed him before within the Falconer's Stairs.

It took all the effort he could muster, but Julian forced his eyes away from the inviting pool. He turned a full circle, casting about for any hint of the enemy that had so doggedly pursued him and Tolburt. But no matter where he looked, he could see no sign of them. Indeed, the entire area around the pool was clear of obstruction in every direction for at least the twenty yards' distance to that next copse. Except for the path they had taken to this place, that was.

Directly behind them stood a single monolith of granite, standing atop a small grass-covered mound. The monolith contained the doorway they had just come through, and through it Julian could see the inner room of the building they had just fought to the death to keep.

But how was it that they had come through that doorway into this place, and not the courtyard that had been in front of the building at first?

Even as he contemplated that question, the doorway seemed to shimmer and blur, like waves of heat rising from the distant stones of a paved road on a hot day in the depths of summer. And then, a moment later, the doorway was gone, leaving only the bare grey stone of the monolith atop the green mound in this idyllic place.

"No one here,' Tolburt said. "Has to be magic." And Julian immediately knew that for truth.

Had not this entire place been one magical trap after another? Was this not a single sick and twisted test, from beginning to end? Of course they couldn't count on anything to be constant from one moment to the next!

Irritation—outrage really—welled up within Julian, borne of the idiocy of this entire endeavor. Some bastard couldn't bring himself to love or trust his own son without setting up some sadistic test for him, and they had to pay the price for it? Never mind that they had willingly come here to pit themselves against the Lord Magus' test for his heir, this was demented. It was wrong.

How DARE he set up a farce like this, and how DARE Feirhard willingly take part in it!

They should both have known better. Too bad Hevergod couldn't be made to pay for his arrogance anymore.

Feirhard, though…

Julian found his lips drawing back into a bloodthirsty grin.

"Have no fear. Take your ease, and accept these gifts as recompense for your troubles. Recover your strength, for you will need it."

Julian turned at Tolburt's words and saw him standing next to the edge of the pool, looking down at one of the stones that lined its edge. "Come again?"

Tolburt looked back at him and shrugged, then gestured down toward the stone. "Feirhard left us a message."

Julian grunted. "I'll trust gifts from him as far as I can throw that rock." He jerked his free thumb over his shoulder toward the monolith for emphasis.

Another shrug from Tolburt. "If it's meant to harm us, it's meant to harm us. But he hasn't done anything without leaving us a way out. Besides," he swept his hand around, taking in the entire area, "if this is a trap, it's the nicest one I've ever seen." He shook his head and, bending over, laid his axe down on the grass beside the paving stones. Then he squatted down and dipped his hands into the pool.

"Jared, don't - " Julian began.

But Tolburt moved too quickly. He brought his cupped hands to his mouth and drank from the pool's water.

Julian froze, watching Tolburt intently, that creeping dread that had been shadowing his psyche for what seemed like days surging forward within him. If it was poison, or some sort of magical elixir, it would probably show itself quickly…

Tolburt remained motionless for several long seconds. Then, all at once, he dropped his head. His body pitched forward and he rolled into the pool.

"Oh crap!" Julian hurried forward, dropping his sword into the grass as he ran as quickly as his much-abused feet would let him toward the water's edge. There wouldn't be much time to fish Tolburt out, if it was even possible. He would -

The water rippled, then Tolburt popped up to the surface, his long hair flinging up over his head as he threw his head back and exhaled mightily. "Ah, gods, that feels great," he said, and he looked at Julian with a broad grin on his face. "Why Julian, if I didn't know better, I'd say you were worried about me."

Julian drew up short and scowled in irritation, but after a second or two found he just couldn't muster the energy for it. He gave a little snort instead. "Well, I guess it's not poisoned," he said, lamely.

"Would you just shut up and get in here? You look like you've rolled through a dozen butcher's shops."

Julian looked down at himself, and winced. He was covered, practically head to toe, in blood, some of it his own but most from those men they had fought. His muscles ached, his feet were rubbed so raw it was painful to even stand let alone run, and he hurt in about a dozen places. A dip in cool water would do wonders, if only to get the muck off.

Still…

Tolburt rolled his eyes, then submerged himself again. He came up a few minutes later, treading water half a dozen feet further out into the pool and looking for all the world like a contented fellow without a care in the world. He began to stroke toward the other side of the pool, about fifteen feet away. When he reached the other side and took hold of the stones that made up the water's edge without incident, that decided it.

Shaking his head at the sheer stupidity of what he was about to do, but honestly not able to come up with a compelling reason why he shouldn't do it except for suspicion, Julian stepped up to the water's edge and jumped in.

The water, cool, clear, and apparently clean, enclosed him, and immediately Julian felt his weariness, his aches, and his stress wash away. He suspended in the water's embrace for a short, cleansing eternity, then floated up to the surface. When his head broke and he drew in that next breath of air, it was like a back rub and a long nap all rolled into one.

He felt…great.

"Wow," he said. "I guess I needed that." He breathed deeply, treading water slowly as the strength seemed to flow back into his limbs, then he ducked his head beneath the surface and gulped down a mouthful of the clear fluid.

And it *was* clear, too. Despite the fact that the blood and muck had begun to wash from his body, the water of the pool showed no sign of it.

Great. More magic.

Of course.

Right then, that didn't seem like such a bad thing.

Letting out a little whoop, Julian kicked his torso higher out of the water, then he plunged headfirst back into the water and kicked downward, losing himself in enjoyment.

He could just stay here forever.

It flashed through his head that if this was, after all, a trap, he just might end up doing that. But right then, he didn't care. The sheer bliss of being washed clean by the pool's water overcame any concern that thought might have brought on at a different time.

Finally, after an untold amount of time soaking without a care in the world, he noticed Tolburt hoist himself up out of the pool. Julian looked over as he pushed himself to his feet, and winced at what he saw. Tolburt had been washed completely clean of blood and dirt, and as far as Julian could tell he was not even scratched. But his back was crisscrossed by a multitude of long, thin white-pink scars. Old wounds, by the look of them, long since healed. But still…

"What happened there?" he said. When Tolburt glanced back at him over his shoulder, Julian waved his hand toward the man's back.

Tolburt's eyes flickered down, as though to look through the meat of his shoulder to the scars, and his lips turned downwards into a frown. "What's it look like?"

Julian stroked to the edge of the pool and, placing his palms onto the stones at its edge, pushed himself out of the water. As he rose to his feet, he gave Tolburt a level look. "A flogging."

"There you go." He turned away from Julian and took a step toward the closer of the two chests. "What do you think's in these?"

Nice attempt to change the subject. Perhaps Julian should just let it go, but a thought entered his mind, a near-certainty that, just then, he needed to confirm. "Was that after…"

He trailed off, but Tolburt turned back to him and finished the thought. "After you made your escape and left me behind?" His nostrils flared and his eyes narrowed. Julian saw a flash of deep-seated anger in them for a second.

Oh hell no. He did not get to be angry over that. "Better than you deserved after what you did to the rest of us."

Tolburt stared daggers at him for a long couple of seconds, then nodded. "I suppose that's true." He rolled his shoulders slightly as though remembering the sting of the lash. "Well, I paid for it. Several times over." He held Julian's eyes for another second, then turned back to the chest. "Let's have a look in here."

He bent over, and the scars on his back twisted sickeningly. Then he opened the chest's latch and lifted its lid.

"Well," Tolburt said, sounding surprised, "that's a sight for sore eyes." He flipped the lid fully open.

Julian looked away from Tolburt's back to the chest, and blinked in surprise. Within were all of Tolburt's things. His clothes, sword belt and weapon, his boots…all the things that had been taken back before the chamber of torture, seemingly a year ago.

He looked back up at Tolburt and saw the bearded man was grinning at him. "Still think this is a trap?"

Julian shrugged.

Now, he was certain of it.

39

PARTING IN SORROW

No surprise, the other chest contained all of Julian's gear, even down to the coins in his purse and the lint in his pockets.

As he withdrew one item after the other, verifying they really were his and doing an inventory in his head, Julian found himself growing more and more nervous. His shoulders clenched as though expecting an arrow to strike his back at any second.

And why not? Not only was all his gear here, but he, like Tolburt, was completely restored physically. All the various cuts and scrapes, the aches and pains, the bumps and bruises, and the extensive damage to the soles of his feet were healed as though the injuries had never been.

He hadn't noticed it when he first climbed out of the pool, so deeply had Tolburt's scars and then the contents of his chest taken Julian's attention. But within the first step toward the other chest, the lack of pain from his foot drew him up, shocked. Tolburt confirmed it a moment later, after looking him over: he was completely healed.

That pool was magical in more ways than one.

Which meant that whatever they were to face next was bound to be worse than anything they had come across yet. And wasn't that a depressing thought?

Julian pulled the last of his gear from the chest and completed his mental inventory. Then he was surprised to see another item within.

He reached down and picked it up, and the slight curve of the short sword's blade gleamed in the sunlight. Julian's eyes widened. This was the weapon he had taken from the torture chamber and left embedded in their attacker's armpit near the crystalline dome between the trio of stone buildings. Without thinking about it, he took hold of the grip and once again marveled at its perfectly textured construction, the contours that seemed to so naturally fit his hand and that promised to never betray his grasp.

"How did this get here?" he asked aloud. Then he snorted out a half-laugh as the absurdity of the question struck him. How did any of this get here? The whole place was magical, why should anything surprise him at this point?

Julian turned to look in Tolburt's direction and found that he had gotten mostly dressed; he was just pulling his tunic over his head. Julian waited for him to get the garment situated, then he whistled softly, drawing Tolburt's eyes to himself.

"Did you find any extra gifts?"

Tolburt's eyebrows rose as he saw the short sword, and he looked down at the collection of gear around his feet. He did a quick scan, then shook his head and looked back at Julian. "Guess Feirhard likes you," he said with a little shrug and a grin.

Julian snorted again. "I doubt that." More likely there was an angle to his having the sword that he couldn't see, but would bite him in the behind.

All the same, it was a *nice* blade. Very nice.

He shrugged and put the weapon down, then started donning his clothing and equipment. If there was a snare of some kind, he could deal with it later. For now, it was just good to have his stuff back. And to not be hurting anymore.

A few minutes later, he rose from lacing up his boots and felt like a new man. He hefted his pack and slung it over his shoulders, shrugging to get it settled, then shoved the short sword through his belt opposite his longsword and turned to face Tolburt.

"All set, Jared?"

Tolburt looked up from where he was squatting next to the pool. He was fully clothed and equipped, and held his water skin into the water. "Can't hurt to bring this with us, right?" he said with a grin.

That was actually one hell of a good idea. Julian returned the grin, nodded, then pulled out his own skin. A minute later, filled skins stowed and both feeling refreshed and if not eager to meet the next challenge, at least ready, they met at the message stone and looked around for any indication on which way to go next.

Alas, it was all pleasant grassland and copses, rolling hills and blue skies as far as the eye could see. There did not appear to be any other signs or guidance anywhere.

Finally, Julian shrugged and looked back at the monolith that they had stepped out of not so long ago. "Straight away from that thing, from the other side of the pool?"

Tolburt frowned slightly, then shrugged. "Might as well."

They strolled around the pool—this was not a place where hurrying seemed even remotely appropriate, or even necessary—and, once they were opposite the monolith, turned and walked straight away.

The ground slowly rose as they walked, and a few minutes later they found themselves cresting a modest hill and looking down at a very different landscape.

Past the hilltop where they stood, the grass, the wildflowers, and the lush copses of trees all stopped. The descending terrain abruptly turned brown and gray, rocky and cloven with crevasses. The occasional scraggily tree or bush, with leaves so withered that it was impossible to tell their types, strived mightily to grow in the blasted land, but seemed doomed to failure. The sky, which had been pleasant and blue, turned grey and overcast, with boiling black clouds in the distance promising storms to come. The temperature had dropped considerably, grown unpleasantly chilly, and the air carried a hint of sulfur and something else, a sweet-sour odor that Julian could not quite put a name to.

Julian halted, the relaxation that had filled him dropping away in an instant, replaced by wary apprehension.

"Well, this can't be good," Tolburt said, lightly, but with just a hint of tension in his voice.

No. No it cannot.

Julian looked over his shoulder. He half expected their resting area and the pool to have vanished, but they still stood, invitingly. He felt a powerful tug within himself, a call to turn back and take his ease some more. There lay safety, and everything he could need for as long as he wanted. Why give that up in exchange for the obvious peril ahead?

Better to choose the pleasant. The safe.

He licked his lips, suddenly feeling the lack of the pool's water on his lips. And were those apples in that tree not so very far away? Surely it wouldn't hurt to go grab a few. Just a short delay, and then the quest could continue. He had struggled enough; he had earned a rest. Why not take it?

Julian had taken a half step back the way they had come before he realized it. Only Tolburt grabbing his upper arm brought him to a stop.

"What are you doing?" Tolburt said, and Julian turned baleful eyes on him, fierce anger rising quickly to full, primal fury surging within him at the younger man's presumption. To lay hands on him? To stop him from going where he willed?!

Julian's hand fell to the grip of his new short sword, and he growled, "Remove your hand, Jared."

Tolburt's eyes narrowed, but he did not let go. "We can't go back there, Julian. Melanie's ahead." He paused, his eyes narrowing. "Remember?"

Melanie.

The word meant something, somewhere. Julian was sure of it, but whatever it was eluded him.

This was foolishness. Stupidity. He jerked away from Tolburt and slid the short sword free. Keeping the tip low, he backed away from the insolent man. He didn't actually want to spill Tolburt's guts, but if forced to it…

Tolburt's eyes widened, and he raised his hands, palms wide and open toward Julian. "What's gotten into you?" he said. He took a hesitant step forward, but stopped when Julian raised his sword. He swallowed. "Ok," his voice took on a soothing, placating tone. "Calm down. What's wrong?"

What was wrong? If he was too stupid to see the folly in what they were doing, Julian had no idea how to explain it. "We have to go back," he said.

"Julian. There's nothing for us back there. The only way is forward."

Nothing for us? Fool! Couldn't he see the fruit, the safety. He preferred…this? Julian cast his eyes toward the blasted landscape and shuddered. No, they were not ready for this. A little more provision first. A little more rest. And then, maybe later…

He took a sidestep toward the clear boundary between the haven and this place. Tolburt's lips turned down into a scowl.

"Damn it, Julian, what about Melanie?"

That word again. It ran afoul on…something…in Julian's mind. It should mean more to him…

But the sunlight reflecting on the water, the ripe fruit on the trees. The scent of honey and flowers wafting into his nostrils, overpowering the stench of this place. How could they even consider remaining here? Julian turned his head to look more fully back at the pool.

"Jared," he began.

He didn't have the chance to get the rest of his thought out. Tolburt's shoulder slammed into his chest, and he found himself crashing to the ground. The wind left his lungs in an unnaturally loud, "Oof," and he fell to gasping. He barely noticed Tolburt falling atop him and slamming the back of his left hand into the ground, and losing the grip on his short sword…

The world seemed to wrench inside his head, and Julian cried out as a thousand tiny daggers stabbed through his skull. Again and again they stabbed, and the pain grew until it encompassed his entire being.

The last thing he heard before unconsciousness claimed him was the sound of his own screams.

🕸 40 🕸

REGAINED SENSES

Julian's eyes cracked open, and he winced. The light was brilliant, so bright it hurt his head just to squint at it. So he closed his eyes again.

The ache did not stop.

Groaning, he pressed his palms to his head and lay there as the rest of his senses, and his memory, returned to him.

"What in the hell just happened?" he managed to say, sounding half-strangled even to his own ears.

A loud snort from above him preceded Tolburt's response. "You tell me." His voice was full of accusation, and confusion.

Tolburt didn't need to elaborate. Julian's actions of a few minutes before—he presumed it was only a few minutes—were clear in his mind, and they made as little sense to him as they apparently had to Tolburt.

He shook his head. "It... It was like we had to go back to the pool. No matter what, we had to. And when you tried to stop me..." He trailed off.

"You found a convenient excuse to off me, like you've always wanted to."

Julian sat up and lowered his hands, looking up at Tolburt in shock, the ache in his head forgotten, or at least pushed to the back of his mind for the moment. "What? No, I didn't - "

Tolburt snorted loudly. "Sure you have." He paused, then

shrugged. "Can't say I blamed you. At first. But after a couple months, it began to get old." He reached down and offered Julian his had.

Julian hesitated for a few seconds, but finally accepted it, and Tolburt helped him to his feet. He took a moment to readjust his gear, unsure how to continue the conversation.

Tolburt came to his rescue. Again. By shrugging. Again. "Like I said, no big deal. I knew you wouldn't really do it." His eyes narrowed as he looked Julian over. "You good to go?"

Julian winced. "Head aches like nobody's business," he said, "but aside from that, I'm good." He rolled his shoulders and spread his hands in a helpless gesture. "Not sure what happened there."

"Well, you started screaming as soon as you lost your grip on that," Tolburt nodded toward the ground off to the left, and Julian saw that short sword lying there, innocent as can be.

If something looks too good to be true, it probably is. Julian scowled. "Feirhard," he growled, and Tolburt nodded agreement. This whole test was getting well past irritating to the realm of the person who conceived it needs to be drawn, quartered, and flayed alive. Slowly. "I've about had enough of this."

"You and me both," Tolburt said. He gestured toward the broken and craggy landscape head and managed a half-grin. "Shall we?"

Julian didn't bother nodding. He just started walking straight away from the little bubble of pleasantness that had seemed so tempting a few minutes ago.

Now the thought of it made him want to hit someone. A very specific someone. Very hard.

Tolburt jogged a few steps to catch up. "Don't want that sword back?"

Julian looked at him sidelong. "You know, I actually *didn't* want to hurt you. But I might change my mind if you say something as stupid as that again."

Tolburt actually burst out laughing. "Will wonders never cease."

Julian stopped and looked at him sternly. "What?"

Tolburt kept on going. "Oh, nothing." He looked back and raised an eyebrow at Julian. "Come on already."

If anything, Tolburt picked up the pace. Julian scowled, but moved to follow him without saying anything else.

It seemed better that way.

❧ 41 ❧

SWEPT AWAY

The smell just got worse.

Normally, after a few minutes trudging along surrounded by the twin noxious odors that seemed to permeate this land, Julian's nostrils would have become used to the scent and he would have noticed it less. But not here, in this place. For whatever reason—and he was sure that reason had a name that rhymed with Feirhard—the odor, if anything, became stronger.

The broken and blasted landscape continued to descend from the hilltop they started atop, and though they often had to change course to avoid a yawning crevasse or a collection of boulders, or some other obstacle, Julian and Tolburt made decent time.

Or they would have, if they had an actual target to aim toward. But since they were, once again, just walking, their progress was lost on Julian. The only real bright side was that as they descended, the terrain became even more broken, which offered cover. And it looked as though they were going to need cover soon; the clouds were growing steadily blacker and thicker ahead of them, and seemed to be blowing straight in their direction. Ever so often, a flash of heat lightning would illuminate the horizon ahead, but Julian could not see any actual forks.

Nonetheless, a storm was brewing. The scented air seemed to grow thicker, more threatening, with each step, and a new odor began to emerge from beneath the sour and sulphuric blend that had been accosting his nose all this time: the scent of water on the wind, of impending rain.

A storm was brewing indeed, and when it broke, Julian didn't think they wanted to be anywhere near out in the open.

"Keep a look out for a cave or something," Julian said to Tolburt. "We're going to need shelter soon."

Tolburt didn't even look like he wanted to disagree. He just nodded, and they continued on. But even looking as carefully as they did, by the time the rain started there was still no sign of shelter more substantial than a narrow overhang of rock or the twisted limbs of a tree barely holding on to life.

The rain came on slowly at first, an almost unnoticeable mist that became a drizzle, and then seemingly between one moment and the next it increased to an annoying and entirely-soaking steady downpour. Water streamed down Julian's face and got in his eyes, and the pattering of drops onto the ground grew into a nearly deafening, continuous drumbeat all around. Rivulets of water came flowing off the ledges and rocks all around, and down the centers of the crevasses they passed, and very quickly visibility reduced to maybe ten feet in front of his face.

And then...lightning. A dazzling flash followed almost immediately by a titanic crack of thunder that left Julian staggering, ears ringing.

Another bolt came. And then another. And all the while, the downpour continued without sign of letting up.

Beside him, Tolburt mouthed something. It looked like "Head back," but the younger man's voice barely carried over the overall din, and Julian shook his head and spread his hands helplessly.

Tolburt rolled his eyes and opened his mouth to speak again. But then he stiffened, his eyes growing wide and his expression turning from one of annoyed misery to one of alarm, then outright fear. He jabbed his finger toward something over Julian's shoulder.

Julian turned to look, and the ground fell out from under his stomach.

The path they had taken downward had been transformed. The flows of water from the multitude of crevasses they had passed, and flowing down the sides of the slopes all around, were merging, and the steady flow of water rushing past their feet had grown to a rushing stream.

But above, that stream was turning into a full-on river, rushing down toward them like a hound chasing a rabbit, slobber spraying everywhere.

They had to get out of there. Right now.

Julian cast about. On either side of them were steep slopes of earth, nearly walls. Streams of rainwater cut through the earth all around, and it would be impossible to gain a purchase to get to higher ground.

There was only one way to go. He turned and grabbed the still gaping Tolburt by the shoulder, spinning him around and giving him a push forward.

Julian had only run a few steps when his feet slipped out from under him and he landed on his backside with a wet splat that went unheard beneath yet another clash of thunder. Beside him, Tolburt slipped also.

But they kept on going, riding the growing tide of water as the stream pushed them on downslope. Soon they were moving faster than they could have run, without risking breaking their necks anyway, and the stream had become a torrent.

Their gentle downward slope deepened into a crevasse of its own, and the current swirled as it rebounded against the earth and rocks on either side. Julian found he could no longer touch the bottom, and it became a struggle to keep his head above water. Every few seconds he would plunge beneath the waves, and he had to kick himself back up.

He shrugged off his pack, letting it sink, but the force pulling him downward hardly abated. He needed to lose the boots, or they would be the end of him. To say nothing of his mail.

Julian gasped in a breath as he broke the surface again, and saw Tolburt off to his left, stroking like mad toward the side of the crevasse. Then he looked forward and blanched.

It looked like just a wall of rock looming before them, but somehow the flow of water continued into it, or through it. There had to be a cave of some sort, and if they got sucked down there...

Icy fear chilled him even more than the water all around, and he kicked furiously, following Tolburt's line toward the side. If they could find something to brace themselves on, to keep from being sucked down, they might have a chance.

It was hard going. Though the wall was only maybe twenty or thirty feet away, it seemed he made no progress at all, and the weight of his gear settled heavily on him, dragging him downward.

He couldn't make it.

Ahead and downstream, Tolburt had managed to wedge himself into place, and he turned to look back Julian's way.

Julian stroked again, kicking for all his might, but he went under again.

As the river took him, he flashed back to a bit more than a year ago, when he and Raedrick first arrived in Glimmer Vale. They had almost immediately been accosted by a group of brigands, just above Silver Falls. During the ensuing fight, Julian had hurled the leader of the band into the icy waters of the Westflow, and stood there watching as the man got pulled under by the weight of his gear and then swept over the Falls.

Turn about really is fair play, it seemed.

He tried one last time to get back up to the surface, but he knew it was pointless. There was only darkness, punctuated by the occasional flash of lightning, and he couldn't even be sure which way was up.

His lungs burned, and he yearned to drawn breath. The blood pounded in his ears in time with his heartbeat.

Not long now.

Something struck him from behind, and then grabbed onto him firmly. Julian turned his head but could not see, and anyway he had no more strength to do anything.

Breathe. He had to breathe.

But he could not.

It took all his self-control to prevent that fatal inhalation, and he hardly noticed something flexible but firm being drawn around his torso.

Then his progress downstream was abruptly halted, and that something dug painfully into his armpits. The force of the current pushed him up, aided by the whatever-it-was that still held onto his back.

Julian didn't believe it at first when he broke the surface. But that didn't stop him from taking the breath he had been yearning to.

A wave slapped him in the face, and he immediately started coughing. The rope—of course it was a rope—around his chest felt like an iron band, so strong was the current trying to pull him along. But he was up, able to breathe.

"Would you get moving?!" he heard in his ear, and he recognized Tolburt's voice.

The younger man had one arm looped over Julian's shoulder, and he was stroking for all he was worth with the other.

Julian could see they were not very far from the crevasse wall now, and the rope was tied off somewhere upstream. Summoning energy he forgot he had, he kicked with all his might. Entangled with Tolburt as he was, it was hard to stroke, but he did it anyway.

And then they were at the wall, and he was able to find hand and footholds. Between those and the rope, it almost became comfortable to cling there after a moment.

Almost.

"Don't know about you," Julian said, his words interspersed with coughs, "but I am truly sick of this place."

❧ 42 ❧

DRIED OUT

They clung to the rock for hours, it seemed, muscles straining against the weight of their gear and against the pull of the current both. Had they not been tied off by the rope Jared had so quickly anchored, Julian felt certain he could not have stood it.

As it was, by the time the rain stopped and the waters began to recede, he could feel neither his arms nor his legs; they resembled nothing besides quivering weights that hung from his body. When finally his foot touched ground beneath the water, it felt like a boost from the gods.

When the waters had receded enough that he could flop down onto his back without fear of being swept away, it was sheer paradise, and never mind the chill of the water that remained.

Finally, after a small eternity, Julian roused himself enough to sit up, and he looked around.

The crevasse they had been swept into was deep, the walls maybe forty feet high on either side, the ground fairly level. The flowing water had bitten into the lower ten feet of the walls, burrowing out the loose earth and rounding the walls out so they were no longer sheer, except, interestingly, where he and Jared had clung. Everywhere else the walls overhung the floor so that, although the walls were only fifteen or twenty feet across from each other, the floor of the crevasse allowed about thirty feet of walking room.

The sky had cleared somewhat, also. The clouds still roiled, but they were higher, less oppressive, and more light made it through them to illuminate the land.

Jared was just sitting up, about ten feet away from where Julian sat, and he looked like hell. His pack was gone, and he had a big gash over his right eyebrow where he had scraped across the rocks at some point. His hair was a tangled, sopping wet mass of black that drooped everywhere, and he had an expression of utter exhaustion on his face.

Still, he managed a little grin. "Well that was not fun at all."

"This whole place is no fun," Julian muttered. He really wanted to just lie back down and give a pass on this whole stupid quest. But that was not an option, so instead, he placed his palms on the ground and, slowly, forced himself to his feet.

That hurt. A lot. He did it anyway.

"You ok?"

Jared nodded and followed Julian to his feet, moving no less slowly than he had. "Good as I can be."

Julian looked at him for a moment, then sighed. "Guess I owe you another one." He grinned ruefully, or tried to. "Thanks."

"Don't mention it." But Julian could tell he felt rather pleased with himself.

Their eyes met, and after a second Jared gave a little nod, which Julian returned.

"Right," Julian said. "Let's see what hoop Feirhard wants us to jump through next."

The water had continued to lower; it was now maybe an inch deep except in a few depressions here and there. So it was easy to quickly ascertain that they stood in a box canyon, albeit one that had been rounded out by the flowing water. The wall that had reared up in front of him as Julian got swept downstream remained there, and it was just as imposing, and impassable, as it had appeared.

And sure enough, just as he had suspected, down near the floor of the canyon, the wide black maw of an open cave lay beckoning to them.

After all, it wasn't as though they had anywhere else to go.

"Could he be more blatant about it?" Jared quipped, and Julian could not suppress a quick, amused chuckle.

"It's probably a trap."

Jared looked sidelong at him and shrugged. "Everything else has been."

"Well," Julian said, squaring his shoulders as best he could despite the continuing fatigue in his limbs, "let's go set it off."

And so they tromped forward through the puddled water toward the cave mouth. Julian could not help think, as they stepped within, that it really did look like a mouth, with worn down teeth in the ceiling just waiting to snap shut on them.

❧ 43 ☙

THE CAVE

The cave was wide, about fifteen feet across, and unnaturally smooth, the floor rising slowly on either side in an exact mirror of the ceiling's downward arc, forming a perfect oval, or near enough.

This was certainly made by a man; even running water could not have made the floor, ceiling, and walls so smooth, yet at the same time keep enough texture to the stone that Julian never once felt as though he was in danger of losing his footing.

"This gives me the creeps," Jared said after they had gone a couple dozen paces and yet somehow found the light undiminished despite their distance from the entrance and the lack of any obvious source of illumination.

Julian snorted. "Not sure why, after everything else we've gone through." He glanced back at the entrance, behind and above them, and wondered at their rate of descent. The floor did not seem to be at that much of an angle. "Still," he added, "can't hurt to be careful."

With that, he drew his sword.

Jared looked sidelong at him as though wondering what he was about. And frankly, Julian couldn't quite put his finger on it. But just then he had the distinct feeling on impending menace, as though all of the perils they had faced were merely a taste of what was to come.

He met Jared's stare and returned it, and after a second, the younger man nodded and drew his own weapon.

233

The path ahead continued to appear level, but occasional glances back over their shoulders showed the entrance continuing to rise higher, as though they were walking on a steep grade.

And then the entrance vanished from sight completely, obscured by the ceiling behind them. And still the light did not change.

The air grew chilly, and Julian soon began to shiver in his wet clothes. A strange odor lingered, growing stronger as they descended: musty dampness but something else, deeper down. Sweet, almost like honey.

Julian wet his lips despite not needing to, his feeling of unease growing. The entire world had condensed down into this single passageway, and he was fairly sure that -

"What odds do you give if we were to turn around, we would never find the entrance?"

Jared took the words right out of Julian's head. He shivered, and not just from the cold. "I wouldn't take that bet."

Onward they continued, and Julian lost track of time. He only knew that the muscles of his legs hurt from their earlier strain, and now his ankles and knees were beginning to echo that ache.

Almost as though they really had been on a steep downward slope.

Nothing changed, and aside from the sound of their breathing and the clomping of their boots on the stone there was no way to tell they were actually moving. Julian began to wonder if perhaps they had erred, and this was not the proper path at all, but instead an infinite tunnel leading nowhere, a final punishment for some test failed.

Then, between one step and the next, the tunnel widened without warning. One second it was the same monotonous passageway it had been, and the next…

The ceiling swept away upwards until it was lost in darkness overhead. The walls spread out and the floor actually took on a real downward slant until after about ten paces the walls were no longer visible on either side and they had descended almost ten feet from the narrow confines of the tunnel.

And then the floor, too, fell away. Only a raised lip, about a foot and a half high, signaled its end, and then the floor fell away into a sheer cliff face that stretched downward into infinity.

A collection of water remained on their side of the lip, evidence of the earlier deluge. Julian stepped cautiously into the puddle and looked down the cliff. His stomach gave a little hop in his belly and he edged back.

"Yikes," he said softly, and turned to peer left and right. "Where did that come from?" Although he knew the question to be pointless —where had any of the things they'd encountered in this magical place come from?—he still could not help but voice it.

Jared snorted. Standing back from the lip a few feet, he craned his neck and leaned forward to look over the edge, then swallowed visibly. "Better question is how do we get past it?"

That was a valid point. Of course, looking across the gulf, Julian could see nothing but gloom past the edge: no hint of another side, or of any bridge or conveyance to get them across.

If there was even something to cross to.

Again he wondered if this wasn't just the end game prison for folks who failed to measure up. But he cast that thought aside. The other challenges had immediate, and final, consequences for failure. He rather suspected that this would be no different.

"There must be a mechanism or something. We just need to find it." Julian looked around, then shrugged. "I'll take left, you take right?"

Jared nodded, but his smirk gave away the fact Julian had already considered: did it really matter who went which way?

"Let's not get separated. No more than a hundred paces, so we keep in sight of each other." Julian paused, considering. "I can't imagine Feirhard would have put the way across all that far from the entrance - " he gestured toward the tunnel they had come in and his eyes followed his hand.

He froze in shock, then muttered a salty curse.

Jared's eyes widened and he followed suit.

The tunnel was gone. Completely, as though it had never been.

The floor still sloped up to where the entrance had been, but now the stone was unbroken as it met the ceiling descending to meet it.

There was no going back.

That thought made him snort out a laugh. Where the hell were they going to go back to?

"No way out except forward," Jared said, and Julian nodded agreement.

"Success or death. Bloody wonderful."

They looked at each other for a second. Then Jared turned away to search his side.

Julian cleared his throat. "Be careful."

Jared looked back at him and grinned. "You too."

❧ 44 ❧

A BRIDGE TOO FAR

A hundred paces passed quickly, despite the slow pace Julian made and his frequent stops to look back and make sure Jared had not vanished.

Fortunately, he didn't.

Unfortunately, Julian could find not even a hint of any sort of mechanism or a way across. The cliff face just stretched on and on into seeming infinity, without offering a clue what to do now.

He stopped, scowling in annoyance and frustration. He had picked a hundred paces because it seemed a nice round number. But really, the crossing, if there even was one, could be miles ahead. Or miles in the other direction. Or maybe there wasn't a way across, but they were supposed to climb down. Or maybe they were supposed to take some damn fool leap of faith. Or maybe…

Enough of that. A man could drive himself nuts pondering too many maybes. It was time to link back up with Jared and put their heads together.

But just as he was about to turn around, he saw something in distance ahead. Movement of some kind; it was difficult to make it out.

Julian had sheathed his sword when he began his search. He drew it again now as a surge of adrenalin flooded his system.

He started forward.

The movement grew more distinct after a few paces. It was man-shaped, and coming in his direction at a slow walk. He couldn't make many features out, but he thought that was a scabbard hanging from the person's belt. And whoever it was didn't seem to be looking in his direction, more out toward the space past the cliff.

Julian increased his pace and moved higher on the slope toward where the ceiling and floor met. If he could get up on the person quick enough, he might be able to take him without much of a struggle.

And maybe they could get some answers.

The person quickly became more clear. He was skinny, tall, and looked decidedly rumpled. He stopped and squatted down, peering over the edge of the drop-off, and when he stood again Julian could make out his face.

He stopped cold. What in the - ?

"Jared?"

The person—Jared—gave a jerk and spun around in Julian's direction, moving to draw his sword at the same time. His eyes were wide with alarm, and then went wider with surprise as he saw Julian.

"Wha - "

His left foot came down awkwardly in the water and mud collecting along the lip and slipped right out from underneath him. Jared's question turned into a shout of chagrin, then alarm, as he flailed about for a second.

Then he fell over the edge.

Julian bit off a curse and, tossing his sword to the side, dove forward. He landed belly-first on the slope and slid down toward the lip, quickly becoming re-soaked in the cold water and mud that had collected there.

A single hand grasped the top of the lip.

Julian crashed into the lip and grabbed at the hand. He felt his momentum continuing forward, and he thought for a heartbeat he was going to go over also.

Then he stopped, balanced on the edge of the lip such that he feared to even move. But he had Jared's left arm gripped tightly in his right hand.

"Got ya. Give me your other hand," Julian said through gritted teeth.

Jared looked up at him, wide-eyed, and swung his right hand up. Julian caught it with his left.

"Julian," Jared began, and his voice sounded...confused?

"Later. Can you get a foothold or something?" Julian's arms were beginning to burn from holding him up.

"I...think so." Jared scrabbled around with his feet and a second later the force of his weight eased on Julian's muscles. Jared looked back up at him. "How are you doing this?"

Julian looked askance at him. "What?"

Jared's eyes left Julian's and moved left, toward where his legs lay atop the lip.

Julian followed his gaze, and his stomach dropped.

His legs were not balanced on the lip. Well, his right leg was. But his left... It was resting on nothing. Only it wasn't nothing, because he sure felt stone-like hardness beneath it. And water and mud were dripping from his leg onto the surface, whatever it was, pooling, and then running down and off. He could clearly see the edge of it, right near his hip.

"Feirhard," he all but spat. Of course the cussed mage would make his bridge invisible. He shook his head and looked back at Jared. "Let's get you up. Ready?"

Jared met his eyes again and nodded.

"One. Two. Three!"

A full-force heave of his shoulders combined with a helpful push up from Jared, and they had the younger man's arms and shoulders up over the lip. A bit of squirming later, Jared was safely back on solid ground and wiping mud and water from himself.

"Thanks," he said, and it sounded heartfelt.

"Guess that makes us even," Julian said as he turned around to find his sword.

A loud snort presaged Jared's response. "Not quite, by my count."

There it was. Julian bent over and scooped his blade up out of the muck. He turned around to face Jared, and shook his head. "Yes. It does." He gave Jared a hard look, one that said, "I haven't forgotten," and the younger man blanched.

Julian held that look for a long second, then grinned and clapped him on the shoulder with his free hand. Jared looked confused, then angry, then bemused all in the space of two blinks, then he returned the grin.

"Come on, let's get the hell out of here."

There was no cleaning the sword off. All of Julian's clothes were covered in muck and with his pack gone there were no other options. So he wiped the mud off as best he could before sliding it back into its scabbard. Then he turned to the spot where the bridge should be.

Sure enough, the water and mud that he had left atop it was still there, plain as day and clearly marking the nearest edge of the structure. As for the rest of it…

Julian squinted, concentrating. He could almost make it out. If he -

"He made the bridge invisible?" Jared sounded incredulous, but considering all they had seen in their time within this test, that seemed silly.

Oh well.

"That's actually impossible," Julian said with a quick shake of his head that never removed his eyes from the bridge. "Back when we first came to Lydelton, Melanie explained you can't actually make something invisible. Cloaking spells are just a suggestion to your brain to not notice it." He pursed his lips; the damn thing still would not come fully into view. "But she also said if you know a thing is there, you ought to be able to see it plainly, because the spell can't overcome your certainty. Or something."

"Ok, so why can't I see it?"

"No idea. Maybe Feirhard's spell is just really strong?" Julian sighed. "Who knows? And does it matter? We know it's there, so we can cross it."

He stepped toward the lip where the bridge lay, squaring his shoulders to step off. But Jared grabbed at his arm, holding him back.

"How do you intend to cross if we can't see it?"

Julian looked back at him and raised an eyebrow. Then he shrugged off Jared's hand and drew his sword. He lowered the tip until it struck the bridge with a soft ting of metal striking rock. After a second, he slid the weapon across the hidden bridge, the steel scraping noisily until it reached the edge, where it dipped into the empty air beyond.

"Same way a blind man walks anywhere, Jared."

Jared's eyes widened, and he looked from Julian to the splattered mud on the bridge, and then beyond into the seemingly endless gloom where the bridge led.

"That's going to take forever."

Julian snorted softly. "Do we have anything better to do?"

That didn't bear answering, and Jared didn't. He sighed, nodded, and drew his own sword. He shifted his blade into his left hand and stepped around Julian to stand with his right shoulder touching Julian's left.

Julian turned his head and met Jared's eyes. He saw uncertainty laced with a hint of fear, but more determination that, no doubt considering how Julian felt about this whole situation, was being driven by supreme annoyance.

Jared nodded, and they stepped together onto the hidden bridge.

❦ 45 ❦

WALKING THROUGH INFINITY

To say it was slow going is to say that a typhoon is a small rainstorm.

At first, Julian was hopeful that they would prove Jared's prediction wrong. After all, he had seen blind men walk at a fairly impressive pace, probing the road ahead with their staffs and maneuvering based on touch with seeming ease.

Of course, they had lots of practice at it. And for the most part, they were on familiar terrain. Not so in this circumstance, in either respect.

Still, they almost managed a normal walking pace, until the moment, about a quarter hour after they departed the ledge, when Julian's leading foot came down on nothing but empty air. Overbalanced, he came damn close to falling over the side, but a quick tug from Jared combined with Julian all but throwing himself to the side to halt his forward momentum saved him from a long fall into...what?

He shuddered as he lay on the invisible bridge and contemplated the seemingly endless void below them. Would he have ever hit bottom? Or would he have just fallen and fallen until eventually he died of thirst?

He shuddered again and tried to force himself to calm, but it took a minute. When he finally regained himself and got to his feet, Jared had completed a survey of the bridge around them.

243

"Damn thing turns to the left at a right angle." The tremble in his voice said it all. He knew as well as Julian how close a call it had been, and he was coming to the realization that there may be any number more of these sudden changes in direction.

Traps within traps within tests within puzzles.

Julian was growing extremely sick of them.

Moving on once more, they reduced their pace considerably, through unspoken consent. Each step forward came only after an exhaustive survey of the bridge ahead. They caught many more sudden shifts that way, and managed to avoid another close call.

But once again the geometry of the place became baffling. At one point, after the third left turn in a row, Julian expected they would soon recross their earlier steps, but the width of the bridge never changed, and they never came to any sort of junction with the place they had been before.

Two more rights, and logic told him they had doubled back on themselves, but again if that was the case there was no sign from the bridge itself.

Nor was there any sign from the surroundings. The sourceless illumination remained, for all the good it did. Even after what had to be a couple hours walking on it, Julian still could not focus in on the bridge itself, not visually anyway. And there was nothing else to look at. The cliff the entrance had been atop had long since recessed into infinity, and there were no other features to behold anywhere.

It was like they were walking on nothing, in a complete void.

Even the air was non-descript: completely still and devoid of any odors except the ones he and Jared brought with them. Nor was there any sound besides that of their footfalls and their swords dragging across the stone as they probed the bridge ahead.

Julian cringed to think of how much time he was going to have to spend with a sharpening stone to get his sword back to respectable condition after this.

But that sure beat stepping off this bridge into nothingness, didn't it?

Julian lost track of time; the monotony of their surroundings completely played havoc with his senses. But fatigue began to set in, and his muscles, already taxed by the long struggle against the deluge, began to scream at him to stop. And then his stomach began to rumble, and he realized it had been a good long time since they'd had a decent meal.

"You don't have any food on you do you?" Julian asked, not really expecting a positive response. All of his supplies had been in his pack, and that was long gone. But maybe Jared -

The younger man shook his head. "It was all in my pack."

"Great."

There was nothing for it but to push on.

Finally, after some unknown but miserable amount of time, things changed. A hint of a breeze brought a smell of freshness, like a meadow in Spring, to Julian's nostrils. He felt his spirits buoy.

Beside him, he could tell Jared felt similarly, and without speaking they picked up the pace a bit. Surely they must be getting near the end.

Surely.

Some time later, Julian found himself blinking to ensure he wasn't seeing things. Was that...an actual physical shape...ahead?

He gave Jared a nudge with his elbow, and when the younger man looked at him quizzically, pointed with his sword. "Tell me you see that."

Jared squinted for a few seconds, then a look of joy combined with relief crossed his face. "About time," he said, but his tone made it more a celebratory statement than complaint.

Julian could only nod agreement.

They pushed on, and over the next several minutes the whatever-it-was ahead became more plain to see: a cliff face rising up from the depths, and a ceiling descending from above and meeting together just beyond the edge of the cliff.

It looked exactly like the place they had first come from, but in his bones Julian knew it was a different location.

And...there back from the cliff face a bit, was that little bit of darkness there an opening? An exit from this place?

Hope surged through him, and he had to restrain himself from throwing caution to the wind and rushing forward to that destination. Only the memory of his near miss with eternal falling stopped him.

And good thing it did, too. Not ten paces farther on, the bridge bent to the right. Then fifteen paces farther along it bent back left. Then left again, then right.

It continued on that way, zigzagging its way toward the approaching cliff face at a maddeningly slow rate now that the objective was in sight. Feirhard surely planned it that way on purpose. A more weary or less wary person traversing this expanse would almost inevitably speed up as the end came into view. And this being test and trap all melded into one, now would be the ideal place to weed those sorts out.

Hevergod must really have not liked his son at all.

Their paces seemed slower than a snail's but slowly and surely the distance closed. As it did each step became easier than the one before, as though just the thought of leaving this expanse behind was enough to relieve the fatigue from aching muscles.

And perhaps it was, because when, finally, Julian stepped off the hidden bridge onto the lip overtop the cliff edge—and it was built exactly as the lip over the other cliff edge, except without the water and mud deposits from the deluge—he felt he could jump all the way up to the ceiling, at least thirty feet above.

"Man it's good to be off that thing," Jared said, hopping down off the lip eagerly. "Never realized how good solid ground feels." He grinned broadly, and the fatigue he must have been feeling seemed to wash away from his features.

"Yeah," Julian replied. He determinedly did not look back at the bridge. It wouldn't do any good anyway, and he halfway suspected the cussed thing would truly not be there if they were to try to get back on it, at this point.

There never was a path of retreat here, only of advance.

Instead, he turned his gaze on the opening in the rock before them.

Just as was the case in the tunnel they entered through, this passage lead away from an area about fifteen feet up-slope from where they were, and directly in front of the bridge, where the ceiling and rising floor met. Also as before, it was a perfect oval, and the stone appeared completely smooth while retaining good traction for a man's footing.

The hint of a breeze was stronger here, though, and the smell of growing things more pronounced. It sent a feeling of well-being through Julian, almost in the same way their pool of respite had.

Yeah, this had to be a trap.

But as always there was no choice but to move onward.

Julian sighed. "Let's get this over with."

Then he trudged up the slope toward the passageway. Jared followed.

46

A FATEFUL CHOICE

The passageway was dark when Julian looked at it from the cliff face. But as soon as he stepped within, it lit up. As before, the source of the illumination was impossible to determine, but this time the light was brighter, more inviting, almost like that on a warm Spring day without a cloud in the sky.

For that matter, the chill that had seemed to imbue all of existence within the interminable cavern, or whatever, that they had traversed on Feirhard's hidden bridge vanished, replaced by the sort of comforting warmth that seemed to go hand-in-hand with the light.

Julian hadn't even realized how cold he was, he had become so accustomed to it.

It felt good. Damn good.

He looked around at the smooth but otherwise nondescript walls, exactly as the first cave passage had been, and felt a strange sense of comfort in that. Then he looked ahead.

The passage was short, opening maybe fifty feet ahead into another larger chamber that seemed alive with light and from which the breeze flowed. The smell of life was almost overpowering, after where he and Jared had just been. In a good way.

The chamber ahead beckoned, welcoming him in.

Julian replaced his sword in its scabbard. Yeah, there could be something lurking ahead, but for some reason he just couldn't bring himself to believe that, the way he felt right then. Glancing aside at

Jared, he had done the same, and looked even more eager than Julian did.

They set off.

Stepping into the chamber ahead, Julian at first had to blink away tears at the brilliance of the light. But after a moment, the illumination receded—or perhaps he merely became accustomed to it—and he could see normally again.

Before them lay a virtual cornucopia.

A field of green grass, with the sun overhead and not a cloud in the sky, and wildflowers of all hues growing everywhere. The ground sloped upwards slightly to the left, forming a low hilltop. To the right, it descended into a forest of maples and elms, from the look of them.

But it was to the hilltop that Julian found his eyes fixed. A long wooden table, unstained and constructed with a simple but elegant beauty, stood at the crest of the hill. Foodstuffs of every variety lay piled atop the table, their odors wafting down to him and Jared irresistibly.

Pork, beef, apples, melons. Goblets sitting beside a half dozen bottles of what could only be wine. On the other end, pastries and sweets of all kinds.

Against untold hours without a bite to eat, that was a temptation too great to ignore.

But even better, to the right of the table lay a trio of chests with their lids thrown open. Gold coins, gems of every kind, sculptures, and other works of art, seemed to pour from the chests there was so much of it. And at the top of the heap of treasure in the largest of the chests: a great golden crown, inlaid with colorful jewels of every kind.

"By the gods," Jared said, his voice subdued, awed.

Julian swallowed hard. He couldn't disagree at all. Every part of his being screamed at him to go up there, eat and take his ease. And take his fortune.

Which was why his mind screamed at him not to.

"It's a trap," he said to Jared.

A voice boomed out from behind them, "Not so."

Julian whirled around and drew his sword with practiced smoothness. He recognized that voice.

Feirhard.

The ancient sorcerer had changed clothes. Instead of the grey and blue robes he wore when they first met, he had on tight-fitting black pants and a loose, ruffled white shirt beneath a vest the color of a well-aged wine. His beard was neatly trimmed, and his hair gathered back from his face by a dully-polished metal band above his forehead.

He still had his staff, clasped in his left hand, and his eyes were as piercingly hard as they had been before.

Feirhard walked out of the tree line to the right of the chamber entrance and marched directly toward them, his gait steady, purposeful, and strong. He certainly did not look his years at all, not from the tone of his muscles or the way he walked.

Julian took him in at a glance, then started forward to meet him, moving quickly on the balls of his feet. He flourished his blade in the air and made ready, all fatigue swept away at the sight of the man he had been wanting to throttle for the gods only knew how long; as long as he and Jared had been in here, anyway.

He felt Jared taking up station to his left and readying his own weapon as much as saw him. Good to know he was onboard.

Feirhard didn't slow, but looked at them with a level of contemptuous dismissal that Julian had never seen before.

"Don't be foolish," the sorcerer said, and made a quick gesture with his right hand.

Julian slammed face-first into something very invisible, very solid, very hard, and very very painful. He staggered backwards, his free hand going to his nose, which hurt like it had been smashed flat, and thankfully found it still in basically the correct shape.

It still hurt like nobody's business, though.

"Son of a bitch!" he growled, and turned baleful eyes on the sorcerer, who had stopped a few paces away and stood facing them seemingly without a care in the world.

"Do calm down," Feirhard said, his tone even, controlled. But stern. "Much as you may wish otherwise, there is nothing you can do to me. So I propose you just - "

"Bugger your proposals," Julian replied. "When I get my hands on you, I'm going to - "

"Do nothing." Feirhard's eyebrows lifted. "For that is all you can do, if you value your life."

Julian just glared at him, seething because he knew Feirhard's words for true. He had neutralized the three of them without even raising a sweat. He could have killed them all if he'd wanted to, and though it pained him to admit it, there would not have been a damn thing Julian could have done to stop it.

Nor could Melanie, apparently.

And where the hell was she?"

Julian opened his mouth to demand an answer, but Feirhard beat him to the punch.

"I am actually impressed. I did not expect you to do so well.' He shook his head slowly. "The first challenge should have done for the likes of you, yet somehow here you are."

"The likes of us?" Jared sounded at least as offended as Julian was. "You miserable bastard, you have no - "

"I know who my parents were quite well, young man. Can you say the same?"

That had to sting; Julian knew for a fact Jared had never known his father. Of course, it was because he had died while Jared was just a baby and not because of illegitimacy. Still…

Jared ground his teeth, going beet red in the face, but held his tongue.

Feirhard looked between the two of them for a second as though weighing something. Finally, he spoke again. "I am a man of my word, and while you were enjoying our little dance I took the time to test you at yours." His eyes darkened, and Julian thought he saw something very close to pain cross his features for a second. "The Lord Magus is dead, and his prince with him. You did not lie about that."

With his free, right hand, Feirhard gestured toward the laden table and chests atop the hill. "There is what you seek, yes? The wealth of the Lord Magus' domain, his crown?" The sorcerer drew a quick breath as though steeling himself. "Very well. My prince is dead. and you have passed the test meant for him. Take it. It is yours."

Julian felt his eyes grow wide in shock. Beside him, Jared went through the same shock but more quickly, moving quickly to an expression of avaricious glee. He took a step toward the slope of the hill.

"Or," Feirhard said, halting Jared in his steps, "you may have the life of your sorceress."

At another gesture from the sorcerer, the tree line behind him and to his left shifted as though the trees had grown legs and were adjusting their formation in response to his command.

And maybe they had, at that.

From deeper within the forest, a platform moved into view. The trees parted way before it, and very quickly it was plain to see. The platform appeared made of steel. It hovered half a foot above the ground as it travelled, but once it was clear of the trees it settled down onto the ground with a barely audible swish of protest from the grass that was crushed beneath it.

Julian took the platform itself in at a glance, but his entire attention was on the figure perched upon it.

Melanie was frozen in place exactly as she had been when Feirhard placed the spell on her. But there was something different. Her features were sunken slightly, as though she were collapsing in on herself. Clearly the preservation that her encasement afforded her was not infinite, and she was beginning to wither away.

"Enough of this game, Feirhard," Julian hissed through clenched teeth. "Release her."

The sorcerer chuckled. "That is entirely up to you." He gestured again at the treasure. "The treasure." Then he pointed at Melanie. "Or the woman. You cannot have both."

Julian finally tore his eyes away from Melanie's face, and he looked at Feirhard directly. The sorcerer's expression was firm, his eyes mercilessly cold.

He meant it. And there was not a damn thing Julian could do to change the situation.

Well, that was no decision at all, was it?

He turned toward Jared, and was astounded to find actual indecision on the man's face.

"You're kidding me, right?"

Jared looked back up at the treasure, just waiting for them, and licked his lips. "Julian, imagine what we could - "

Julian bounded across the distance between them and grabbed him by the lapel of his shirt with his free left hand. He raised his right to strike with his sword, the tip, marred by scraping against rocks though it was, pointed right at his heart.

One thrust was all it would take.

"Don't even *think* about it. So help me, I'll - "

Jared threw his hands up in a gesture of surrender. "I know, I know." He lowered his eyes, and Julian saw shame there. "It's just, well…" He trailed off, but Julian knew exactly what he was trying to say.

Gods help him, part of him felt the same way. But only a part.

Julian slowly released his grip on the younger man's shirt. He nodded. "Yeah, I know." Gently reaching out for Jared's shoulder, he guided him into a turn away from the treasure. Jared seemed to resist for a second, but then, once it was fully out of view he straightened and moved of his own accord.

Casting a look of defiance at Feirhard, Julian walked with Jared to the platform, then stepped up onto it next to Melanie.

Feirhard watched them in silence until they had climbed up onto the platform.

No sooner had Julian and Jared taken up position than the chamber seemed to shake. But there was no feeling of motion and no noise to go along with the shaking, just a quivering in the world that made Julian's head spin.

The little hill where the table and chests were laid out in particular began to shimmer. The green of the grass faded into a dull off-white, and the trees at the edge of the clearing similarly became ghastly in their wilting.

And then it all vanished, and they found themselves in a large oblong chamber that appeared carved out of solid granite. The platform where Melanie, and now Julian and Jared, stood was unchanged, but the little hill was gone, vanished completely.

In its place was only a gaping hole in the earth, from which the flickering orange-red light of a roaring fire and a substantial column of smoke emanated.

Had they tried to climb that hill, he and Jared would now be falling to what almost certainly would be an agonizing, and he had no doubt very prolonged, death.

Feirhard spoke.

"You have chosen," the corners of his lips turned upward ever so slightly, "wisely."

47

BIRTHRIGHT

The air surrounding Melanie shimmered, and Julian backed away as far as he could without leaving the platform. After what had just happened, he neither trusted the rest of the floor in the chamber nor knew what to think of the shimmering around Melanie.

He could only pray it was for the best.

The shimmering continued for several long seconds, and gradually was joined by a low humming that grew in pitch until it made Julian wince and want to press his hands to his ears.

But before he could do that, it ceased, and with it the shimmering.

Melanie collapsed limply to the floor of the platform, free of her prison.

Jared moved to help, but Julian beat him to it. Almost at the speed of thought, he was on his knees next to her, his sword left behind thoughtlessly. He reached beneath her head and shoulders and, cradling her gently in his left arm, lifted her head toward his own.

"Melanie," he said as gently as he could, but even to his ears it sounded too loud.

She stirred, moving slowly at first. It was like her limbs had forgotten how to work together, the way they shuffled around. But after a few moments, her movements became more coordinated. Her breathing quickened, and she cracked her eyes open.

The blue of her irises expanded rapidly from thin bands to wide circles as her pupils contracted in the chamber's light, and she pressed her eyelids shut for a moment. Her tongue flicked across her lips, which Julian could see were cracked from lack of water, and she shuddered.

Then she opened her eyes fully and met his. She smiled weakly.

"Julian," she said. A spasm of coughs obliterated whatever else may have come out of her mouth right then. When she regained herself, she said, "Do you have any water?"

Julian felt around with his free hand, but he had lost everything except his weapons when his pack washed away. He looked up at Jared, and blinked in surprise as the bearded man held out a waterskin.

"It's the water from that pool." He paused, then added, "I think."

Flashing a grateful grin, Julian took the waterskin and unstoppered it, then held it up to Melanie's lips. She drank slowly at first, but after the liquid made its mark on her, she grasped it with her left hand, pressing the skin to her mouth far more forcefully that Julian would have.

When finally she lowered it, she looked one hell of a lot better, more or less her regular self. Julian supposed the pool's water hadn't been diluted by the deluge much at all, if any.

He marked that in another of the things he owed Jared thanks for.

"I thought I'd lost you," he said softly, moving his right hand to brush the hair back from the left side of her face.

Melanie looked up at him with a strange expression for a long several seconds, then she lifted her head up toward his and he felt her lips on his cheek.

"You should know better than that," he heard in his ear.

And then she sank back down, and her expression was all business. "You were successful, I take it?"

"They were indeed." Feirhard's voice was louder, and when Julian looked up he saw the sorcerer standing at the side of the platform. The cold sternness had left his features; he now only had the look of a weary man who was nonetheless looking at a hard road ahead. He flashed another hint of a smile. "Though I wish they were not."

The cold rage that Julian had been holding onto ever since Feirhard's initial attack on them erupted to full life. He tensed his muscles to launch himself at the old man. But then he felt Melanie's warm weight on his arm and he stopped, not wanting to drop her while she was still regaining her strength.

Turns out, he didn't need to. Jared did all the leaping forward and throwing a punch—with the point of a dagger leading the fist—that Julian could have wanted to.

He met the same result Julian had when he first rounded on the sorcerer: he smacked hard into an unseen wall and rebounded, landing on his backside and looking like he had been poleaxed.

Feirhard rolled his eyes and looked from Jared to Julian and back, then focused fully in on Melanie. "They never learn, do they?"

Melanie sniffed and pushing herself up to a sitting position, extricated herself from Julian's care. "Can you blame them?" A simmering anger bubbled beneath the surface of her cool tone, causing Julian's hackles to go up. He had only seen Melanie truly enraged a few times, but it was not something he wanted to face himself, if he could help it.

Feirhard looked at her for a moment, then shrugged. "I suppose not. Are you better?"

"Very much better, thank you." She pushed herself to her feet, all the while continuing to scowl at him.

Julian rose as well, eyeing her with confusion. "You talk as though you know each other."

"We have had a number of conversations during my time here," she said, not taking her eyes off the old sorcerer. But she must have seen the look of incredulity on Julian's face because she added, "I don't know how either."

Feirhard shook his head with a soft snort. "It is quite simple, my dear. Had your Magestirium - "

"They are not *my* Magestirium."

He paused, then nodded. "Of course. Forgive me. Regardless, had they a modicum of true understanding of the art, it would not be a mystery." He sighed, then looked away toward the pit where the fire still burned. "So much lost,' he murmured, just barely loud enough to hear.

"So what happens now?' Julian said. He didn't try to keep his tone diplomatic; the bastard didn't deserve it. But he could recognize futility when he saw it, so he made an effort to not put "Come over here and let's fight" into his tone.

Feirhard looked back at him and raised one eyebrow. "Now we go our separate ways. As I said, I had time to look out into the world and see the truth of what you said." His shoulders drooped slightly. 'My liege is long dead, my duty is done. So I will go find a way in the world. And you will go home."

"Wait," Jared said, but when Feirhard's eyes came to rest on him, he floundered, his words not coming. Finally he looked down, cleared his throat, and began again. "The note said Kalem's birthright was here. And the history said the purpose of the test was to recover the key to his father's kingdom." He looked around, befuddled.

"You are wondering where the key is?"

Jared nodded, and the sorcerer laughed. It was the first genuine sound of mirth Julian had heard from the man.

Feirhard pointed at his chest. "It is here." Then at his head. "And here."

Jared continued to look perplexed. Feirhard sighed again.

"Ask yourself, what is required to be a good, strong ruler of a healthy nation?" He paused for a second. Then he held up a finger. "Courage. Creativity. Loyalty. Integrity. A fighting spirit. Determination. Respect. Willingness to sacrifice."

"But," Julian said, "the histories said Kalem was all those things, and the people loved him." He glanced at Melanie. "Right?"

She nodded, an expression of interest on her face.

"It is easy to gain the loyalty of the crowd," Feirhard replied dismissively. "Any fool can do that, but still be a fool. And the crowd is fickle, easily lead. They are not where a ruler should focus his attention." His eyes narrowed. "The Lord Magus had no desire to deny his son access to his birthright. But he loved his nation and his people too much to turn it over to him unless he was absolutely sure Kalem not only had the character and skill for it, but that he, and his closest advisors and friends, was fully ready." He spread his right arm wide, taking in the chamber and, by extension, the rest of The Falconer's Stairs. "And so the test. This was merely the final step, designed to test his followers' mettle as much as his. Loyalty must go both ways, up and down. Sacrifice can be demanded of anyone. But above all, they must have been willing to place another's need above their own petty greed." His eyebrows rose.

"So Hever - " Julian stopped, clearing his throat at a stern look from Feirhard, then started again. "The Lord Magus would have let his son die in...that," he gestured at the still-glowing pit they had escaped by choosing correctly, "if he chose wrong?" He shuddered. "He really didn't like his son at all did he? No wonder they called him a butcher."

Feirhard looked stonily at Julian for a long few seconds, then shook his head. "You still do not see. This was to be a final test, of his followers as much as of Kalem."

Melanie blinked, surprised. "You would have imprisoned Kalem as you did me, and then watched to see what his followers did to rescue him."

Feirhard nodded. "If they were properly loyal—if he inspired such proper loyalty—they would pass the test. If not..." He shrugged, as though the deaths of such men were of no import.

"If they," Melanie gestured toward Julian, then Jared, "had chosen wrong?"

"Then you and I would be having this conversation alone, and I would be offering you my deepest condolences."

In other words, Melanie had never been in any true danger. She was just made to appear that way, the carrot that kept him and Jared running through the test. That set Julian's teeth on edge. Though it should have come as some relief, in a sense, it just made him despise Feirhard all the more.

The room was silent for a long moment, and perhaps Feirhard sensed the animosity heading his way. Because after a few seconds he gave a quick bob of his head, as though waking himself from some reverie, and turned away.

"I will take my leave of you now," he said, and lifted his staff. The ball at its head flashed brilliant red for a second, then the chamber wall opposite where they had entered—Julian was surprised to see the entrance passage still in existence—split and then opened, revealing the scene of a mountain vale, dominated by a crystal clear lake, with a forest on one side. And on the other, a peak that looked distinctly like a bird of prey perched atop a rock.

The Raptor's Ascent, back where they started.

"Take whatever trifles you will from this room. When you leave, the doorway will close behind you, and you will not be able to return. Your animals should have been guided back to the lake by now, so you should have little difficulty." He looked back at them and raised an eyebrow meaningfully. "Fare well."

Feirhard strode toward the door, not looking back until Melanie said, "Wait!"

The old sorcerer fixed her with a questioning look.

"Will you go to the Magestirium then?"

He shook his head. "From what I've seen in my views of the world, and what I've learned from my discussions with you, they seem...rather boring. Obsessed with trivialities, when they could do things of grandeur."

Julian hadn't had all that much interaction with the Magestirium, but that seemed a bit unfair. They could be stuffy, and certainly they were full of themselves, but...

But Melanie was nodding in agreement, so what did he know?

Feirhard spoke again, and this time he smiled. It was not a kindly smile, but neither was it threatening. It was just...unsettling. 'You have promise though, young sorceress. Perhaps I shall come pay you a visit someday, to see how you've developed."

He turned then and stepped through the doorway, leaving them alone in the chamber, and in silence.

48

TRIFLES

They remained silent for a while after Feirhard left. Julian wasn't sure about the others, but he frankly found it difficult to believe their ordeal was over, just as suddenly as that.

He had become so used to being constantly on edge in this place, he wasn't sure how to respond to the release.

"Ok, I don't believe for a second he's done with us. Not until we're out that door and miles away from here," he said finally, only realizing as he said the words that it was entirely what he had been mulling over in his mind without realizing it.

He stepped forward off the platform, steeling himself for a trap, but nothing happened. So he looked back at the others, grinned, and jerked his head toward the door. "Let's get the hell out of here."

But Jared and Melanie didn't look as eager as he felt to be leaving. Jared was looking around at the chamber as though trying to see into every nook and cranny, and Melanie just appeared thoughtful.

"There is no rush, Julian," she said.

He snorted. "He could change his mind and come back at any time to try and finish us off. We need to get while they getting's good."

She just sniffed. "If he wanted to 'finish us off' he could have, without difficulty, at any time he pleased." Melanie shook her head. "No, we are quite safe, I expect."

"Yeah," Jared said, finally stepping off the platform and walking over to the other side of the chamber, where the pit lay. The glow had begun to fade, but it still was not inviting. "Besides he said we could take whatever we want." He flashed Julian an annoyed look. "Might as well get *something* for our efforts."

Julian could understand his annoyance. Jared had worked up in his mind that whatever lay here at The Falconer's Stairs would set him up, maybe for life. And, he had to confess he had felt some of that pull as well. But he hadn't come for that; he'd come to make sure Jared didn't do wrong by Melanie.

Clearly that was no longer a concern.

Or, really, Julian finally believed it had never been a concern. Jared had changed. Or he had changed in how he viewed Jared.

Whatever.

So the guy had a point. Could be there was something worth keeping here. But Julian couldn't shake the feeling that they were missing some grand axe that was about to fall, and they needed to get moving immediately.

"I agree with Jared," Melanie said, and also stepped off the platform.

Clearly there would be no reasoning with them. So he might as well join them, and set to searching.

The chamber was not as featureless as he had initially thought. Although, to be honest, he hadn't really taken the time to look around earlier.

It was oval-shaped, and the long side held the entrance passage and the door to the lake. The pit took up about half of the left side of the room. The other half of that end had shelves carved into the stone of the walls, and what looked to be a similarly-carved desk as well. The walls around the platform were bare, except for a few discolored yellowish spots here and there. But there was a wooden table with a single chair against the wall, and next to it a darkly-stained wooden cabinet as tall as Julian's shoulder.

Julian went straight to the cabinet, and was unsurprised to find it full of foodstuffs: salted pork, cabbages, carrots, apples, smoked beef, and on the upper shelves several bottles of wine.

"We've hit the mother lode," he called, and turned toward the other two, holding up one of the bottles in his left hand and grinning as he bit into a round, red, delicious apple that he held in his right

Jared and Melanie were across the room, fiddling with the carved bookcase. They looked up from what they were doing, and Julian could see the hunger in Jared's eyes. He licked his lips as he watched Julian eat, but Melanie was less impressed.

"Good. See if there's a satchel or something so we can - Ah-ha!" That last came with a sound of triumph as she twisted her arm, which she had stuck almost elbow-deep into a nook above the desk, activating something.

A solid crack echoed through the chamber, and the wall next to the left-most book case pushed outward and then swung open.

Julian felt the puff of air that escaped from the newly-opened side chamber from across the room.

That was interesting.

He put the bottle back, took up another apple, and hurried across the room to join Melanie and Jared.

They didn't wait for him, but strode quickly into the side chamber. Julian was about to call out for them to be careful when Jared called out, "Found our stuff!"

Julian stepped into the side chamber, and gawked.

Yes, his and Jared's packs were there, looking as though they had been freshly cleaned and dried out. He had a strong suspicion they would find every item accounted for, down to the pocket lint, just as had happened at their pool of relaxation.

But what really caught his eye was the knee-high iron-banded chest sitting against the far wall, and above it, hanging from mounts on the wall, the short sword he had taken from the torturer and one of those neat curved swords the desert warriors had carried, and between them a silver medallion with an intricate engraving of some sort on the centerpiece. The medallion was sized such that it was clearly intended for a woman.

Customized gifts?

Or a trap.

"This looks promising," Julian said levelly. "Here." He handed Jared the second apple, and the younger man bit into it eagerly.

Melanie looked askance at Julian for a second, but her severe expression quickly gave way to a little grin of amusement. "Seriously, Julian, I highly doubt you need to worry."

Then she stepped up to the chest, reached out, and threw the top open.

Surprisingly it was unlocked, but then again burglars weren't exactly likely in this place. Still, why would -

That train of thought fled Julian's mind completely as he took in the chest's contents. The right half held books, of course. What else would a sorcerer, mage, whatever treasure highly? The left, though. Well, that *was* the mother lode. There was probably a hundred marks worth of coins, a couple little engraved boxes that looked to be carved from polished bone of some sort, and if he wasn't mistaken a few gems thrown in as well.

"Whoa," Jared said. His eyes were popping out of his head.

And he wasn't kidding. The average family in Glimmer Vale got by on maybe ten marks in a year. So they were looking at ten years' worth of pay.

Not a bad haul at all.

It made Julian quite curious what not a trifle was, in Feirhard's world.

Getting their trifles out of the chamber posed a bit of a challenge, because the chest was heavier than it looked, and Jared and Julian struggled to move it, even together. But more than that, Feirhard had said the door would close as soon as they left. But did that mean when all three of them left, or would it key on any exit at all?

If the latter, they really could only take what they could carry, because throwing a book through, for instance, might inadvertently trap them inside this place forever.

That was not a concept worth risking for any reason.

Fortunately, there truly was no hurry. Even Julian began to see that as true as time went on and nothing bad happened to them.

"In that case," Melanie said, when he finally admitted it, 'why don't we eat first?"

You didn't have to ask him twice.

A half hour later, with a full belly, the task looked a whole lot less daunting to Julian. Still, there was one thing that had to happen first.

"You know, I'm about done with these clothes," he said, picking at his thoroughly muddied, torn, and generally destroyed clothes. "I'm going to go change."

He retreated to the side chamber so Melanie wouldn't have to witness that act, and replaced his clothing with spares from their packs. Julian e-settled his mail down over his shoulders before donning his dark green jacket, then he stepped back into the main chamber, feeling much, much better about life, and ready to tackle the job.

In the end, they decided it was better to leave some things behind than to risk being trapped, so Jared and Julian dumped their packs and discarded several extra garments each.

After all, Jared quipped, "We can always buy new ones."

Then, into the extra space that left, they moved as much of the money as they could. It wasn't all of it, but it was enough; they probably only left behind ten marks total.

Melanie took the books herself, and pocketed the medallion.

The packs were quite a lot heavier, but tolerable. And anyway they only needed to make it back to their campsite. So after donning his pack and slipping his new short sword into his belt, Julian looked around the chamber with a certain satisfaction.

"Don't know about you, but I'm about ready to get out of here."

"Damn right," Jared replied, and Melanie merely nodded assent.

Turning to the doorway, they lined up shoulder to shoulder. Then, as one, they stepped out of The Falconer's Stairs and back onto the shore of the lake beneath The Raptor's Ascent.

❧ 49 ☙

HOMEWARD

They reached their old campsite by the northern shore of the lake, and Julian was surprised—though he shouldn't have been, he supposed—to find their horses back, and not just back but hobbled in the same picket line he and Jared had set up when they first arrived.

Feirhard was true to his word, it seemed.

Again.

And didn't it really burr Julian up to have to recognize that.

Melanie and Jared unburdened themselves, and Julian followed suit. He dropped his pack to the ground and sat down beside it. The sun was drawing low in the sky and approaching the peaks to the east, and weariness seemed to flow from his every pore.

It crossed his mind that they maybe ought to think about setting a watch, but before he could muster the notion to do anything about it, he drifted off to sleep.

When he woke, the sun was high in the sky—it looked to be a bit before noon—and the smell of woodsmoke and cooking beef wafted through the air. Groaning softly, he pushed himself up onto his elbows and looked around.

Melanie was sitting on a little stool next to a cheerful little camp-fire about ten feet away. She had erected a cooking spit, and was slowly turning a hunk of meat as it cooked over the flames. A small tent where she had no doubt spent the night stood off to Julian's left.

Jared still lay sprawled in the grass on the other side of the fire, soft snores coming from his prone figure.

The fact that Jared was still asleep made Julian feel like less of a slacker.

He sat up the rest of the way and rolled his shoulders; he had a crick in his neck from a rock or something during the night. "Morning," he managed to croak out.

Melanie looked away from the meat toward him and smiled warmly. "About time you came back around. There's tea in the pot." She nodded toward a small teapot and a trio of cups that she had set on one of the stones lining the fire site.

"Thanks." He stood, his left knee popping audibly as he straightened, and moved over to the fire. He picked up a cup and filled it from the pot, then took a long drink. Exhaling contentedly, he looked away toward the lake and The Raptor's Ascent on the far side. "Hard to believe it's all over."

"It was an…interesting…experience."

He winced. She probably had had at least as rough a time as he and Jared. Julian looked back at her and found her looking firmly at the meat. "What was it like?"

She shook her head. "Difficult to describe. I was aware, but felt nothing. No pain, no sense of time. Feirhard…spoke with me, and I was able to respond. From time to time he would show me images of what you and Jared were doing." A little shudder rippled through her. "It wasn't entirely unpleasant, I suppose, but all the same I'd rather not repeat it."

"I can understand that." He wouldn't want to go through it even once. Probably it was best to tackle another subject. "Something's been bothering me since the start in there." He gestured toward the seemingly sculpted rock structure across the valley.

Melanie looked at him and raised an eyebrow.

"Feirhard survived over five hundred years. He said time flows differently in there." He paused to swallow another mouthful of tea, then said, "It felt like just a couple days at most, but I wonder how long we were really inside."

"About a month and a half."

Julian blinked, surprised. "Come again? How do you - "

"Last night after you two collapsed and left me to set up camp, I took some observations of the stars. Based on their positions, and a few hints Feirhard dropped during our conversations, that is my best guess."

"Oh." He supposed that made sense, come to think on it. Everyone knew the stars shifted as the seasons passed. "Alright then."

Melanie looked at him strangely for a second, then burst out laughing.

"What?"

"You're impossible to please sometimes."

He decided not to answer that.

Jared awoke a few minutes later, conveniently just as Melanie declared the meat ready. An unhurried meal later, sitting in the grass around the fire pit, Julian felt quite a lot more human.

"Guess we'd better get packed and make some time today."

"Is there any real rush?" Jared asked. He still looked fairly sleepy. "I mean, not like we're on a schedule." He grinned broadly. "The money's not going to spoil, after all."

Julian looked askance at him. "I'd like to get home if that's all the same to - " he interrupted himself with a big, loud yawn, and both of his companions chuckled. He rolled his eyes. "Fine, but let's get started at first light tomorrow, at least."

Jared nodded agreement, then leaned in closer to the fire, an eager expression on his face. "Well, ninety crowns split three ways."

"Two," Melanie said. "I have no interest in it."

Jared looked at her like she was daft for a second, then shrugged as though to say, "However you want it." Then he grinned broadly at Julian. "Forty-five each then."

Julian shook his head. "Thirty. Raedrick gets a share."

"What are you talking about? He didn't come on the trip."

Julian just stared at him for a long moment, and Jared dropped his eyes. "Right. Good point." He perked up again after another couple seconds. "What are you going to do with your cut? I'm going to build myself a nice house right down by the lake, maybe my own private dock, too."

Julian cocked his head to the side. "So you're planning to remain in Lydelton then."

"Yeah, no better place to be for guys like us, right?" Jared's brow furrowed. "That going to be a problem?"

A week ago, just the idea of Jared staying in Glimmer Vale would have made Julian grind his teeth until they ached. Now, though…

He shook his head. "Nah. Just don't bring any more magic maps our way." He downed a swallow of tea. "Please."

Jared chuckled. "Can't make any promises on that."

Julian snorted, but after a second joined Jared in his laughter.

Melanie had been watching their interchange, an unreadable expression on her face. When Jared got up to attend to nature, she watched him depart for a moment, then turned frank eyes on Julian. "Good to see you two have made peace."

"Yeah well, just so long as he doesn't let it go to his head."

Melanie rolled her eyes and chuckled softly. "You really are incorrigible, you know that?"

Julian shrugged. "Part of my charm, I guess."

Her mirth faded and she looked at him for a long few seconds, then she nodded. "I suppose it is, at that."

What the hell did that mean? Julian was going to respond with a teasing quip but when he looked back at her, he saw that Melanie's expression was completely serious. And…open. In a way he had seen only a few times before.

"I was very worried about you," he said. And he cursed himself for it, because it seemed such a silly, tiny thing to say right then.

"I know."

She reached across the distance between them and took his hand, and he felt a little jolt. He squeezed her fingers gently, and she returned it.

Jolly whistling announced Jared's return a moment before he came into view from around the tent Melanie had erected for herself. Just before he did, she pulled her hand away and it felt like a great chasm had opened up between them.

Jared blew out the last of his whistle and sat back down on the other side of the fire. He grinned at them. "Did I miss anything good?"

Melanie looked back at Jared and shrugged. "Not particularly. We were just discussing how to load the horses, now that we have one fewer than we came with."

Julian didn't counter her lie, and just like that, the moment was gone.

They passed the rest of the day in relative ease and retired early.

Julian could not have remained up late even if he had wanted to. In the morning they climbed the rise leading west out of the valley just as the sun was creeping over the mountains. Julian spared one look over his shoulder as they reached the crest.

The Raptor's Ascent reflected in the mirror-like stillness of the lake below, and for a second it almost looked as though the great rocky bird was waggling one wing at them, like it was waving goodbye.

Julian felt a shiver go down his spine. He shook his head, and the illusion vanished.

He almost told the others to stop, to determine whether they could see the effect or not. But instead he resolutely turned away, placing his back to the Falconer's Stairs and all the tribulations that had befallen him and his friends there.

But as he rode down the far side of the hill and the great structure vanished behind the rising mountains of the Saddleback Range, Julian could not help but wonder about the place they had left behind, and the man who had occupied it for so long.

He felt certain they would see Feirhard again someday. He did not look forward to that, not one bit.

MESSAGE FROM THE AUTHOR

Thank you for reading my book. I hope you enjoyed reading it as much as I enjoyed writing it.

Every review helps an author out, so whether you loved this book, hated it, or something in between, please take a minute to tell other readers what you thought. All of the online retailers make it very easy to do, and I would really appreciate it.

Feel free to come say hi at my website or on Gab. I always enjoy hearing from readers, especially since you all are, collectively, my boss.

I also have a weekly podcast, Story Time With Michael Kingswood, where I read stories and talk through some of the latest goings on in my world. I'd love to see you there.

Thanks again. My best to you and yours.

Warm Regards,
Michael Kingswood

MAILING LIST

If you enjoyed this book and would like word on new releases and special deals from Michael Kingswood, sign up for his newsletter on his website. Guaranteed to be spam-free, you can opt out at any time. And you can rest assured he will not share your information with anyone, for any reason.

https://michaelkingswood.com/newsletter-signup/

MEMBERSHIP

Michael would like to invite you to become a supporting member of his website. Similar in concept to Patreon, a few dollars a month will give you access to exclusive content, and help him to focus more of his time to writing fun and exciting stories for your enjoyment.

Sign up at his website:

https://www.michaelkingswood.com/membership/join/

ABOUT THE AUTHOR

Michael Kingswood is 20-year veteran of the US Navy submarine force and a lifelong fan of science fiction and fantasy literature. His work has appeared in numerous collections and anthologies, to include the Fiction River Anthology series from WMG publishing. He holds a bachelors degree in Mechanical Engineering as well as a Master of Engineering Management and a Master of Business Administration. He has four children and currently resides in San Diego.

Find Michael Kingswood online at:

www.michaelkingswood.com

www.facebook.com/michael.kingswood

twitter.com/michaelkingswd

MORE BOOKS BY MICHAEL KINGSWOOD

GLIMMER VALE CHRONICLES

Glimmer Vale

Out-Dweller

Tollard's Peak

Robbed Blind

The Falconer's Stairs

Glimmer Vale Omnibus Edition #1

STORIES FROM GLIMMER VALE

Legacy

Hidden Magic

Captive Hearts

Wedding Gifts

Lost Credit

THE PERICLES CONSPIRACY

Passing In The Night

The Pericles Conspiracy

DAWN OF ENLIGHTENMENT

Masters Of The Sun

NOVELLAS

What Lurks Between

The Necromancer's Lair

The Champion

Veritas Morte

STORY COLLECTIONS

Stories From The Great Challenge

Tales Of Adventure #1

Tales Of Adventure #2

Short Story 10-Pack

A Jar Of Mixed Treats

Short Mystery 10-Pack

Stories From Glimmer Vale, Volume 1

SHORT FICTION

Michael has also published a number of shorter works, links to which can be found on his website.

9 780999 806 8404